CHAPTER ONE

"This Cabernet is simply divine."

Jacob Hunt wasn't sure if Margot Gottlieb could even taste it anymore. She'd knocked back at least one of the twelve bottles he'd brought along in the space of an hour.

"You must tell me where you sourced it from," she added.

"That, my dear is strictly top secret," Jacob said and tapped his nose. "If I tell you I shall have to kill you."

Margot laughed her shrill laugh and drained yet another glass.

It was mid-summer, and the temperature had reached its peak on the island of Guernsey. The Gottliebs were hosting their annual summer soiree, and the guests were now suitably fed and enjoying the late afternoon heat. A few of them were splashing in the pool in front of the main house. Others had gone to walk off the feast that had been put out, and the atmosphere was jovial.

The Gottlieb summer event was a big thing, and it was something everyone in their circle of friends never missed. In fact, it was said that should a person on the guest list fail to make an appearance, it was tantamount to social suicide.

"I feel peculiar," Naomi Potter announced and immediately sat down on the bench overlooking the clifftop.

Naomi was one of the guests who had decided to take a walk in the grounds of the Gottlieb estate.

"How much have you had to drink?" her fiancé, Mark asked.

"A couple of glasses of wine with lunch," Naomi replied. "No more than usual."

"Are you sure?"

"Of course I'm fucking sure. I'm not an idiot. Why are you looking at me like that?"

"I'm not looking at you like anything," Mark said. "And since when did you start cursing like a sailor?"

"What?"

Naomi's eyes bored into his. There was a fire in them he hadn't seen before.

"Are you alright?" Mark said. "You look a bit strange. Are you feeling alright?"

"I'm feeling just fucking fine. Why don't you trot off and join your little hussy. I saw how you and Sasha were all over each other back there."

"I don't know what you're talking about."

"I don't know what you're talking about," Naomi repeated in a derogatory tone. "Just fuck off."

"I can't talk to you when you're like this. I don't know what's got into you."

Mark turned and started to walk away. He didn't know what was happening – Naomi's behaviour was extremely out of character. He'd only taken a few steps when he heard something behind him.

"Don't you fucking walk away from me."

It was Naomi, and the fire burning in her eyes was now so intense that Mark's instincts were telling him to run.

He didn't get the chance. She was on him in an instant. She wrapped her arms around his neck and when he threw her off, she began pummelling his back hard with her fists. A hand found his face and sharp nails slashed at the skin on his nose and cheeks. The other hand cupped his forehead and one of her nails found an eye and tried to gouge it out.

Mark was screaming now. Blood was running down his face from the damage that had been inflicted to his left eye, and he'd lost the vision in it. He found a burst of energy and managed to shake his crazed fiancé off, and then he ran.

He ran like he'd never run before. He dared to look behind him, and his good eye told him that Naomi had fallen to the ground and was now bashing the path with both fists. Mark kept on running. The pain in his eye was something he'd never experienced before and the sting from the wounds on his nose and cheek was making him feel ill.

He slowed when the gigantic house came into view. There was safety in numbers here, and he would be able to call an ambulance. He reached the tennis court and headed straight towards the group of people. Then he stopped in his tracks. Something was wrong – something was terribly wrong.

He could hear the sound of raised voices. A man and a woman were screaming at each other. Margot Gottlieb was hurling abuse at Jacob Hunt. Jacob retaliated with a slap to her face so loud that Mark could hear it twenty metres away. Another slap sounded and Margot leapt in the air and latched onto Jacob's neck. Mark was too far away to see exactly what she was doing but it looked like she was trying to take a bite out of Jacob's face.

Peter Gottlieb was crouched on the edge of the swimming pool. He was holding someone's head under the water. Mark couldn't see who the drowning figure was. There were a few other guests by the pool and none of them were doing anything to help the thrashing person underneath the water.

Everywhere Mark looked, fights had broken out. Husbands were attacking wives – sisters were mauling brothers, and close friends were behaving like mad people. Mark's good eye was struggling to comprehend what was happening.

Then something happened that Mark would never forget. The crack of a gunshot sounded and everything went quiet. The guests stopped dead – it was as if this was part of an action scene in a movie and the film had been paused.

CHAPTER TWO

Detective Inspector Liam O'Reilly was in a great mood. He was sitting at a table at his favourite restaurant and his new wife was sitting opposite him. For the past couple of weeks, O'Reilly and Victoria had been on a strict diet, and now both of them were looking forward to ordering whatever they wanted from the menu in The Red Snapper.

"What do you feel like?" O'Reilly asked.
"I haven't decided yet," Victoria said. "What about you?"
"That seafood platter special looks grand."

Victoria had been diagnosed with laryngeal cancer and the treatment had gone well, but she'd decided to increase the chances of beating it by cutting out anything the cancer might use against her. This included alcohol and unhealthy food. O'Reilly had reluctantly agreed to join her in the latter and he hadn't enjoyed it one little bit, but now, after two weeks of a strict healthy food regime he'd lost five pounds, and he was determined to do something about putting some of that weight back on.

"I'm going to have the steak," Victora decided.
"Good choice."
Neither of them had noticed the man standing next to the table, which was surprising as Bertram Pink, the head chef was over six feet six.
"It's good to see you again," Bertram said. "Where have you been hiding?"
"We've been on a diet," O'Reilly said. "Veggies, fruit and brown rice, can you believe it?"
"Good for you. I have to say you look good for it."
"The diet's over for now," O'Reilly told him. "How's the seafood platter?"
"Too much food for one person," Bertram said.
"I'll have one of those then."
"And I'll go for the fillet steak," Victoria said. "Medium rare, thanks."

"I'll put the order in," Bertram said. "It really is good to see you again."

O'Reilly's phone started to ring inside his pocket. He took it out, looked at the screen and rejected the call.

"Work?" Victoria guessed.

"Nothing that can't be handled by someone else," O'Reilly said. "Here's to good food and even better company."

He raised his beer in the air. Victoria reciprocated with her glass of water.

"Have you given any more thought to the promotion?" Victoria asked out of the blue.

"I'm not interested," O'Reilly told her.

"But it's been offered to you on a plate. Detective Chief Inspector in the Border Agency. It'll mean a huge pay increase."

"I'm really not interested," O'Reilly said. "The GBA is not my idea of a dream job, pay rise or no pay rise. I'm happy right where I am. I love my job – I have a grand team, and even Andy is starting to grow on me."

* * *

"He's not answering," DC Andy Stone said.

The rat-faced detective put his phone back in his pocket and sighed.

"He probably didn't hear it," DC Katie Owen said.

"He rejected the call," DC Stone said. "The line went dead before the voicemail kicked in."

"We'll have to do without him," DS Will Skinner said. "What a mess."

A call had come in about a gunshot in Rousse in the far north of the island. Uniforms were dispatched and what they found on the luxury estate was something none of them would ever forget. The grounds of the Gottlieb property resembled a war zone, with casualties all over the place. The more seriously injured had been taken to hospital, and they would be questioned later, but there were still a lot of confused people mulling around the estate, and the three detectives were tasked with finding out exactly what happened on the Gottlieb estate.

"So far," DS Skinner said. "We have a man with serious injuries to his face and neck. He has deep lacerations to his nose and mouth, and one of his eyeballs has been gouged out of its socket."

DC Stone winced. "Nasty."

"A woman almost drowned," DS Skinner continued. "She was barely alive when the paramedics arrived but they managed to resuscitate her, and she was taken away in an ambulance. A few more people sustained less serious injuries, but they too have been taken to hospital."

"Look at them," DC Owen pointed to the group of people gathered by the house.

Some of them were sitting on the ground. Others were pacing up and down, and more were standing, stock still as if they'd been captured in time.

"What do you think happened?" DC Stone asked. "Some kind of argument that got out of hand?"

"It must have been quite an argument," DC Owen said.

"Katie," DS Skinner said. "I don't know what happened to these people, but I don't like it. It's possible they're in shock so we need to tread carefully. We'll be formally interviewing every one of them in due course, but right now I suggest we just have a casual chat with them."

DC Owen walked over to a man who looked to be in his late-fifties, early-sixties. He was dressed in just a pair of swimming trunks and he had a towel wrapped around his shoulders. His thick, white hair was dry so DC Owen guessed he'd been out of the pool for a while.

"Are you OK?" she asked him.

"Who are you?"

"DC Owen. I'm from the Island Police. What's your name?"

"Gottlieb," he said. "Peter Gottlieb. This is my property."

"Can you tell me what happened?" DC Owen said.

"You tell me," Peter said.

"What were all the people doing here?"

"What do you think they were doing here?" Peter said. "We have a summer party this time every year."

"Did some kind of fight break out?" DC Owen asked.

"I really don't know."

"People were seriously injured, Mr Gottlieb," DC Owen said. "Many of them had to be taken to hospital. We need to know what happened."

"I don't know. One minute I'm enjoying a dip in the pool and the next thing I know I'm staring down at bodies on the ground. The police and the ambulances arrived, and I had no idea what had happened. I remember the gunshot though."

"That's why we came out here," DC Owen said. "Somebody phoned us about a gunshot."

"Was anybody shot?"

"I don't think so. Do you have any idea what could have happened?"

"Madness," Peter said, matter-of-factly. "Absolute madness."

CHAPTER THREE

"Everyone we've spoken to so far has told us the same thing."
DS Skinner was speaking to the team the next morning. O'Reilly was back on duty. The seafood platter at the Red Snapper was the best he'd ever tasted, and he promised Bertram Pink he would be back again soon to sample another one.

"All in all," DS Skinner carried on. "Nine of the guests at the Gottlieb party were injured. Some of those injuries were more serious than others, but nobody seems to know how the guests were hurt."

"Somebody must know something," O'Reilly said.

"All we know at this stage," DS Skinner said. "Is a number of altercations broke out, but nobody can tell us what caused the fights. A woman almost drowned, but none of the guests seem to know how it happened. And a man suffered serious injuries to his face, but nobody saw what happened to him either. We'll be speaking to him as soon as we can."

"What do we know about these Gottliebs?" O'Reilly asked.

"The family have been on the island for generations," DC Owen said. "Their initial wealth came from banking, but that wealth has increased substantially in recent years with investments in property and the Internet."

"There is far too much money on this island," O'Reilly mused.

"The estate is owned by Peter and Margot Gottlieb," DC Owen said. "And their summer soirees are high on the list of social events for the well-heeled of the island."

"I want everyone who attended that party brought in and questioned," O'Reilly said. "Experience has taught me that different rules apply when we're dealing with the filthy rich. It stinks, but that's the way it is. No doubt they'll come armed with lawyers, but there's nothing we can do about that. Do we know who fired the gun?"

"We don't, sir," DC Stone said. "But we do know that none of the guests suffered a gunshot wound."

O'Reilly was finding this difficult to comprehend. A group of friends attended a party at a luxury estate – numerous fights broke out at roughly the same time, and nobody could tell them what caused the violence.
"What did the officers first on the scene have to say?" he asked.
"It was PC London and PC Hill, sir," DC Stone told him. "Kim said she'd never seen anything like it. Carnage was how she described it."
"Did they speak to any of the guests?"
"They did, and they all said the same thing. It was like they were all plunged into the inky depths of madness at precisely the same time."
"Inky depths of madness?" O'Reilly repeated.
"Sorry, sir," DC Stone said. "I've been doing an online creative writing course. I thought it might make me more of an equal in Assumpta's eyes. I know how much she likes to write."
"Never going to happen, Andy," O'Reilly said. "Never in a million years."

The door to the room opened and PC London came inside.
"Sorry to interrupt," she said. "But I've got a man waiting by the front desk who claims to know something about what happened at the summer party yesterday. I thought you'd want to speak to him."
"Thanks, Kim," O'Reilly said. "Can you tell him I won't be long?"
"Will do, sir," PC London said.

"Are we treating this as a series of assaults?" DC Stone said.
"Until I know exactly what happened," O'Reilly said. "We're not treating it as anything. I'd better go and speak to the witness before he develops a sudden memory block too. I want everybody who was at that party yesterday questioned before the end of the day. Could you get onto it please."

He left the briefing room and made his way to the front desk. A middle-aged man was the only person sitting in the waiting area and O'Reilly assumed he was the one who'd come in with the information. O'Reilly introduced himself and was told the man wasn't one of the guests at the party. His name was Walter Thorpe, and he owned the catering company that had provided the food. O'Reilly suggested they talk in his office.

"Take a seat," he said.
Walter did. O'Reilly sat opposite him at the desk.
"What did you want to tell me?"
"I was there yesterday," Walter said. "At the Gottlieb estate."
"So I believe," O'Reilly said.
"I own a catering company – *Exclusive Eats*, and we were hired to provide the food yesterday."
"Do you know the Gottliebs?"
"Everybody knows the Gottliebs," Walter said. "I mean, I don't know them personally – I don't mix in those kinds of circles, but everyone knows about them on the island."
O'Reilly had never heard of them. He kept this to himself.

"What is it you wanted to tell me?" he asked instead.
"I've never seen anything like it," Walter said. "I was overseeing the serving of the dessert when all hell broke loose."
"What happened?"
"At first it was just a few raised voices," Walter said. "I think it was Margot Gottlieb and a man, but then he slapped her. He hit her really hard and she went berserk. She jumped on him and tried to bite his face."
"Do you know who this man is?"
"I'm afraid not. But that wasn't the end of it. The next thing I knew, Peter Gottlieb was fighting with a woman in the pool. He had her head under the

water, and he was keeping it there."

"Did you do anything to help her?" O'Reilly said.

"I didn't know what to do. There were quite a few people around the pool, and none of them were moving. They were all staring at what Peter was doing as though they'd been glued to the spot."

"What happened then?" O'Reilly said.

"A man came out of nowhere," Walter told him. "His face was covered in blood and one of his eyes looked like it had been ripped out. That's when I heard the gunshot."

"What did you do then?"

"I hit the deck," Walter said. "What do you think I did?"

"Did you see who fired the gun?"

Walter shook his head. "No, but one of my waiters did. He told me later that it was Barbara Gottleib."

"Is she the daughter?" O'Reilly asked.

"Granddaughter. Barbara is six years old."

CHAPTER FOUR

"This just gets more and more bizarre," O'Reilly said.

He told the rest of the team what Walter Thorpe had told him.

"It was a six-year-old girl who fired the gun," he said. "Barbara Gottlieb is the granddaughter of Margot and Peter."

"Where on earth did she get a gun?" DC Stone wondered.

"Where indeed?" O'Reilly said. "Not only are we dealing with a number of simultaneous assaults, now we have a little girl with a firearm."

"Did we retrieve the weapon?" DC Owen asked.

"Not as far as I'm aware," O'Reilly said. "And we need to do something about that. I want that property searched until that gun is found. Where are we at with the people on the guest list?"

"Peter Gottlieb isn't playing ball, sir," DS Skinner said. "I asked him for a list of people who attended the party, and he refused. He said something about respecting the privacy of his guests."

"I expected as much," O'Reilly said. "We'll have to go another route."

"What other route is there, sir?" DC Stone said.

"Find out if any of the Gottliebs have a firearms license, Andy," O'Reilly said. "If they don't, we threaten them with that."

"What if one of them does have a license for the gun?" DS Skinner said.

"We threaten them with a violation of the safe storage laws. Not only was that weapon clearly accessible to a little girl, but it was also obviously loaded, and that is against the law."

"It'll be difficult to prove, sir," DC Stone pointed out.

"We're not actually going to arrest them for it," O'Reilly said. "It'll be a long, drawn-out process that will most likely come to nothing. No, I just want to rattle them a bit. We'll get that guest list – you mark my words."

It wasn't going to be that easy. Two hours later, the weapon Barbara Gottlieb had fired was found. Neither Margot nor Peter had a license for a firearm, but it didn't make any difference because the shot that rang out came from a starting pistol. There was probably some violation of the law they could be charged with – a six-year-old shouldn't have had access to a starting pistol, but O'Reilly couldn't be bothered with the effort. He would have to find another way to get a list of the guests from the party.

He was on his way to the briefing room when his phone started to ring. He looked at the screen and saw that it was a number not in his contact list. He answered it anyway.

"O'Reilly."

"Liam." The voice was one he wasn't expecting to hear.

It was Chief Officer Robert Johnson.

"What can I do for you, sir?" O'Reilly asked.

"Have you got a minute for a chat?"

O'Reilly sensed that this wasn't a question.

"Of course, sir," he said. "I'll be right there."

He ended the call and made his way upstairs. He wondered what the man in charge of the Island Police wanted to talk to him about. He could only assume it was something relating to the Gottlieb family, and he wondered if the chief officer and the affluent family were acquainted. He hoped not – in his experience, when someone involved in an investigation thought they could call in favours from someone in their old boy network, it only caused headaches.

The door to Chief Officer Johnson's office was open so O'Reilly went straight in.

"Close the door," CO Johnson said.

O'Reilly pushed it shut and sat down opposite him at his desk.

"What is it you wanted to see me about?"

"Have you given any more thought to the GBA position?" CO Johnson said. O'Reilly wasn't expecting this.

"No, sir," he said. "There isn't much to think about – I'm very happy where I am."

"It's a highly sought after post, Liam," CO Johnson told him. "The salary increase aside – the position comes with very attractive perks."

"I'm aware of that, sir," O'Reilly said. "But a job in the border agency really isn't for me. My forte is detection – it's all I know, and I'm pretty good at it."

"I would seriously ask you to reconsider."

"With respect, sir," O'Reilly said. "My talents are better put to use where I am."

"Your name is at the top of the list. In fact, it is the only name on the list. That is unprecedented, and the men and women who put your name down are expecting you to accept the position."

"I see," O'Reilly said, even though he didn't.

"I'm glad we're on the same page."

O'Reilly thought about this for a moment. Was the chief of the Island Police telling him he didn't have a choice in the matter? He didn't think so. He hadn't applied for the DCI job in the border agency, and he certainly didn't want it.

"I'm flattered, sir," he said. "But I'm not the right person for the job. I'm sure they'll be able to find someone more suitable."

"Your file makes for interesting reading," CO Johnson said out of the blue.

"Sir?"

"Your record in the special detective agency of the Gardai is exemplary," CO Johnson added.

"I worked with a great team."

"I couldn't help but notice that there are gaps in your record. Prolonged gaps in fact."

"I was forced to take some time off for personal reasons, sir," O'Reilly said.

CO Johnson looked him in the eye. "Personal reasons. I spoke to your old chief superintendent recently. Jasper O'Hagan."

"He didn't like me very much," O'Reilly admitted.

"Chief Superintendent O'Hagan spoke about your personal problems. Your time off wouldn't have anything to do with your association with some people high up in the criminal fraternity, would it?"

"Is that what O'Hagan told you?" O'Reilly said.

"He mentioned someone known as *The Man*."

"I can't say I remember anyone by that name, sir."

CO Johnson nodded his head. "Good to hear it. I would urge you to reconsider the GBA position, Liam."

"I'll give it some thought," O'Reilly lied. "Will there be anything else?"

"I think that's all for now."

O'Reilly got to his feet.

"Enjoy the rest of your day, sir."

"Very good," CO Johnson said as the phone on his desk started to ring.

CHAPTER FIVE

O'Reilly needed some fresh air. He wasn't quite sure what the meeting with the chief officer had been about. If he didn't know any better, he would think the CO had issued some kind of veiled threat, and O'Reilly wondered why he'd been in contact with Chief Superintendent O'Hagan. And why did he mention *The Man*.

The Man had a hand in most of the criminal activities in Dublin back in the day. Whenever there was a drug bust or a gang-related murder in the city you could guarantee that *The Man* was involved. Nobody knew his real name and very few people had actually met him. He was a phantom who remained in the shadows. O'Reilly had made a stupid mistake one night. His intentions had been honourable, but the road to hell is often paved with those kinds of intentions, and O'Reilly had ended up in a particularly nasty kind of hell. He found himself indebted to a dangerous man. That debt had long been paid off, but once you've entered into a deal with someone like *The Man*, the deal is never quite done.

Why had Chief Officer Johnson brought it up now? O'Reilly couldn't think of an explanation for that, and why was he so keen for him to accept the GBA job? O'Reilly didn't have an answer for that either.

He crossed the road and headed north on the beach road that ran parallel to the esplanade. His belly was telling him he hadn't eaten anything since the seafood platter, and he needed to rectify that. The sun was beating down and the beach was packed. Summer was in full swing, and it was O'Reilly's favourite time on the island. He realised that this was his second summer on Guernsey. Two summers in, and the place already felt like home.

The café where he usually bought his cheese and ham sub was busier than usual and O'Reilly considered going somewhere else. He had work to do, and he couldn't afford to waste time waiting for his food. Fortunately, the waiter who usually served him was on duty and a simple *thumbs up* from both of them indicated that O'Reilly would like his usual, and the waiter would get onto it right away.

O'Reilly sat at a table at the back of the café. The window seats were all occupied with people he didn't recognise – tourists, probably. The sub was brought out five minutes later, and O'Reilly polished it off in record time. He paid the bill and added a generous tip for the waiter's prompt service.

He'd no sooner stepped outside into the sunshine when his phone started to ring. It was DC Owen.

"Katie," he said. "I'm just on my way back."

"We've got a body, sir," DC Owen said.

"Go on."

"A man was found over in Vazon," DC Owen said. "The woman who called it in was in quite a state. The words she used were *maimed beyond recognition*."

* * *

The man had been discovered on the rocks below the ancient walls of Fort Hommet. The popular tourist spot attracted a host of visitors in the summer, and O'Reilly wondered why the man had been left in that particular location. It didn't make any sense.

He got out of DC Stone's car and took a look around. It was mid-afternoon, and the area around the fort was relatively quiet. Most of the tourists were probably grabbing a bite to eat. The officers first on the scene had already secured the fort with police tape, indicating that it was strictly off limits. O'Reilly had been told that DI Peters and his team were on their way, and the first responders knew that nothing was to be touched until the forensics officers arrived.

O'Reilly walked over to DC Owen and DS Skinner. They were both standing a few metres away from the outer cordon. O'Reilly realised something – the twinge in his leg that had plagued him for months was not there anymore. The motorbike accident that had resulted in a broken femur had put him out of action for quite some time, but now the bone had returned to how it was before and there was no longer any pain when he walked.

"What do we know?" he asked DS Skinner.

"A couple found the body while they were exploring the rocks below the fort, sir," DS Skinner said. "The man got sick as soon as he saw what had been done to the man, but the woman handled it a bit better. She called it in straight away."

O'Reilly made a mental note to inform DI Peters about the vomit at the scene.

"This place is a popular tourist attraction," DC Owen said. "It's a strange place to dump a body, so I think this is probably where he was attacked."

"I'm inclined to agree with you, Katie," O'Reilly said.

"There's a broken wine bottle on the ground halfway between the clifftop and the fort," DS Skinner said. "You can still see the stain the wine made on the path."

O'Reilly looked out past the police tape at the sea beyond the clifftop. The water seemed different today. The brilliant blue was now lined with stripes of green and the chop was non-existent. It was a perfect postcard shot.

DI Peters arrived with DC Glenda Taylor. The Head of Forensics walked over to O'Reilly and joined him in admiring the scene in front of them.

"It really is something special, isn't it?"

"Picture postcard stuff," O'Reilly said.

"I was born on this island," DI Peters said. "And I never get tired of the views on days like this. What do we know?"

O'Reilly told him and it didn't take very long.

"One of the people who found the body lost the contents of his stomach," he added.

"I'll bear that in mind," DI Peters said. "Do we know if anyone else has been down there?"

"I don't think so."

"Did they touch the body?"

"I very much doubt it," O'Reilly said. "They found him, the bloke puked, and the woman called it in. I'll leave you to it. I need to speak to the poor bastards who found him."

CHAPTER SIX

The couple who had made the grisly discovery were sitting on one of the benches overlooking the cliffs. They introduced themselves as Jack and Kerry Wilson and told O'Reilly that they were on holiday on the island. Jack didn't look well at all. His eyes were puffy and red, and the skin on his face looked like the blood flow had been cut off to it. O'Reilly explained who he was and asked if either of them needed medical attention.

"It was just such a shock," Kerry said. "Jack and I were scrambling on the rocks and there he was. It was like something you'd see in a horror film."

"How long are you on the island for?" O'Reilly asked.

"Another week," Kerry told him.

"We're going to need you to come in and make a statement, but we can arrange a convenient time for that, and we can also get someone to come and pick you up."

"There's no need for that," Kerry said. "We're staying at the Royal on La Grange – the Island Police HQ is a five-minute walk away."

"I appreciate it," O'Reilly said.

Jack started to cough. He stood up and walked away. O'Reilly heard him clearing his throat, then he spat something onto the rocks.

When he came back, he looked even worse than he did when O'Reilly first saw him.

"Sorry about that," Jack said.

"Are you sure you're alright?" O'Reilly said. "Shock can be nasty."

"I've always had a weak stomach," Jack said. "And I'm terrified of the sight of blood. Did you see what had been done to that poor man?"

"I think you should get yourself checked over by the paramedics," O'Reilly suggested. "There's no shame in it."

He walked up to DC Owen and asked her to escort Jack to the ambulance.

"Could you talk me through what happened?" O'Reilly said to Kerry.

"We'd just finished walking around the fort," she said. "And we decided to do a bit of exploring on the rocks."

"Were there any other people around?"

"Hardly any. I read an online guide, and it said the quietest time to visit the fort was around noon. Most of the tourists usually go somewhere for lunch."

"Are you saying you had the place to yourself?"

"Not entirely. We saw a few other people when we were doing the tour of the fort."

"What about down by the rocks," O'Reilly said. "Was there anybody else down there?"

Kerry shook her head. "Nobody. He didn't get like that by taking a tumble, did he?"

"No," O'Reilly said. "It doesn't appear so."

Jack returned with a paper cup filled with hot tea.

"I'm fine," he said. "They told me to drink this, and not to drive for a while."

"Do you need a lift somewhere?" O'Reilly offered.

"We've got a hire car in the car park," Kerry said. "I can drive."

"If you could come in and make that statement," O'Reilly said. "It doesn't have to be today."

"We'll be there first thing in the morning," Kerry said. "The folks back home are not going to believe this. What a thing to happen on holiday."

"You'll definitely have a story to tell."

A grey-haired woman was talking to DC Stone next to the walls of the fort. O'Reilly walked over to them.

"This is Margaret Jones, sir," DC Stone said. "She's in charge of the fort."

Margaret started to laugh. It was a hearty laugh, and it was contagious. O'Reilly realised a smile had formed on his face.

"In charge of the fort," Margaret repeated. "It makes me sound like some kind of medieval relic. I'm not that old. No, I'm one of the many volunteers affiliated with the tourist trust who help out with the maintenance and upkeep of the fort. It's a listed protected monument and the upkeep isn't cheap. We have a collection box if you'd care to make a donation."

"I'll do that," O'Reilly said.

"They have CCTV, sir," DC Stone said.

"You have cameras?" O'Reilly asked Margaret.

"Two of them," she said. "One on the Martello Tower looking onto the old bunkers, and another facing out from the west side of the fortification."

"Can I ask why you might need cameras?" O'Reilly said.

"We've had some trouble with vandalism," Margeret explained. "Petty stuff mostly, but this fort is a national treasure, and it needs to be protected. And we've had the odd incident where kids have tried to get into the bunkers. Most of them were sealed off years ago, but you know what kids are like."

"Would you be able to show us the footage?" O'Reilly said.

"I'm afraid not."

"We can get a warrant if necessary," O'Reilly said.

Margaret laughed again. "I didn't mean it like that. I can give you the entire history of the fort from its construction in 1680 through to the end of the Second World War when the British forces stripped the artillery and the blast doors, but what I know about computers can be written on the back of a postage stamp. I'll ask Harold to get in touch with you."

"Is he your IT guy?" DC Stone said.

"He's a lowly volunteer like me," Margaret said. "But he has youth on his side."

"Could you get hold of him now please?" O'Reilly asked. "That CCTV footage is very important."

"What happened to the poor man on the rocks?"

"We're not sure yet," O'Reilly said. "Where is that collection box you spoke about?"

"In front of the entrance to the shrine of the Sacred Heart," Margaret said.

CHAPTER SEVEN

Harold Michaels was a man who firmly believed that when opportunity knocked you had to grab hold of it with both hands and keep hold of it. And now, with his eyes glued to the screen of his laptop, opportunity was knocking, harder than it ever had before. Harold had been informed by Margaret Jones that the Island Police were very keen to get hold of the CCTV footage from Fort Hommet – Harold got the sense that the camera footage was important to them, and he wasn't mistaken.

"This is pure gold," he said to the laptop.
He'd watched the footage from 9pm the previous night, and now he was viewing it again. The sun had recently set, but there was still a glow of half-light to see by.

At 9:15 the camera on the west side of the fort picked up a flicker of movement by the rocks at the top of the cliff. Two figures approached and for a brief moment both of them were caught beautifully on camera. It was two men, and the stagger in their gaits suggested that they were both drunk. The shorter of the two raised a bottle in the air and looked straight at the camera as if he was aware that he was being filmed.

The men disappeared from view for a few minutes and then they appeared once more. This time they were further away, and it was difficult to make out what they were doing. Harold knew that the cameras were only mid-range models and when he tried to zoom in, he cursed the person responsible for buying them. The pixilation was terrible, and the image was so blurred it was impossible to see what was happening.

But then the men moved closer. The short man was gesturing wildly with both hands. His friend clearly didn't appreciate this, and he backed away a few paces. The two men remained like this for over a minute, and then the Mexican standoff was broken when the short man rushed at his friend like a rhino charging a car. The tall man was knocked to the ground and that's where he stayed. The bottle was brought down on his head three times, and the mouth of the short man opened wide. If the CCTV could record sound, it would have captured a noise so guttural and primal it would have chilled the marrow in Harold Michaels' bones.

The short man didn't stop there. Harold watched as he smashed the bottle on the ground and proceeded to ram the jagged glass into his taller friend's face. It made for disturbing viewing, but Harold didn't look away. The short man's arms were now raised skywards, and he mouthed another silent scream. The bottle fell from his grip and landed on the path.

Then something strange happened. The short man froze in his tracks for so long that Harold had to check that he hadn't paused the footage by mistake. The time display at the bottom of the screen told him he hadn't. After a couple of minutes, the short man's hands were placed on his face, and he crouched down next to his dead friend. Then he took hold of one of the other man's feet and dragged him out of the shot.

"Pure gold," Harold said.

He opened his browser and sought out the contact details of the island's top two newspapers. The details for the Guernsey Gazette and the Island Herald were easy to come by. Harold sent an identical email to both of them: *What would you be willing to pay for CCTV footage of a murder?*

* * *

"What's taking him so long?" O'Reilly said.

Margaret Jones had promised to inform Harold Michaels that the Island Police needed the CCTV footage quickly, and he in turn had agreed to get onto it straight away, but it had been three hours and there was still no sign of it.

"Get hold of him," O'Reilly said to DC Stone. "Explain the urgency."

"I've tried," DC Stone said. "He's not answering his phone."

"Keep trying."

The forensics team were still busy at the scene by Fort Hommet, but DI Peters had informed O'Reilly about an interesting find. There was a broken wine bottle on the path between the fort and the cliff and he'd found what appeared to be blood stains on the ground. There were also shoeprints in the dirt and two indentations on the path that ran all the way to the rocks where the body was found. DI Peters deduced two things from this – the injuries the man sustained were caused by the broken bottle, and his body was dragged away from the path and down to the rocks.

"The fekkin' camera was pointing at the exact spot where the wine bottle was found, Andy," O'Reilly said. "Which means it'll have probably caught the whole thing on tape. I want that footage now."

DC Stone called Harold Michaels for the tenth time and got the same result. The voicemail message informed him that he was unable to take the call at present.

"Still nothing," DC Stone said.

DC Owen came inside the office.

"Peter Gottlieb has had a change of heart, sir," she said. "We've got a list of the guests who were at the party yesterday."

"What made him change his mind," O'Reilly said.

"He didn't say."

"How many are we talking about?"

"Nineteen."

"Prioritise them," O'Reilly told her. "Some of the guests weren't injured in any way, and those are the ones I want to concentrate on. Why were some of them spared? The evidence of the violence on display yesterday is very disturbing, but why were some of the guests left alone?"

"I've also heard from the hospital," DC Owen said. "The man who was badly maimed is out of surgery and he's up to talking to us."

"I'll take care of that myself," O'Reilly said. "Andy, you can come with me – I need a driver."

"I thought you were allowed to drive now, sir," DC Stone said.

"That's neither here nor there, Andy. As the old saying goes - you don't buy a dog and bark yourself."

"Sir?"

"Never mind. Are you ready to go?"

CHAPTER EIGHT

O'Reilly wasn't sure what to expect when he and DC Stone went inside Mark Spring's hospital room, but he really didn't anticipate someone who resembled an Egyptian mummy. Mark was sitting up on the bed drinking water through a straw. His entire face was swathed in bandages. Gaps had been left for his nose, mouth and one of his eyes, but the rest of the face was covered up. The doctor they'd spoken to had informed them that Mark had been lucky. It had been touch and go as to whether he would lose his left eye, but even though the eyeball had been dislodged from its socket, the medical team had worked quickly and managed to reattach it. Whether he would lose the sight in it was something that only time would tell. Mark had suffered lacerations to his nose, mouth and cheeks - some of them were quite deep, but most were superficial, and they would heal in time.

O'Reilly pulled up a couple of chairs and he and DC Stone sat down next to the bed.
"How are you feeling?" O'Reilly asked.
"Utterly confused," Mark replied. "I'm still trying to come to terms with what happened yesterday."
"The docs said you were lucky."
"I don't feel lucky. Would you feel lucky if your fiancé put you in hospital? Would you consider yourself fortunate if the woman you've known for ten years suddenly turned into a monster and tried to kill you?"

O'Reilly didn't reply to this.
"Can you talk us through what happened yesterday?" he said.
"It was a great party," Mark said. "As usual. The Gottlieb affairs rarely disappoint. The food was top notch, and there was plenty to drink for those who are that way inclined."
"You're not a drinker then?" DC Stone said.

"I used to be," Mark told him. "Until things hit rock bottom. It's a long story, and I've been three years dry."

"Good for you," O'Reilly said. "How are you acquainted with the Gottliebs?"

"I've known Peter and Margot for about five years. I assist Peter with the financial side of his business interests. He's a good man – he's firm but fair, and that's why I couldn't believe it when I came back to the house and saw what he was doing to Sasha."

"Sasha?" O'Reilly said.

"Sasha Ballantyne, sir," DC Stone said. "She was the woman who nearly drowned."

Mark reached over to pick up the bottle of water on the table.

"Jesus."

"Are you alright?" O'Reilly said.

"Every inch of my face burns," Mark said.

DC Stone grabbed the bottle and handed it to him. "Try not to move too much."

"You were talking about what Peter Gottlieb did to Sasha," O'Reilly said.

"I thought I was imagining it," Mark said. "I couldn't see out of my left eye, and I thought my mind was playing tricks on me. Peter Gottlieb was on the edge of the pool, and he was holding someone under the water. I didn't know it was Sasha at the time, but Naomi told me about it when she was here earlier."

"Naomi is your fiancé?" O'Reilly said. "She's the one who did that to your face?"

"She can't remember doing it."

O'Reilly thought about this, and he didn't know how to interpret it. The only person who attended the Gottlieb party who had any recollection of the events that spiralled into violence was sitting in the hospital bed in front of him, and he wasn't sure why that was.

"Can you remember the events that led to your fiancé becoming violent?" he asked.

"It was shortly before the dessert was due to be served," Mark said. "Neither Naomi nor I are dessert people, so we decided to take a walk around the grounds. A few other people did the same."

"There were others who walked with you?" DC Stone said.

"We didn't all head in the same direction. Naomi and I took the path that led up to the clifftop, and the others opted for the gentler route on the west side of the estate."

"It sounds like quite a large property," O'Reilly said.

"Peter and Margot own twenty-two acres," Mark said.

"What happened then?" O'Reilly said.

"Naomi told me she felt funny, and I asked her how much she'd had to drink. Perhaps that was a mistake."

"Does your fiancé like to drink?" DC Stone said.

"Not excessively," Mark said. "She told me she'd had a couple of glasses of wine with lunch, and I asked her if she was sure?"

"Why would you ask that?" O'Reilly said.

"Because two glasses of red wine wouldn't normally affect her like that. That was when she started to scare me."

"What did she do?" DC Stone said.

"She became aggressive. And she started swearing at me. Naomi hardly ever swears."

A nurse entered the room.

"Is everything OK?"

"Could I get some stronger painkillers please?" Mark asked him. "The ones you gave me aren't working."

"I'll sort something out for you."

The nurse checked the drip next to the bed and left them to it.

"What did you do when Naomi became aggressive?" O'Reilly said.

"I told her I couldn't talk to her when she was like this, and I turned to walk away. She screamed at me and the next thing I know she's on my back with her fingers clawing at my face. I shook her off, but she came back for more. She started punching me on the back and then she gouged out my eyeball. That's when I knew I had to get out of there."

"Has Naomi ever been violent in the past?" O'Reilly asked.

"Never," Mark said. "She's the kindest soul you could ever meet. She's a big softie."

"You said she came to visit you earlier," DC Stone said.

"That's right. She can't remember doing any of this to me."

Mark raised a hand and place it gently on his face.

O'Reilly's phoned beeped to tell him he'd received a message. He glanced at the screen and saw it was Assumpta. The message was brief.

Call me now.

O'Reilly knew something serious had happened.

"Mr Spring," he said. "I have to ask you this – do you wish to press charges?"

"What?" Mark said.

"Your fiancé assaulted you," DC Stone elaborated. "She put you in hospital. Do you want to take it further?"

"Of course not," Mark said. "I don't know what happened yesterday, and neither does Naomi."

"Do you have any idea what could have caused the people at the party to behave in the way they did?" O'Reilly said.

"I don't," Mark said. "I've known most of them for years, and in all that time I've never known them to act like that. It was as if a wave of madness descended and washed over them. It carried them along and left a trail of destruction in its wake."

CHAPTER NINE

"I wonder if he's been doing the same online course as me," DC Stone said in the car park of the hospital.

O'Reilly looked up from his phone and frowned. "What?"

"A wave of madness descends," DC Stone said. "It washes over them all and leaves a trail of destruction in its wake. I reckon he's subscribed to my creative writing course."

"Shut up, Andy," O'Reilly said. "I need to make a call."

He walked away from the shifty-eyed detective and called his daughter. Assumpta answered immediately. "Have you seen the latest Herald post?"

"You know I don't care about the drivel that Viking puts out," O'Reilly said.

"You'll want to see this, Dad," Assumpta said. "The Gazette received an email earlier asking how much we'd be willing to pay for CCTV footage of a murder. Of course, we ignored it, but it seems that the Island Herald didn't. You need to take a look at their online forum, Dad."

"I'll do that. Is it bad?"

"Somehow, someone got hold of footage of the murder up by Fort Hommet. Fred Viking has put it out for the whole world to see."

O'Reilly thanked Assumpta and ended the call. He walked back to where DC Stone was smoking a cigarette next to his car.

"We've got a problem, Andy."

"What is it, sir?" DC Stone said.

"Can you bring up the online thing for the Island Herald on your phone?"

"Of course."

DC Stone took out his phone and swiped the screen. He tapped a few times. "What the hell?"

He shifted the phone so O'Reilly could see the screen too. A mobile phone wasn't the ideal device to watch the footage that had been posted on the

Island Herald's site, but it was sufficient. O'Reilly could make out the path where the broken wine bottle had been found earlier, and he recognised the view beyond the cliffs. The level of violence on display was not something that ought to be available for public viewing, and O'Reilly was determined to make the people responsible for airing it pay the highest price possible.

He called DC Owen.

"Katie, I want you to find the address for Harold Michaels. He was the man who was supposed to get us the CCTV footage from Fort Hommet."

"What's going on, sir?" DC Owen asked.

"It looks like the fekkin' idiot has sold the footage to the Island Herald," O'Reilly said. "And it's already live."

"You're kidding me?"

"I'm afraid not. And I want Fred Viking arrested. Can you arrange for some uniforms to bring him in."

"On what grounds, sir?" DC Owen said. "Freedom of the press is a grey area in terms of the law."

"Make something up," O'Reilly said. "Perverting the course of justice. Public indecency. I don't care – I want Fred *the Ed* hauled in and I want it done now."

O'Reilly was furious. He'd had his fair share of run ins with the editor of the Island Herald, but Fred Viking had outdone himself this time. O'Reilly didn't think he could stoop any lower than he had done in the past, but clearly there were no limits to how low he would go for the sake of a juicy story.

"What are we going to do, sir?" DC Stone asked.

The message notification tone on O'Reilly's phone prevented him from answering. He read the message and put the phone back in his pocket.

"Do you know La Mare Road in Castel?"

"I do, sir," DC Stone said. "I know most of the roads on the island."

"That's where we're going. As quick as you like."

* * *

Fred Viking was a naturally self-opinionated man but he was feeling particularly smug right now. A piece he was supposed to be having a final read through regarding the unusually high influx of tourists this year had been sidelined so Fred could keep an eye on the ratings on the online version of the Island Herald. The article on the increasing numbers of people flocking to the island in the summer months paled into insignificance compared to the piece of journalistic gold dust that had fallen into Fred's lap earlier in the day.

When the email had landed in his inbox, Fred had sensed there was something authentic in the tone of the message. His instincts were telling him that this message was genuine, and he'd replied immediately.

Let's talk.

The reply had come back within a minute.

Make me an offer.

Fred had to think quickly. Even though his gut was telling him that this was the real deal, he would be derelict in his duty if he didn't get some kind of confirmation.

I'm interested, but I need some kind of proof that this is genuine.

This time the reply took longer to appear.

I don't want anyone to know where you got this. I don't want the police to come calling.

Fred assured the sender that he would keep it anonymous, and he couldn't help adding:

The Island Police don't know their arses from their elbows – especially the dickhead who thinks he's in charge. Chief Officer Robert Johnson is an imbecile.

Fred felt especially pleased with himself now. He waited for a reply, and it didn't take long to materialise.

Consider this a taster.

This message came with an attachment. Fred's hands were shaking as he clicked on it. The clip wasn't long – no more than fifteen seconds, but it served to whet the appetite. Fred knew he was on the verge of something very special. He thought hard about how much he would be willing to pay, and he decided to take a gamble.

How much?

When the figure appeared on the screen, Fred knew his gamble had paid off. The sender of the email had demanded much less than Fred had been willing to pay. The funds were transferred, and Fred composed a short email guaranteeing that the identity of the sender would remain anonymous, and the full video clip was promptly sent over.

It was posted to the online forum within the hour and Fred Viking was feeling very smug indeed. The ratings were soaring. In the space of an hour the number on the top of the screen had already surpassed the record ratings for a single post, and Fred knew he was in possession of something extremely valuable.

He wasn't mistaken. When the door to his office burst open and a red-faced Gary Powers came in with two uniformed police officers, Fred Viking began to understand how valuable the CCTV footage actually was.

CHAPTER TEN

"Fred Viking has been arrested," O'Reilly said.

They'd just arrived at La Mare Road in Castel, and DC Owen had sent him a message to let him know.

DC Stone turned off the engine. "Do we have enough to hold him?"

"Probably not, Andy," O'Reilly said. "But a police interrogation ought to inconvenience him a bit."

"That video clip was pretty gruesome. Surely there are laws about broadcasting such graphic media. Kids can log onto that site."

"Will and Katie know what they're doing. They'll put the wind up him."

"It's a shame the DCI isn't back until next week," DC Stone said. "He knows the law better than any lawyer on the island, and he'd be able to nail Viking for something."

DCI Tom Fish was still on leave. He and Superintendent Anne Hayes were still getting to grips with the joys of parenthood. Superintendent Hayes had given birth to a baby girl a few weeks ago, and neither she nor DCI Fish had set foot inside the station since the birth.

"No doubt Viking will come up with some freedom of the press bull," O'Reilly said. "But's he's outdone himself with this one. Posting footage of an actual murder is sick, even by his standards."

"How are we going to play it with Mr Michaels?" DC Stone asked.

"Aggressively. When a vital piece of evidence is leaked to the press it makes my blood boil."

Harold Michaels wasn't what O'Reilly expected at all. Margaret Jones had described him as someone with youth on his side but the man standing in the doorway of number 88 Rue La Mere looked older than the Irish detective. If O'Reilly were to describe him, he would use the word *thin*. Everything about him was thin. He was very tall, and his spindly arms were unusually long. He was wearing a pair of shorts, and his stick-like legs looked like a decent kick would break them in half. Even his head was thin. It wasn't much wider than the long neck it was attached to. When he looked down at the two Island Police officers on his doorstep, he resembled a stick insect inspecting a leaf.

"Can I help you?"
"Harold Michaels?" O'Reilly said.
"That's me."
"I'm DI O'Reilly, and this is DC Stone from the Island Police. Can we come in for chat."
"I assume you have some kind of identification," Harold said. "You don't look like police detectives, especially him."
This was directed at DC Stone.
"He gets that a lot," O'Reilly said and took out his ID.
DC Stone did the same.

They sat outside in the small space that passed for a garden.
"I believe you're a volunteer for the tourist trust," O'Reilly said.
"That's right. I like to do my bit for the island."
"That's very commendable of you. What do you do for a living?"
"IT," Harold said, rather vaguely.
"Computers?" O'Reilly said. "I'm afraid my knowledge of modern technology is rather limited, but you must know your stuff."
"I do alright."
"Can you explain to us why it is you haven't managed to forward the Island Police the CCTV footage we asked for hours ago. I was led to believe you would get to it right away, and a man with your expertise ought to have done it pretty quickly."
"What exactly are you doing here?" Harold asked.

"I asked you a question," O'Reilly said. "Where is that CCTV footage?"

"I got a bit sidetracked. I'll get onto it right away for you."

"It's a bit late for that," DC Stone said.

"Do you subscribe to the Island Herald's online site?" O'Reilly said.

"I don't really follow the news," Harold said.

"I'm going to ask you to cut the crap now," O'Reilly said. "How much did Viking pay you?"

"I have no idea what you're talking about."

"I don't believe you. You sent an email to the Island Herald asking them how much they would be willing to pay for CCTV footage of a murder. Does that ring any bells?"

Harold got to his feet. He stretched his weedy arms and looked down at O'Reilly.

"How? How did you trace it back to me?"

"Come on, Mr Michaels," O'Reilly said. "You may be an expert in IT, but you seem to be somewhat lacking in the commonsense department. Who else could have sold the footage? It doesn't take a genius to figure it out. How much did he pay you?"

"A grand," Harold whispered.

"I didn't quite catch that."

"A thousand pounds," Harold said, louder this time. "Am I in trouble?"

"You should be," O'Reilly said. "We could bring you in for wasting police time but, ironically all that would achieve would be to waste even more police time. We could have you for attempting to pervert the course of justice though. What's the maximum sentence for that, Andy? My memory isn't what it used to be."

"Five years, sir," DC Stone said. "Or a fine of up to fifty thousand pounds. Sometimes both."

"You can't be serious?" Harold said. "I'll give the money back."

"It's a bit late for that," O'Reilly said. "Although there might be a way you can make things right."

"I'll do anything. I can't go to jail. It would kill me."

O'Reilly told him what he had in mind.

* * *

Less than a mile away, an argument was brewing between an elderly couple sitting on the rocks to the southwest of Cobo beach. Otto and Frieda Klein had enjoyed a relaxing lunch and a few drinks at the beachfront restaurant, and they'd taken a stroll along the beach in the late afternoon sunshine. Frieda was reminding her husband about the one time in their marriage when he'd strayed. The affair lasted no longer than a week and the adultery had occurred over thirty years ago.

Otto didn't know why Frieda had decided to bring it all back up now – he certainly wasn't expecting it, nor did he anticipate the blow to the head from the rock he didn't realise his wife was holding in her hand.

CHAPTER ELEVEN

When O'Reilly went inside the station, he was instantly aware of a pungent stench in the reception area. It was a blend of something sickly sweet and a reek that reminded him of sour milk. The expression on PC Woodbine's face behind the reception desk told him that he could smell it too.

"Who died?" O'Reilly asked him.

"A man came in just now, sir," PC Woodbine said. "He was dressed like an old tramp, and he stank like nothing I've ever smelled before. The stench lingered even after he'd gone."

"What did he want?"

"He came in to confess to the murder by Fort Hommet. He stank of booze, and that stink you can still smell."

"Where is he now?" O'Reilly said.

"I sent him on his way, sir," the giant PC said. "He was just a drunken timewaster."

"A man comes in to confess to a murder," O'Reilly said. "And you dismiss him because of his appearance. What were you thinking?"

"You didn't see him, sir."

"What exactly did he tell you?" O'Reilly asked.

"He said he killed someone, but he can't remember doing it. He kept shoving his mobile phone in my face the whole time. I promise you - he was a real nutcase."

O'Reilly looked around. There was nobody else in the area by the front desk.

"You fekkin' idiot," he said to PC Woodbine.

"Sir?"

"What did he look like? What was he wearing?"

PC Woodbine described him, and O'Reilly hurried out of the station.

It didn't take him long to catch up with the man. He could smell him before he saw him. O Reilly followed him until he stopped by the railing on the esplanade. He took out a cigarette and lit it. O'Reilly put his hand over his nose and took a deep breath with his mouth. The stench really was disgusting. The man responsible for the stink looked to be around the same age as O'Reilly. His hair looked like it hadn't been washed in weeks and it stuck to his scalp like it had been glued in place. His face was blotchy and the visible blood vessels on his cheeks and nose suggested he was a very heavy drinker. He wasn't very tall, but he was stockily built, and he'd walked with the swagger of an ex-boxer. He was dressed in a pair of filthy jeans and a T-shirt.

O'Reilly made his way over to him.
"Excuse me."
The man turned to face him.
"Can I have a word?" O'Reilly said.
"I'll move on in a minute."
"There's no need for that," O'Reilly told him.
"I know you. I've seen you in the papers. You're police. You need to train your youngsters better."
"I have no idea what you're talking about," O'Reilly said.
"That makes me smarter than you then, doesn't it?"

The reek of the man was starting to make O'Reilly feel ill. Tourists were walking by, but they were all giving them a wide berth.
A filthy hand was extended. "Mike Trunk at your service, sir."
O'Reilly didn't shake the hand.
"You came in to confess to a murder," he said. "Is that correct?"
"I might be an occasional drunk," Mike said. "But that doesn't make me a monster. Although I have no recollection of the episode. None whatsoever, and that, my friend has never happened to me before. Do you like a drink?"

"Sometimes," O'Reilly said. "Do you want to tell me what's on your mind? We can do that back at the station."

Mike seemed to be mulling this over. He took a long drag on the cigarette that had obviously gone out and nodded.

"I don't understand it," he said. "If I hadn't seen the video, I never would have believed it, but there's no doubting that it was me in that clip. Bizarre is the only way to describe it."

"Let's talk back at the station," O'Reilly said. "I'll arrange for some food and perhaps a change of clothes for you."

"Much obliged, sir," Mike said. "Lead the way."

Five minutes later O'Reilly went inside his office and booted up his laptop. He switched on the kettle to make some tea while he waited. Mike Trunk had been offered a shower and a change of clothes. It was more for O'Reilly's benefit than the strange drunken man's. PC London had found some clean clothes in lost property, and O'Reilly hoped that the stench would be gone when he interviewed the man later. O'Reilly had also asked someone to go and fetch some food for the drunkard.

He made the tea and sat down in front of his laptop. He opened the file containing the CCTV footage from Fort Hommet and started to watch. Harold Michaels had given him a copy of the footage, and he'd also given him a copy of the email thread between him and Fred Viking. The editor of the Island Herald was also somewhere in the station but the hospitality he was receiving was nowhere near as pleasant as what had been offered to the rank-smelling sot.

There was something in the words Mike Trunk had spoken that made O'Reilly believe him. He was a drunk, but he'd been lucid when he spoke about the murder. He claimed he couldn't recall the events surrounding the murder, but he'd seen himself in the video footage, so it had to be true. O'Reilly had to agree with him – bizarre was the only way to describe it.

O'Reilly watched the footage from start to finish, then he watched it again. He hovered the cursor over the pause option and clicked it when the faces of both men were captured in the footage. The taller man looked slightly older than the short, squat man but there was little doubt in O'Reilly's mind that Mike Trunk was the person who had maimed the man found on the rocks by Fort Hommet. His grimy face was staring right back at him. O'Reilly could almost smell the funk of him.

CHAPTER TWELVE

O'Reilly was pleasantly surprised when he and DC Owen went inside the interview room. Mike Trunk looked like a totally different man to the one he'd spoken to on the esplanade. His hair was washed, the clothes he'd been given were clean, and there was no trace of the offensive odour he'd brought in with him earlier. If O'Reilly passed him on the street, he would think this was just another tourist on the island.

The CCTV footage was damning. There was no doubt the person who killed the man by Fort Hommet was the same man sitting in the chair in his borrowed clothes, but O'Reilly needed more than that. Mike Trunk had come to the station to confess to a murder he had no recollection of committing, and this made O'Reilly curious. The murder was brutal, but why did the killer not remember it?

O'Reilly turned on the recording device and got the formalities out of the way.

"Mr Trunk," he said. "Can you tell us why you came to the station earlier today?"

"Please, call me Mike. I saw my ugly mug on the Internet."

"Could you elaborate on that?" DC Owen said.

"I'll do my best, love. I like to keep abreast of the news. It pays to know what's going on in my line of work."

"What do you do?" O'Reilly said.

"Finance," Mike said. "Of sorts. I'm a very adept financial adviser. Basically, I advise them to invest in my drinking habit, and I used to be a lot better at it than I am now."

"Mr Trunk," O'Reilly said. "Mike, you come across as a well-educated man. How the devil did you end up like this?"

"Circumstances," Mike said. "An unfortunate series of events. I got tired of the corporate world before they got tired of me, I suppose. I like to drink, you see. Sometimes I might not touch a drop for weeks, but when I fall into the old ways, I can binge a week or two away. I'm not a mean drunk though. There's nothing I hate more than a mean drunk."

"Can you remember anything at all about last night?" O'Reilly asked.
"What are you saying?" Mike said.
"You told me you can't recall the events captured in the CCTV footage."
"That part is correct."
"Do you remember what happened earlier on?" DC Owen said.
"I do."
"The man you were seen with," O'Reilly said. "Who is he?"
They still had no idea who the dead man was. He didn't have any form of identification on him, and nobody had come forward with any information about him.

"He's an acquaintance of mine," Mike told him. "Our paths cross every now and again."
"Do you have a name for us?" O'Reilly said.
"Woody."
"Woody?" DC Owen repeated.
"That's all I can tell you," Mike said. "That's all I got out of him, and it was sufficient."

"How did you end up by the fort?" O'Reilly said.
"That was Woody's idea," Mike said. "We'd had a bit to drink on the beach and he suggested a trek up to the fort. Who was I to argue?"
"I'm not following you."
"Woody provided the booze," Mike explained. "So I could hardly disappoint the man, and pretty decent booze it was too. Cabernet Sauvignon – excellent vintage."
"How much did you have to drink?" DC Owen said.

"The same as usual."

"Could you explain what you mean by that?" O'Reilly said.

"I apologise," Mike said. "It's an old boozer joke. *How much did you have to drink? Same as usual – all of it*. In this case it was four bottles. It's all that Woody could manage to nick."

"He stole the wine?" DC Owen said.

"I happen to know a bit about wine," Mike said. "And reds like that must easily go for a hundred quid a bottle. Of course he stole it. Drunks like us don't pay that kind of money to achieve oblivion."

"OK," O'Reilly said. "You had a drink on the beach, and you made your way up to the fort. What happened then?"

"There was only one bottle left," Mike said. "Which is probably for the best. I don't mind admitting that I started to feel a bit peculiar. Woody too."

"You felt sick?" DC Owen said.

"Not sick, really – more not quite myself. It's hard to explain."

"What did you do when you started to feel unwell?" O'Reilly said.

"I have no idea."

"Is that when you blacked out?" DC Owen said.

"I don't recall blacking out," Mike said. "If that makes any sense, but I must have because there is a gap in my memory between the time I realised there was something wrong with me, and coming to my senses on the beach below. It was daytime then, and I wondered where Woody had ended up. It was only afterwards when I saw the video footage that it dawned on me what had happened."

O'Reilly didn't know what else to ask him. The description of the events leading up to the murder were very clear. Mike Trunk recalled everything up until the time of the murder, but he had no recollection at all of killing this Woody character.

"Mike," O'Reilly said. "Do you think you had any reason to want Woody dead?"

"None at all," Mike said. "We weren't especially close friends, but we always got on. We enjoyed a drink together. That's why I got the fright of my life when I saw what I'd done to him, and that's why I came straight here to confess."

"Why exactly did you do that?" O'Reilly said. "Is it because of the CCTV footage? Did you realise that the game was up, and it was only a matter of time before we found you?"

"That didn't even cross my mind," Mike said. "I came to confess because it was the decent thing to do. I have no idea what made me kill Woody but kill him I did, and I needed to do the right thing."

CHAPTER THIRTEEN

"I'm flummoxed, Katie," O'Reilly said.

"You're not the only one, sir," DC Owen said.

"We've got a man in hospital with serious facial injuries. The wounds were inflicted by his fiancé, but he refuses to take it any further. The fiancé can't remember hurting him. We have a woman who almost drowned, and we have a witness who saw the man who held her head under the water. But Peter Gottlieb can't remember doing that either, and now we have a man confessing to a murder he has no recollection of carrying out. What's going on, Katie?"

"I'm as lost as you," DC Owen said.

"Whatever next?" O'Reilly wondered.

He was about to find out.

DC Stone came inside the office with a grave expression on his face. "What's up, Andy?" O'Reilly asked him. "Did you fail your first creative writing module?"

"Very funny, sir." DC Stone wasn't laughing. "We've had a report of another murder. An old woman was found wandering aimlessly on Cobo Beach. She was confused, and she claimed to have killed her husband."

"Was she telling the truth?"

"Unfortunately, she was. He was found a couple of hundred metres away on the rocks. His head has been bashed in."

"Jesus," O'Reilly said. "Where is she now? Where is the old lady?"

"She was taken to hospital. She's very confused."

"What is this madness?" O'Reilly said. "What the hell is happening to the people on this island?"

"Do you think these events are linked, sir?" DC Stone said.

"How? How can a spate of violence at an upper-class party be connected to a drunkard killing his friend and an old lady bashing her husband's brains in?"

"It's just odd, that's all," DC Stone said. "That it's all happened within a short space of time. I've never seen anything like it."

"How is Mr Viking bearing up?" O'Reilly changed the subject.

"He's not impressed, sir," DC Owen said.

"Good."

"The threat about the insult to CO Johnson seemed to have the desired effect," DC Owen added. "Fred has promised to take the CCTV footage off the site."

"I thought that might work."

"I hinted that the email thread between Fred and Harold Michaels might end up in the hands of the Guernsey Gazette," DC Owen said. "And he fell for it."

"The Gazette wouldn't print something like that," DC Stone argued. "Assumpta and Fiona have more integrity than that."

"Fred *the Ed* clearly didn't want to take the risk," O'Reilly said. "You do not call the chief of the Island Police a dickhead on paper. I assume Fred has been allowed to go."

"He has," DC Owen confirmed. "I doubt he'll pull a stunt like that again in a hurry."

"Don't underestimate the man, Katie."

"What now, sir?" DC Stone said.

"What now?" O'Reilly mused. "Now we all go home. We go home and distance ourselves from the insanity that seems to have taken a hold of the island. At least for a few hours anyway. We'll crack on in the morning."

"Are you alright, sir?" DC Owen asked.

"Grand, Katie. Just grand. Get yourself off home. I'm planning on getting a bit drunk tonight – if there was ever a time when I needed a few drinks in me, it's right now. I'll see you both in the morning."

O'Reilly left the station and turned onto La Grange. He carried on for a hundred metres or so and stopped so abruptly, a man walking behind him almost collided with him.

"What the hell is wrong with you?"

"Sorry about that," O'Reilly said to him. "I forgot where I lived for a moment."

The man observed him as though he'd suddenly grown another nose and made a hasty departure.

O'Reilly had told the truth. For a brief moment he still thought he lived in the apartment in the capital. Even though he'd been living with Victoria in her house in Vazon for quite some time, he'd set off on the short walk to his old apartment on Belmont Road out of habit.

"This damn madness is contagious."

He spoke the words out loud, and a young couple up ahead crossed over the road.

He made his way back to the station just in time. DC Owen was heading for her car.

"Can I trouble you for a lift, Katie?" O'Reilly asked her.

"No trouble at all, sir," she said. "Where have you been?"

"Can you believe I set off for my old place like I used to. My mind is on other things."

"We'll figure it out. When don't we figure it out?"

"Wise words, Katie Owen," O'Reilly said.

The drive passed in silence for the first mile or so. O'Reilly gazed out of the window as they headed inland. The traffic was heavier than usual, but it always was in the summer.

"Do you think the recent events are connected?" O'Reilly asked the question DC Stone had put forward as they were passing the green of the nature reserve in Kings Mills.

"I really don't know," DC Owen said. "It is strange that it's all happened so quickly. And the fact that everyone involved seem to have acted so out of character makes me think that there is some kind of link."

"Tomorrow is another day."

"What are your plans for this evening?"

"Another meal out," O'Reilly decided. "Even though I ate a seafood platter for two last night, and a cheese and ham sub that would feed an army, there seems to be a hole in my belly that I need to fill."

CHAPTER FOURTEEN

The Cobo Beach Hotel was a ten-minute walk from Victoria's house in Vazon so they decided to go there on foot. It was a glorious, warm evening without a puff of wind in the air, and O'Reilly reckoned a walk would do them good. It didn't cross his mind that the leisurely stroll would take them past the scenes of two brutal murders until he gazed across at the stone walls of Fort Hommet and he remembered the old man who had been beaten to death on the rocks two-hundred metres further north. He realised he and Victoria would have to walk past those rocks on their way to the hotel.

A quick glance to the left told O'Reilly that the forensics team were still busy at the scene. DI Peters' car was parked at the south side of the pavilion, and O'Reilly wondered what they were still doing there. Surely it was an open and shut case – the old lady had confessed to killing her husband, so what else was there to say on the matter? O'Reilly didn't dwell on it. The meal out was supposed to be helping him take his mind of the investigation.

"Are you OK?" Victoria asked.
"I'm fine," O'Reilly said.
"You seem a bit preoccupied."
"You know me too well."
"I married you, Liam," Victoria said. "Of course I know you well. Penny for them."
"The thoughts inside my head right now are not worth a penny."
O'Reilly reached down and took hold of Victoria's hand.
"Let's pretend we're here on holiday," he said. "Nothing else matters this evening but sea air, good food and even better company."

The hotel had an outside terrace facing onto Cobo Bay and that's where O'Reilly and Victoria chose to sit. A waiter handed them two menus and asked if they wanted something to drink. O'Reilly ordered a *Scapegoat* and Victoria settled on a mineral water.

"This is nice," Victoria said. "I haven't been here for ages."
"This is the first time I've been," O'Reilly said. "The view is spectacular though. How are things at work?"
"Getting back to normal. Tommy isn't treating me like I might break any second."
"That's big brothers for you. Wasn't it about this time last year when the bike rally was here?"
"The *Grunt*," Victoria said. "It was, but it's been cancelled this year. There's talk of it being a permanent cancellation."
"Because of what happened last year?"
"People are still talking about that madman."
"At least something good came of it," O'Reilly said. "That's where we met."
Victoria smiled. "It is an unusual tale to tell. Where did you two meet? Oh, I was a suspect in a murder investigation, and I fell in love with the lead detective. You couldn't make it up."
"You were hardly a suspect," O'Reilly reminded her. "Not in my eyes anyway."
"That's good to know."

The waiter came back, and O'Reilly ordered two fish and chips, plus another round of drinks. He looked out to sea and something in his peripheral vision made him turn his head. Two uniformed officers were approaching their table. As they got closer O'Reilly saw it was the PCs Hill and Woodbine.
"This is all I need," he said.

"Evening, sir," PC Hill said.
"Evening, Greg," O'Reilly reciprocated. "PC Woodbine."
He had yet to learn the giant PC's name.

"It's Martin, sir," PC Woodbine said as if reading O'Reilly's mind.

"Martin," O'Reilly obliged. "What brings you here?"

"We were told to retrace the old couple's steps, sir," PC Hill said. "Apparently they had lunch here before they took a walk to the rocks."

O'Reilly really didn't want to discuss the investigation right now, but he couldn't help himself.

"Did you get anything useful?"

"Nothing, sir," PC Hill said. "The waitress who served them couldn't tell us much apart from the fact that they're German tourists and the woman insisted that they bring her a particular brand of wine."

"Germans can be very demanding," O'Reilly said.

"The waitress said the hotel doesn't stock the wine she asked for but one of the bar staff knew where to get hold of some and he went to fetch a bottle."

"That's service for you," Victoria said.

"We won't disturb you any longer," PC Hill said. "Enjoy your evening."

The food arrived, and O'Reilly tucked in. He didn't give the ongoing investigation any more thought. Victoria finished her fish and chips before him, and it dawned on O'Reilly that it was the first time she'd beaten him.

"Your appetite is definitely improving," he said.

He finished the remaining fish on his plate and put down his knife and fork. Half of the chips were left untouched.

"I feel great," Victoria said. "Do you want to talk about it?"

"Talk about what?"

"Whatever it is that's responsible for the pile of chips still on your plate. I've never known you to leave food."

O'Reilly sighed. "It's a long story."

"I haven't got anywhere I need to be in a hurry. Let's order another round of drinks."

"Something very strange is happening on this island," O'Reilly began. "Yesterday, the guests at a well-heeled function all became aggressive at the same time. Spontaneous violence broke out, and all but one of the guests have no recollection of any of it. Later last night, a drunk man killed a friend of his in an extremely brutal manner. He too doesn't remember doing it. And this afternoon an elderly German woman bashed her husband's brains in for no apparent reason. There's madness on the island and I'm struggling to rationalise it."

Victoria started to laugh and it caught O'Reilly off guard.
"What?" he said.
"I'm sorry," Victoria said. "I shouldn't laugh at you, but what you just said is rather contradictory. You can't rationalise madness – insanity is surely the total opposite of rational thinking."
"You're right," O'Reilly said. "I don't know where to look next. These crimes are not normal. What made usually sane individuals crack like they did?"
"You said all but one of the guests have a memory blank of what happened at the party?"
"That's right. It's the man who was attacked by his fiancé. He remembers everything."
"Why do you think that is?"
"I have no idea. Hold on, I'm an idiot."
"I wouldn't go that far."
"No," O'Reilly said. "Would you excuse me while I make a few phone calls."
"What are you thinking?"
"I'm apologise for doing this – I know I said I wouldn't think about work this evening, but I think I know what made these people crack."

CHAPTER FIFTEEN

"We've got our first real lead," O'Reilly told the team the next morning. The phone calls he'd made from Cobo beach had confirmed his suspicions. The first call had been to Walter Thorpe. The owner of the catering company who had provided the food for the Gottlieb party told him that the drinks served at the function weren't his responsibility. The wine that was served with lunch was provided by one of the guests. His name was Jacob Hunt, and he'd brought along a case of Cabernet Sauvignon – *Chateau La Folie* to be precise.

The second call was to DI Peters. O'Reilly asked about the broken wine bottle found close to the body by Fort Hommet. The bottle had been smashed but the label was still intact. It was *Chateau La Folie*.

The clincher had been when O'Reilly spoke to the waitress who'd served the German couple yesterday lunchtime. The wine the old lady had insisted on was also a *Chateau La Folie* Cabernet Sauvignon.

"Coincidence?" O'Reilly said. "I don't think so."
"Are you saying there was something in the wine that made those people go berserk?" DC Stone asked.
"I don't know, Andy," O'Reilly said. "But when I look at the facts, that's the conclusion I come to. It's yet to be confirmed, but I believe everybody at the Gottlieb function drank some of that wine, apart from Mark Spring. When I spoke to the man yesterday, he told me he hasn't touched a drop of alcohol for three years, and he's the only guest who remembers anything about the altercations that broke out."

"This is unbelievable," DS Skinner said.
"But it makes sense," O'Reilly said. "We've had a series of seemingly random acts of madness. Momentary lapses of reason, and the only common

denominator is those identical bottles of wine. It has to be important."

"How did you even come up with a theory like this?" DS Skinner said.

"I rationalised madness, Will," O'Reilly said. "By definition madness is an irrational state of mind, but what if there is method in this particular madness?"

"Do we have any way of testing this theory of yours, sir?" DC Owen asked.

"I've asked DI Peters to see if he can scrape together enough of the remaining wine from Fort Hommet for testing purposes. He's going to see if he can find anything useable in the empty bottles from the Gottlieb party too. Unfortunately, even if there is some residue in the bottles, the testing process is a lengthy one, but those bottles of Cabernet Sauvignon are very relevant here."

"We have a lot of questions to ask a lot of people," DC Owen said.

"We certainly do, Katie," O'Reilly agreed. "We need to speak to everyone who was at the Gottlieb soiree on Saturday again."

"None of them can remember anything," DC Stone reminded him.

"They can't recall the violence that broke out," O'Reilly said. "But they might remember what happened at the estate before that. They might remember drinking some of that wine."

"Why did the German woman demand a bottle of that particular wine?" DS Skinner wondered.

"Why indeed?" O'Reilly said. "That's the first question we'll be asking her when we talk to her later. We'll also be speaking to our drunk friend again. Mike Trunk told us that his friend Woody helped himself to four bottles of that wine. Where did he get it from?"

"I'm still finding it hard to get my head around this, sir," DC Stone said. "Let's say the wine is the cause of the uncharacteristic violence – are we talking about some kind of poisoning?"

"It's possible," DS Skinner said. "It's happened before. Certain brands of food have been targeted and subsequently had to be taken off the shelves."

"That's why it's imperative that we locate the source of that wine," O'Reilly said. "And get it off the market."

"What did you say the wine was called again?" DC Stone said.

"*Chateau La Folie*," O'Reilly said

"Madness," DS Skinner said.

"It most certainly is," O'Reilly agreed.

"No, sir," DS Skinner said. "*Chateau La Folie. La Folie* in French means madness."

"Very appropriate."

    "The CCTV footage from Fort Hommet has been taken down from the Island Herald's website," DC Stone said. "That's something at least."

"Too little, too late," O'Reilly said. "Half of the people on the island have already seen it."

"How are we going to play this, sir?" DS Skinner asked. "Are we treating it as a series of separate incidents or are we going to focus on the contamination of the wine assuming a single perpetrator is responsible?"

"Until we know exactly what was in that wine," O'Reilly said. "We'll concentrate on the background information. But if whatever was put in that wine is the reason for the irrational behaviour of the people involved, it complicates things somewhat."

"Diminished responsibility," DC Owen said. "It means that Mike Trunk and the German lady are just as much victims of this as the people they killed."

"I'm not quite sure how this is going to play out in terms of the law, Katie," O'Reilly said. "But you may have a point there. We won't dwell on that aspect of it – how the powers that be decide to punish them is not our problem. We'll stick to looking into who would want to do something like this."

"How long are we talking with the tests on the wine?" DC Stone said.
"A couple of days at least," O'Reilly said. "DI Peters did try to explain the process, but he lost me halfway in. From what I can gather, when we're not entirely sure what it is we're actually testing for things become complicated. Those bottles of wine could have been contaminated with something new for all we know – something that hasn't been tested for before. We're getting somewhere with this – I can feel it in my weary Irish bones."

CHAPTER SIXTEEN

Jacob Hunt looked like he was expecting a visit from the police. When he opened the door of his luxury apartment to see O'Reilly and DC Owen standing there he nodded and sighed deeply.
"I was wondering if you'd be calling round."
"Why is that?" O'Reilly said.
"Because when I spoke to the other detectives yesterday, I got the feeling that it wasn't the end of it. I suppose you'd better come in."
There was a large plaster on his left cheek, and his neck was covered with small scratches.

He led them through the apartment to a set of sliding doors leading out to the back garden.
"Shall we talk outside?" Jacob said.
"We can do that." O'Reilly said.
"Can I offer you something to drink? I can ask Shirley to rustle up some of her famous lemonade."
"That won't be necessary," O'Reilly said.

They sat at a table on the small deck. Through the gap in the trees at the bottom of the garden you could just make out the blue of the sea in the distance.
"What is it you want to talk to me about?" Jacob asked.
"Some new developments have come to our attention," O'Reilly said. "We'd like to ask you about the wine that was served at the Gottlieb function on Saturday. I believe it was you who provided it."
"That's my line of work," Jacob told him. "I import and export wine."
"I wouldn't have thought there would be much to export from Guernsey. I don't recall seeing any vineyards on the island."

"The wine comes in from France," Jacob explained. "And I ship it all over the world from here. I have a warehouse close to the harbour in St Peter Port."

A middle-aged woman came outside. She walked over to their table and stood right in front of Jacob Hunt. O'Reilly realised that she was deaf when she started to communicate in sign language.

"We're fine, Shirley," Jacob said.

He signed something and she went back inside the apartment.

"She was asking why I hadn't offered you anything to drink," Jacob translated.

"Is Shirley your wife?" DC Owen said.

"Housekeeper," Jacob said. "Although she bosses me around like she's my wife sometimes. My sister was deaf, and I learned to sign when I was a kid."

"Let's go back to the wine you provided for the Gottliebs," O'Reilly said. "It was a cabernet sauvignon, is that right?"

"*Chateau La Folie*," Jacob elaborated. "It's a wine I'm particularly fond of."

"Where did you get it from?" DC Owen asked.

"I source it from a vineyard in the Loire valley. It's a quirky little vintage. Why are you asking me about the wine?"

"What made you decide to bring the wine?" O'Reilly asked. "And why that particular variety?"

"It's a tradition. I usually provide a case of something for the summer function."

"You didn't answer my question," O'Reilly said. "Why that particular wine?"

"What is this? Am I being accused of something? Do I need to contact my lawyer?"

"That won't be necessary," O'Reilly said. "I don't know much about wine – I'm more of a beer drinker, but my daughter likes a drop every now and then and I've never come across that brand before."

"It's a rather exclusive blend."

"Expensive then?"

"Not especially," Jacob said. "The retail price for a case is a little under two thousand pounds."

Expensive then, O'Reilly decided.

"OK," he said. "You brought along a case of *Chateau La Folie*."

"I didn't bring along a case," Jacob said. "I had it delivered."

"By who?" DC Owen said. "Who delivered the wine?"

"One of my drivers. It was delivered the morning of the party."

"Where was the wine before that?" O'Reilly asked.

"At the warehouse. Are you going to explain the relevance of the wine?"

"You said it's an exclusive blend," O'Reilly said. "How exclusive are we talking about?"

"I ship small quantities to collectors," Jacob said. "Mostly in the Middle East and the Orient."

"Is it not sold in shops and restaurants on the island then?" DC Owen said.

"I'd have to check that for you."

"Could you do that please," O'Reilly said.

"Now?"

"If you could."

"I'll have to make a couple of phone calls," Jacob said.

"We'll wait," O'Reilly said. "And would it be possible to change my mind about that lemonade? It's rather hot out here."

Jacob stood up. "Of course. Give me a few minutes."

"What do you think?" DC Owen said when Jacob Hunt had gone inside the apartment.

"I didn't get the impression that he was at all fazed when we brought up the wine."

"I didn't either," DC Owen said. "The wine could have been tampered with without Mr Hunt being aware of it. Someone could have laced it while it was still in the warehouse."

"We still don't know if it was spiked with anything," O'Reilly said. "But you're right – I don't think Jacob Hunt is involved at all."

Jacob came back with his housekeeper in tow. Shirley placed a tray of lemonade on the table and filled two glasses.

"Help yourselves," Jacob said.

"Are you not having some?" O'Reilly said.

"I'm not thirsty. Dig in. Don't worry – I'm not trying to poison you."

O'Reilly reluctantly obliged. He took a small sip.

"It really is very good. Did you have any luck with your phone calls?"

"According to the records," Jacob said. "Two cases of *Chateau La Folie* were sold to the boutique wine shop in St Georges, and another case was delivered to the Royal Hotel in Albecq."

"When was this?" DC Owen said.

"Last week," Jacob said. "Thursday to be precise."

He scratched the plaster on his face.

"How is the cheek?" O'Reilly said.

"Itchy," Jacob said.

"Human bites can be nasty," DC Owen said.

"I was given a course of antibiotics," Jacob told her.

"I believe it was Margot Gottlieb who did that to you," O'Reilly said.

"Apparently. I don't remember what happened."

"A witness saw you slap Mrs Gottlieb," O'Reilly said. "You slapped her hard, and she retaliated by biting your face. It's odd that you can't remember it."

"I promise you I have no recollection of it."

"What *do* you remember about Saturday afternoon?" O'Reilly said.

"I've already spoken to the other officers about this," Jacob said.

"Humour me please. What do you recall about that day?"

"I was chatting to Margot. I think she was asking me about the wine. Small talk. That's about all I can remember."

"You weren't the only one who was there that day who suffered injuries," DC Owen said. "Many of the guests were hurt."

"And I can't tell you what happened to them. I was talking to Margot and the next thing I remember is the gunshot. By then there were injured people everywhere and I have no idea what happened to any of them. How many times must I go over it?"

"The Royal Hotel in Albecq, you say?" O'Reilly said.

"Excuse me?" Jacob said.

"That's where one of the cases of *Chateau La Folie* went. And two cases to the boutique shop in St Georges."

"That's right."

"How many cases are there still at the warehouse?"

"A dozen or so," Jacob said. "But all of those are spoken for. I believe they're to be shipped out sometime in the next week."

"Grand," O'Reilly said. "We won't take up any more of your time."

He got to his feet. DC Owen did the same.

"Do you think there was something wrong with the wine?" Jacob asked.

"Are you implying that there was something in that Cabernet Sauvignon that caused the people at the party to behave like they did?"

"If that's the case," O'Reilly said. "We'll find out. Thank you for the chat. I hope the antibiotics help the bite wound. DC Owen is right – human bites can be very nasty."

CHAPTER SEVENTEEN

"The Royal Hotel in Albecq can account for eleven of the bottles of *Chateau La Folie*," O'Reilly began the afternoon briefing. "The other bottle from the case was sold yesterday afternoon to the Cobo Beach Hotel."

"That's the bottle the German woman insisted on," DS Skinner said.

"Frieda Klein," O'Reilly said. "She demanded a bottle of that particular wine. Why would she do that?"

"Germans can be picky," DC Stone suggested.

"Has she said anything yet?" DS Skinner asked.

"We've yet to speak to the woman," O'Reilly said. "And we'll be doing something about that later today."

"Two more cases of the wine were supplied to the boutique wine shop in St Georges," DC Owen said. "I spoke to someone there earlier, and they claim to have sold two of the bottles, but there are only eighteen still in stock, which means that four are unaccounted for."

"Mike Trunk told us his friend Woody somehow got hold of four bottles of the stuff," O'Reilly said. "So, I'd say it's safe to assume that he's the one responsible for the shortfall in the stock at the wine shop."

"How did he manage to steal four bottles of wine?" DS Skinner wondered.

"That's not important," O'Reilly said. "What I want to know is what happened to that wine? We're still waiting for the results of the tests, but I'm convinced that someone spiked that *Chateau La Folie* with something."

"Do we know who bought the two bottles from the wine shop?" DC Stone said.

"Unfortunately, not," DC Owen said. "Both bottles were paid for in cash."

"Those cases of wine go for two grand," O'Reilly said. "My maths isn't that great, but that means each bottle costs about a hundred and fifty pounds a pop."

"A hundred and sixty-six, sir," DC Stone corrected.

"Which is a lot of money to fork out in cash."

"It was two separate transactions," DC Owen said. "Both were carried out on Saturday, but none of the people who work at the wine shop remember who bought the wine."

"What's going to happen to the remaining wine at the hotel and the shop?" DC Stone asked. "Can we confiscate it?"

"Not without a warrant, Andy," O'Reilly said. "And right now we have no grounds for one. We're not going to get a warrant based on speculation. When the results from the lab come back, we'll have more of an idea of what we're dealing with but until then, our hands are tied."

"Can't we just warn the hotel and the wine shop about the possibility that the wine has been contaminated?" DS Skinner suggested.

"That's a complicated one," O'Reilly said. "Once again, we don't have proof that that's the case, and things could get ugly if we start throwing those kinds of accusations around."

"I say we just put it out there," DC Stone said. "Get the word out that there is something wrong with the *Chateau La Folie* wine, and to hell with the consequences."

"I'm on the same page as you, Andy," O'Reilly said. "But we're not going to do that. The Island Police do not want to be slapped with a lawsuit for making unsubstantiated accusations."

"The world has gone mad."

"You're not wrong there," O'Reilly agreed. "There's madness on the island and I have no idea what to do about it."

* * *

"Are you mad?"

Joanne Hawkins looked at the label on the bottle of wine her best friend held up and gasped.

"*Chateau La Folie*," Belinda Cole said with an exaggerated French accent. "Castle of madness."

"We're having a party in the woods," Joanne added. "We're not going for dinner with the bloody queen. That wine must have cost a fortune."

"So what? I took some money from the stash my stepdad keeps in his safe. I know the combination."

"You are mad."

"Relax, Jo," Belinda said. "He won't miss a couple of hundred quid. And if he does, I'll pay him back. In a few days I'll be eighteen, and my Grandfather's inheritance will be on its way to me. Are we ready?"

    The two girls had known each other for more than a decade. They'd grown up two doors down from one another on an exclusive golf estate on the west of the island. They'd attended the same school and the same sixth form college and this was to be their last summer together before they headed their separate ways. In Joanne's case it was to Oxford to study medicine. Belinda was planning on travelling the world and she was planning on doing it in style. The money that she would be entitled to in a couple of days was a substantial amount, and it would allow her to live a life of leisure for the foreseeable future. But none of that mattered now. The two teenagers were determined to make their last few weeks on the island as memorable as possible.

    The walk up to Bluebell Woods didn't take long. The path was busy with tourists coming and going but the two girls expected it to be. The part of the woods they were heading for wouldn't be so crowded. They would have that part to themselves.

    "Are you sure this is the right place?" Joanne asked.

They'd climbed over the fence that was supposed to prevent the public from going any further. There was no path here, and the girls would have to trample through the undergrowth from now on.

"I've been here before," Belinda said. "It's not far now. We just have to be careful of the cliff further along. It sort of creeps up out of nowhere."

"Where are the others?" Joanne asked. "I thought you said two o'clock."

"They'll be here. You worry too much. Drink some of this."

She handed Joanne the bottle of wine.

"There's hardly any left," Joanne said and took a long swig. "You're such a pig."

Belinda snatched the bottle from her. "And you've been fucking Henry Graham."

She started to laugh.

Joanne stopped dead. "I don't know what you're talking about."

"Yes you do," Belinda said. "We're almost there."

She walked off quickly, the dry branches snapped under her feet as she went. Joanne was in two minds whether to follow her. Her gut instinct was telling her to get as far away from Belinda as possible. Something in the tone she'd used when she accused her was unsettling.

And how did she know about her and Henry? That part was bugging her. It had only happened twice, and Joanne was sure that nobody else was aware of it. It had also happened almost a month ago, so why was she only bringing it up now? She took a few deep breaths and headed in the same direction her friend had gone.

She found Belinda in a small clearing close to the cliff edge. She was staring out to sea and she was standing stock still.

"Are you alright?" Joanne dared to say.

Belinda didn't reply.

"Bella," Joanne said. "What's going on?"

Belinda turned around. The vacant expression in her eyes was unsettling. She took a few steps towards her friend and stopped dead.

"I saw you."
"What did you see?" Joanne asked.
"I saw you in the back of Henry's car. Don't even try to deny it."
"I'm sorry," Joanne said. "It just happened."
Belinda's expression softened, and she managed a smile.
"It's fine," she said. "I'm over him anyway. Do you want the rest of this?"
She held out the bottle of wine. Joanne didn't accept it.

"Where is everybody else?" she said.
"There is nobody else," Belinda told her.
"What are you..."
She wasn't allowed to finish the sentence. She caught the wine bottle in her periphery as it was swung towards her face, and there was a flash of light when it connected with her right cheekbone. She screamed out but the second blow cut it short when the bones in her nose were shattered. A series of further blows resulted in more flashes of light, and she fell to the ground. The blow that finally extinguished the light in Joanne's head caused the bottle to smash.

Belinda gazed down at her broken friend and her eyes came to rest on the equally broken bottle in her hand. A sparrow chirped in a nearby tree. "Did you see what I did?" Belinda screamed at it.
The sparrow didn't reply. Belinda walked towards the edge of the cliff – she peered over the edge and dropped the broken bottle down onto the rocks below.

CHAPTER EIGHTEEN

The call came in just ten minutes after Joanne Hawkins' heart stopped beating. A man visiting the wartime graveyards below the Bluebell Woods phoned the police when he came across a young woman wailing like a banshee on the path up to the clifftop. He tried to comfort her, but she didn't respond. She kept repeating the same words over and over again. *I killed her.*

"What do we know?" O'Reilly asked PC London. She was one of the officers first on the scene. O'Reilly and DC Owen had been on their way to the hospital to speak to the German woman who claimed to have killed her husband when the call came in. The wailing teenage girl had been taken to the same hospital.

"The man who found her said she was inconsolable, sir," PC London said. "She was curled in a ball, and she kept screaming about how she'd killed her."

"Who was she talking about?" DC Owen asked.

"We took a look around," PC London said. "And we found a girl on the ground up in the woods by the clifftop. The public aren't allowed up there. She's definitely dead."

"Jesus," O'Reilly said. "What the hell is happening on this island?"

"DI Peters is up there now, sir," PC London said.

"Did the girl say anything else?"

"Nothing, sir. She calmed down a bit when the sedative the paramedics gave her kicked in, but all she kept saying was *I killed her.*"

"Where's the man who called it in?"

PC London pointed to a tall man with a camera around his neck. "I told him to stay where he was."

"Thanks, Kim. We'll go and have a word with him."

The man who made the call to the station was an English tourist called Steven Platt. He was in the middle of a week-long holiday on the island. O'Reilly introduced himself and DC Owen.

"Can you talk us through what happened?" he said.

"I was taking photographs of the gravestones," Steven said. "And I heard this ungodly scream."

"Did you see who screamed?" DC Owen asked.

Steven shook his head. "It came from up in the woods. I've never heard anything like it. It didn't sound human. *Did you see what I did*, that's what she screamed."

"Did you go and check it out?" O'Reilly said.

"I didn't dare. Whoever made that sound was clearly deranged."

"OK," O'Reilly said. "What happened then?"

"Everything was quiet again, so I carried on taking photos. I came here to Guernsey especially for the war graves. My grandfather is buried here."

"I thought these were all German graves," O'Reilly said.

"My grandfather was German."

"Right."

"I was about ready to leave," Steven said. "When I heard the sobbing. It was more of a wail really. I saw her by the bottom of the path that leads up to the cliffs. She was hunched over, and she was clearly in distress."

"What did you do then?" DC Owen asked.

"I went to see if I could help, of course. I asked her if she needed medical attention."

"Why would you ask that?" O'Reilly said.

"Because she had blood on her T-shirt. I thought she was hurt. She wasn't listening to me. She kept on wailing and saying *I killed her*. I didn't know what else to do, so I called the police."

"You did the right thing," O'Reilly said. "Did someone speak to you about making a statement?"

Steven nodded. "The young woman PC mentioned it. She's got my details. Was she telling the truth?"

"Excuse me?"

"Did she kill someone?"

"We don't know what happened yet," O'Reilly said. "I'll let you get on."

DS Earle emerged from the woods. He was holding something in an evidence bag. O'Reilly made his way over to him.

"What have you got there?"

"Broken wine bottle, sir," DS Earle told him.

He held it up. It was the bottom half, and the label was quite clear.

"*Chateau La Folie*," O'Reilly read. "Another one."

"It's almost definitely what was used to kill her," DS Earle said. "And there are still traces of the wine in the bottom."

"Is it enough to be able to test?"

"Should be. What's going on, sir?"

"I have no idea," O'Reilly admitted.

"DI Peters is still up there," DS Earle said. "We haven't been able to find the rest of the bottle, and that might pose a problem. If we're thinking it was used to inflict the damage to the victim, it's logical to assume the person who killed her was holding the bottle by the neck. We're probably not going to get any prints from the bottom of the bottle."

"I don't think that makes much difference," O'Reilly said. "We've got a young woman covered in blood who was found babbling about killing someone."

DI Peters appeared. He spotted O'Reilly and DS Earle and made his way over to them.

"Jim," O'Reilly greeted him. "That was quick."

"There isn't much to see up there," the Head of Forensics said. "It seems pretty cut and dry. Young woman with numerous head wounds – murder weapon next to her body, and another woman who claims to have killed her. I managed to locate the rest of the wine bottle."

DS Earle looked confused. "Where is it?"

"Fifty feet below the clifftop," DI Peters told him. "Smashed to pieces on the rocks."

"Is there any way we can retrieve it?"

"We could get there by boat," DI Peters said. "But I believe it would be a pointless exercise. It won't take long for the elements to destroy any evidence of value on the bottle."

"I think we've got enough anyway," O'Reilly said.

"We should have the results back from the lab later today," DI Peters said. "We'll soon know if there was anything in the bottles retrieved from the earlier crime scenes that shouldn't be there. And once we know what we're dealing with, any further tests should be much easier to carry out."

"Those bottles of wine were tainted with something," O'Reilly said. "Of that, I'm certain. Something in that wine caused normally sane people to flip."

CHAPTER NINETEEN

Frieda Klein greeted O'Reilly and DC Owen with a warm smile. The German women was sitting up in bed in the hospital room. O'Reilly had spoken to the doctor and he'd been told that Mrs Klein had been extremely confused when she was admitted yesterday but she was much more lucid today. She'd refused to take the sedatives she was offered, and she'd expressed a desire to speak to the Island Police about what had happened on the beach.

O'Reilly pulled up a couple of chairs and he and DC Owen sat down.
"How are you feeling?" O'Reilly asked.
"Shocked," Frieda said. "I killed my Otto, didn't I?"
"I'm afraid your husband is dead, yes."
"Oh my. Why would I do such a thing?"
Her English was very good, without much trace of an accent.

"Can you tell us what you remember about yesterday?" O'Reilly said.
"Otto and I had a wonderful lunch," Frieda said. "The seafood here is the best."
"You ate at the Cobo Beach Hotel," O'Reilly said. "Is that right?"
"I had prawns. Otto chose the veal. He's not very adventurous when it comes to food. Why did I kill him?"
"We'll work up to that. You had some lunch, and you ordered a bottle of wine – is that correct?"
"I know you're not supposed to accompany seafood with red wine," Frieda said. "But that's the way I've always been – different, my father used to say about me."
"The wine you requested wasn't on the wine list," DC Owen said. "Can you tell us why you wanted that particular wine."
"*Chateau La Folie*," Frieda said, with genuine fondness. "I first tasted it when Otto and I took a holiday in the Loire Valley. I'd never tasted anything like

it."

"It wasn't on the wine list at the Cobo Beach Hotel," O'Reilly said. "Yet you still insisted on it."

"I did no such thing."

"The waitress we spoke to at the hotel told us you demanded that particular wine," DC Owen said.

"She's a liar," Frieda said. "I enquired as to whether they could source a bottle of *Chateau La Folie* – the waitress told me she would see what she could do, and soon afterwards a bottle was brought to the table. I did not demand anything."

"I apologise," O'Reilly said. "Did you and your husband both drink the wine?"

"Of course not."

"I'm afraid I'm not following you."

"I mean, Otto never would drink wine. Beer is Otto's drink – that man is so painfully German I sometimes worry that one day he will take to wearing lederhosen in public. No, Otto didn't drink any wine."

"What did you do after lunch?" O'Reilly asked.

"I suggested we take a walk along the beach," Frieda said. "I was feeling rather queasy, and I thought the fresh air might be good for me."

"You were feeling sick?" O'Reilly said.

"Not really sick," Frieda said. "More peculiar. It's difficult to explain."

"How much wine did you drink?" DC Owen said.

"All of it of course."

"You drank a whole bottle to yourself with lunch?" O'Reilly said.

"Is that not allowed? I've been drinking wine since I was a girl. I can handle it – or I thought I could."

"You and your husband went for a walk on the beach," O'Reilly said. "Did you have an argument?"

"Why would you think that?" Frieda said.

"I'm just trying to get a detailed picture of what happened."

"I don't remember having an argument," Frieda said. "And I don't remember killing Otto."

"You were found walking aimlessly," O'Reilly said. "And you told the people who found you that you'd killed your husband. Why would you say that if you don't remember killing him?"

"Because it must have been me. Mein Gott."

A solitary tear formed in the corner of her right eye. O'Reilly watched as it rolled down her cheek. Frieda made no effort to wipe it away.

"I realise this must be distressing for you," O'Reilly said. "But we're trying to get to the bottom of what happened yesterday. Is there anything at all you can remember between the time you began to feel peculiar and when you told the people on the beach that you'd killed your husband?"

Frieda shook her head. "Nothing. I recall nothing of that. Why would I do such a thing?"

O'Reilly didn't have an answer for that. Nor did he know why a group of well-heeled people had suddenly turned into rabid maniacs. He wasn't sure why an intelligent drunkard had turned on a friend of his, and he also couldn't figure out why a teenage girl had decided to attack her friend with a wine bottle. None of it made any logical sense.

"What's going to happen to me?" Frieda asked. "Will I go to prison?"

O'Reilly didn't know how to reply to this either. He recalled a case in Ireland when he first joined the ranks of the Gardai. A woman had walked into a police station and confessed to killing her boyfriend. She claimed to have no memory of the event, and she also told the guard on duty that she had no reason to want him dead.

The murder was investigated. The attack took place in a quiet street not far from a nightclub. The man had sustained serious head injuries, and those injuries proved to be fatal. All the evidence indicated that the woman had indeed carried out the attack. Her boyfriend's blood was all over her clothes – her fingerprints were found on the rock that was used to kill him, and traces of her skin were found under his fingernails from when he'd tried to defend himself.

    The case went to trial and the woman was acquitted. A witness had come forward with information that cleared her of any wrongdoing. The man had confessed to putting something in her drink at the nightclub. It was a new, synthetic drug and fortunately for the defence it was a drug that remained in the system for quite some time. A blood test confirmed that the witness was telling the truth, and since in the eyes of the law, a person who does not intend to come under of the influence of a drug, and who does not intend to commit bodily harm cannot be held accountable for events beyond their control, she got away with murder. In a bizarre twist of fate, the witness who came forward was convicted for being an accessory to the murder and the person who carried out the actual murder was allowed to walk free.

    O'Reilly wondered if something similar was happening here. Was there a lunatic out there somewhere who liked to watch from a distance. Did they get a kick out of seeing the results of their actions come to fruition? One thing was for sure – the common denominator in all the recent irrational acts of violence was the bottles of wine. It was the *Chateau La Folie* that was responsible for the wave of madness that had washed over the island, and O'Reilly desperately needed to know what the hell the wine contained that had caused that madness.

CHAPTER TWENTY

The revelation came later that afternoon. DI Peters called O'Reilly to tell him the results were back from the bottles of wine from the Gottlieb party and the broken bottle they'd retrieved from the scene by Fort Hommet. He also had some news about the tests performed on the blood of the people who had recently decided to commit murder. He didn't want to discuss it over the phone, so O'Reilly scheduled a briefing to discuss the findings.

Everyone was already seated in the briefing room when DI Peters came in. The Head of Forensics wasn't alone – a woman with long white hair accompanied him.

"Good afternoon," he said. "I'd like to introduce Dr Gloria Handel. Dr Handel is a specialist in narcotic analysis. I had the pleasure of attending one of her lectures a few years ago – she's one of the leading experts in her field, and she's kindly agreed to assist us today."

"Glad to have you with us," O'Reilly told her.

"I hope I can help," Dr Handel said. "I'm afraid DI Peters has blown my trumpet much louder than he should have. I wouldn't consider myself one of the leading experts in the field, and I'm retired now."

"Don't be so humble," DI Peters said. "When it comes to narcotic testing, you've probably forgotten more than I will ever know."

"I'll try to keep this simple," Dr Handell began. "Layman's terms if you will. I don't know how much you know about drug analysis, but there is no simple test. One size definitely does not fit all where the examination of narcotics is concerned. But in this instance we got lucky. DI Peters gave me a brief rundown of how the suspected drug caused the people who ingested it to behave, and I was able to narrow it down a bit. I believe I've come across something similar before. That's why we were able to have the results much quicker than we expected."

"May I interrupt?" It was O'Reilly.

"By all means," De Handell said.

"Can you confirm that the all the bottles of wine you tested were contaminated?"

"The remaining bottles from the Gottlieb party and the one we retrieved from Fort Hommet all contained traces of the same narcotic," DI Peters confirmed.

"That's grand," O'Reilly said. "I knew it."

"A few years ago," Dr Handell continued. "A new drug hit the streets of Germany. It was something I'd never seen before. It was a synthetic blend of methamphetamines and various psychotropic drugs. The effects of this narcotic were erratic. Some users would describe a high of all highs with an increased sense of awareness and a feeling of invincibility. Others would become extremely anxious, paranoid and delusional. Psychotic episodes and violence was a known side effect."

"Are we looking at the same drug here?" DS Skinner asked.

"We're looking at something similar. The narcotic that was introduced to the streets of Berlin was known as *Brandt*."

"Fire," DC Stone translated.

"You know your German. It wasn't on the streets for long, but it was available long enough to cause a number of violent incidents in the city. And, like fire it is unpredictable. One person might suffer no adverse side effects, and another may suddenly become uncharacteristically violent. It causes anxiety and extreme paranoia. You might believe that everyone is out to cause you harm, and this can lead to retaliation."

"You said the drug in the wine is something similar to this *Brandt*," O'Reilly said.

"That's correct," Dr Handell said. "It bears a close resemblance to the old German narcotic, but I believe this one has been modified somewhat. For instance, the effects of *Brandt* were unpredictable, but here we have a drug that appears to cause the same effects in everyone who takes it. And the breakdown of the drug in the system is much different too."

"How long does it remain in the system?" O'Reilly asked.

"That's difficult to tell, but there were no traces of the drug in the blood of the people you believe were exposed to it. The timescale for *Brandt* was two to three days. It took a long time for the enzymes in the liver to produce an adequate quantity of active metabolites to break the drug down to inactive forms. The absence of the drug in the blood we tested suggests a much quicker breakdown process."

"Can you explain why that is?"

"This narcotic was created in a laboratory," Dr Handell said. "It's possible that chemicals were added to aid rapid breakdown."

"We can't prove that these people did actually ingest the drug then?" O'Reilly figured out.

"Unfortunately, not, but it seems likely, don't you think?"

"I do," O'Reilly said. "This is something we've never come across before. Do you have any idea where this drug came from?"

"That's not Dr Handell's department," DI Peters pointed out.

"Fair enough. At least we have enough to justify seizing the rest of the wine."

"Now we know what we're dealing with," DI Peters said. "We'll be able to test the other bottles much quicker."

"Is amnesia one of the side effects?" DC Stone put forward. "None of the people who were exposed to the drug can remember anything that happened during the violent episodes."

"It's possible," Dr Handell said. "I have to admit, this is something truly remarkable."

"You sound like you're a fan," O'Reilly said.

"From a scientific perspective, this is something very clever indeed. Whoever produced this particular narcotic really knew what they're doing."

"How did the drug get in the wine?" DC Owen asked. "We know now that the bottles of wine were spiked, but how did the drug get there?"

"All of the bottles we tested had tiny imperfections in the bottle caps," DI Peters said. "It's impossible to be a hundred percent certain, but it appears that the narcotic was injected using a syringe with an extremely thin needle. The pinprick holes were then resealed with some kind of waxy substance."

"What about the cork?" DC Stone wondered.

"Corks are rarely used these days, Andy," O'Reilly said. "Most wines have screw off caps. So, now we know how they did it. I want every one of those remaining bottles of wine seized, and I want us to look closely at where the wine has been – from its origin to where it is now."

"Are you thinking it could have been tainted before it landed on the island?" DS Skinner asked.

"I really don't know, but I doubt it was spiked during production. It's more likely it was laced somewhere between Jacob Hunt's warehouse and the places it was sold to. We follow the movement of the wine and we'll get closer to the person who contaminated it."

"There's still one bottle unaccounted for, isn't there?" DC Owen reminded them.

"There is," O'Reilly confirmed. "The wine boutique in St Georges sold two bottles. It's safe to assume that one of them was purchased by Belinda Cole, but there's still one in circulation. I want that bottle located. Check to see if the wine shop has CCTV. The camera might have caught the purchaser of the wine in the shop. It is imperative that we find that wine before someone drinks the damn stuff."

CHAPTER TWENTY ONE

"I'm afraid you're too late."

The man standing in front of O'Reilly didn't look long out of school. His pale skin was riddled with acne scars and his short, black hair looked like it hadn't been washed in a while. A strange smell seemed to follow him around. He'd introduced himself as Billy Foot and he was a forklift operator at the warehouse owned by Jacob Hunt.

"What do you mean we're too late?" O'Reilly asked.

"The remaining cases of *Chateau La Folie* were shipped out early this morning," Billy said.

"That's not possible," DC Owen said. "We spoke to Mr Hunt and he said they were only due to go out in the next week or so."

"I loaded the containers myself," Billy told her. "That was yesterday. The container vessel left the port at first light."

"Is Mr Hunt here?" O'Reilly said.

"I don't think so."

"Find out."

O'Reilly was furious. Jacob Hunt had definitely told them that there were still quite a few cases of the wine in the warehouse.

"Something's going on here, Katie," he said.

"Mr Hunt lied to us, didn't he?"

"He did. He said there were still a dozen or so cases here, ready to be shipped off to the Middle East and the Orient. Why would he tell us that if the wine had already left?"

Billy Foot returned with a woman. She was much older than him, and the way Billy walked a few feet behind her told O'Reilly that she held much more authority here than the young man did.

"Can I help you?" she asked.

"Who are you?" O'Reilly said.

"Melissa Paul. I'm the manager here. Billy tells me you're looking for Jacob."

"Is he at work today?" DC Owen said.

"He's taking some time off," Melissa said. "He was badly injured over the weekend, and he needs some time to recover."

"I see. Billy here told us that a shipment of wine left the docks this morning. Is this correct?"

"It is."

"And a dozen or so cases of *Chateau La Folie* were in that shipment?"

"Yes," Melissa confirmed. "What's this all about? This is a perfectly legitimate business. Why are the Island Police sniffing around?"

"Because something stinks," O'Reilly said. "And it's not just the BO wafting over from the armpits of your man there."

He nodded to Billy. The young forklift driver's face flushed red.

"Where is the container now?" O'Reilly asked.

"On its way to Portsmouth," Melissa said. "From there it will be transported to its final destinations. Why are you so interested in some cases of wine?"

"That doesn't concern you. How long have you been working here?"

"Six or seven years. I assure you, everything we do here is above board. We have all the necessary import and export licenses in place, and we run a respectable operation."

"I've heard that one before," O'Reilly said. "We won't take up any more of your time. Come on, Katie."

He turned to leave and stopped in his tracks.

He turned back around. "Was Mr Hunt aware that the *Chateau La Folie* was due to be shipped out today?"

"Probably," Melissa said.

"Could you do a bit better than that. I was led to believe that this was Mr Hunt's business."

"One of many," Melissa said. "He doesn't take much of an active role here anymore. He has other business concerns to concentrate on."

"I'm not buying that. We're going to need to take a look at your books. I want to know exactly when that wine arrived here, and I want to take a look at the orders and the shipping details."

"I'm sure you're aware that you will need to provide us with a warrant before we can give out that kind of information."

"I was hoping to avoid that," O'Reilly said. "It takes time and it's usually rather unpleasant for everyone concerned – especially you in this instance. Operations will have to be postponed while a full audit is being carried out. Nothing will be allowed to come in, and nothing will be allowed to leave the warehouse."

"Are you threatening me?"

"I'm asking you to be reasonable," O'Reilly said. "I just want to know when the *Chateau La Folie* arrived here, and I want to know who organised the shipment this morning. You would be doing us a huge favour."

Melissa Paul seemed to be mulling this over. Billy Foot was still lingering, and the stench of him was getting worse.

"I'm sure you have work to do, lad," O'Reilly said.

"I'm all up to date," Billy told him.

"The loading bays need cleaning up," Melissa said. "Get onto it."

Billy nodded and left them to it.

"I suppose you'd better come with me," Melissa said to O'Reilly and DC Owen.

She led them across the warehouse and stopped in front of one of three doors at the end. She opened the door and told O'Reilly and DC Owen to take a seat inside the office.

"What's really going on here?"

"We're not at liberty to discuss that," O'Reilly said. "What's Jacob Hunt like?"

Melissa flipped open a laptop on the table and switched it on. "To be honest, he's hardly ever here."

"You said he has some other businesses," DC Owen said. "What else does he do?"

"I don't know the details, Melissa said. "But he has his fingers in a number of pies. Property, the Internet."

"The rich just keep on getting richer, don't they?" O'Reilly mused.

Melissa sat down in front of her laptop. "What is it you need to know?"

"Everything you can tell us about that *Chateau La Folie* wine," O'Reilly told her.

"Here we go," Melissa said. "This is it here."

O'Reilly moved closer to get a better look. "What am I looking at?"

"This is a spreadsheet of the timescale involved," Melissa placed her forefinger on the screen. "This is when the wine landed on the island."

"That's three months ago," DC Owen said.

"April 15th," O'Reilly read.

"An order was placed by a client in Bahrain a month later," Melissa said.

"And the Chinese invoice was created a week after that. Everything seems to be in order."

"I don't know much about the wine game," O'Reilly said. "But was Mr Hunt in the habit of buying stock before he had definite orders placed?"

"The *Chateau La Folie* is a favourite of some of our clients," Melissa explained. "Pretty much guaranteed sales."

O'Reilly studied the screen and did some quick mental arithmetic at the same time.

"According to this," he said. "Eighteen cases were shipped in from France. Two of those cases were sold to the boutique wine shop in St Georges, one to the hotel in Albecq and the clients in Bahrain took eight off your hands. The Chinese customer purchased six. What happened to the other case?"

"Mr Hunt had it delivered to the Gottliebs for the party," DC Owen reminded him.

"Of course," O'Reilly said. "My memory isn't what it used to be. In that case, all the wine that came in can be accounted for."

"I assure you," Melissa said. "Everything is in order."

"We won't trouble you for much longer," O'Reilly said. "We just need to know about the shipment that left this morning. Who was responsible for that?"

"I was, of course," Melissa said.

"Can you remember when this was arranged?" DC Owen said.

Melissa minimised the screen and tapped the keypad to bring up another one.

"The freight docket was created last month," she said. "June 28th."

"And was Mr Hunt aware of this?" O'Reilly said. "Did he know that the wine for Bahrain and China would be shipped out today?"

"Probably."

"But it's possible he wasn't aware of the exact date of the shipment?"

"I suppose so," Melissa said.

"Can you explain why he would be under the impression that the wine wasn't due to leave for another week or so?"

"I can't, no."

"It probably slipped his mind," O'Reilly said. "We won't keep you any longer. Thank you for your help."

"Are you going to tell me what this is all about?" Melissa said. "Is it something I need to be concerned about?"

"Probably not," O'Reilly told her. "We'll see ourselves out."

CHAPTER TWENTY TWO

"We've got a problem, Liam."

It was just after six in the afternoon – O'Reilly was about to call it a day, when DI Peters had called him.

"Go on."

"We're finished testing the *Chateau La Folie* from the hotel in Albecq," the Head of Forensics said. "Now we know what we're looking for, we can carry out the analysis much quicker, but we've come up empty handed."

"What exactly are you saying?" O'Reilly said.

"None of those bottles tested positive for the drug, Liam."

"Are you absolutely sure?"

"Positive. My whole team have been working flat out since the wine was seized. We've checked, double checked and triple checked and that wine tested clean for any narcotic."

"What about the remaining bottles from the boutique shop?"

"We've yet to take a look at those, but I can tell you beyond a shadow of a doubt that none of the wine from the Albecq hotel had any trace of the drug we found in the residue of the Gottlieb wine and the bottle taken from Fort Hommet."

O'Reilly thanked him for keeping him in the loop and DI Peters promised to let him know if there were any developments with the wine from the boutique wine shop. He couldn't understand what any of this meant. It didn't make sense. The bottle of *Chateau La Folie* the German women drank came from the hotel in Albecq. If none of the other bottles in the case were spiked with the mystery drug, why had Frieda Klein gone berserk after drinking the wine with lunch? Perhaps the person responsible for lacing the wine had only contaminated one of the bottles in the case. Was it possible that Frieda Klein had just been unbelievably unlucky?

O'Reilly was certain that the wine from the shop in St George would tell a different story. Mike Trunk's friend, Woody had stolen four bottles, and it had caused the peculiar drunk to turn homicidal. And a girl, just days away from her eighteenth birthday had also killed her best friend after drinking the wine she bought from the same shop. DI Peters would come up trumps when he tested the remaining wine from the shop – of that O'Reilly was convinced.

He left his office and headed down the corridor towards the exit. He was intercepted halfway there by a man he could really do without right now.
"Have you got a minute?" Chief Officer Robert Johnson asked.
Once more, O'Reilly sensed this wasn't a question.
"What's on your mind, sir?" he said.
"Walk with me," CO Johnson said.
He made his way towards the front desk and O'Reilly had no choice but to follow him.

They went outside and CO Johnson made a beeline for the black Land Rover parked in its usual prime parking space. He stopped next to it and turned to face O'Reilly.
"Have you given any more thought to the GBA DCI position?"
"I thought we'd discussed that, sir," O'Reilly said. "I'm not the man you're looking for."
"I've yet to get the measure of you, Liam."
"Sir?"
"You've been with us just over a year," CO Johnson said.
"Something like that," O'Reilly said. "This is my second summer on the island."
"And since you arrived here, a maelstrom of crime seems to have formed around you. Murder and mayhem have gravitated towards you like moths to a flame."

O'Reilly wondered if the chief of the Island Police had signed up for DC Stone's creative writing course too. He didn't ask him about it.

"Is there something you want to say, sir?" he asked instead.

"I believe I may have expressed myself in a rather ambiguous manner the last time we spoke," CO Johnson said.

"A little bit," O'Reilly dared. "I got the feeling there was something you were expecting me to pick up from the tone of the conversation. I'm afraid I'm not too good at reading between the lines. I prefer a straight to the point chat."

"Very good. Perhaps I did beat around the bush a tad. The GBA post has your name on it."

"So you said," O'Reilly said. "And I don't want the job."

"I'll be completely straight with you," CO Johnson said.

About fucking time, O'Reilly thought.

"The situation with the previous DCI in the Border Agency is a delicate one, and it's one that is still shrouded in controversy. That's precisely why the position has only been advertised internally, and it is also why we seek to fill the position ASAP. I'm sure you appreciate that."

"Of course, sir. I know all about what happened to the previous DCI. I was the one responsible for it."

"And that is exactly why you should be the person to fill the gap left behind. The press are not our biggest fans right now, and I believe you taking the GBA post will help to swing public opinion back in our favour."

O'Reilly thought about what the Chief Officer was asking. It didn't take him very long.

"I can't help you, sir," he said. "I don't want the DCI position, and you can't force me to accept it."

"Is that your final decision?" CO Johnson said.

"It is. And before you start with your veiled threats again, I'll save you the bother. I made some unwise decisions back in Dublin and I paid for them. I paid for them dearly. I will not be held to ransom, sir."

CO Johnson observed him with curious eyes. O'Reilly was sure his lips had curled up into a smile.

"DCO Dove speaks highly of you."

"DCO Dove is a good man, sir," O'Reilly said.

This time the smile was more obvious.

"I really can't quite figure you out, Liam," CO Johnson said.

"I get that a lot, sir," O'Reilly said. "Will there be anything else?"

The beep when CO Johnson pressed the key fob in his hand told him the conversation was over.

CHAPTER TWENTY THREE

A few miles north in St Sampson, a couple were celebrating their thirty-fifth wedding anniversary. John and Yolanda Stewart had decided on a quiet, intimate celebration. Both of them were in their early sixties and their days of wild parties were well and truly behind them. John had recently sold the business he'd owned for the majority of their married life – the children had flown the coop, and they were looking forward to life in the slow lane. The sun was making plans to rest its head for the night, and for one of the Stewarts it would be the last sunset they would ever see.

John topped up his glass of wine and offered his wife a refill.
She held out her glass. "Don't mind if I do."
"To the start of a new life," John toasted.
"How does it feel?" Yolanda asked.
"How does what feel?"
"No responsibility. No phone calls interrupting us when we're in the middle of something. Do you realise – we'll be able to take a holiday without having to worry about how the business is doing."
"It's going to be strange," John admitted. "But don't forget it was that business that paid for all of this."
A gesture with his arms took in the large garden and the view beyond it. Passenger ferries were coming and going from the harbour. The lights of the island of Herm were turning on in the distance. John picked up the cheese knife on the table and cut a slice of brie from the cheese board. He spread it onto a cracker and offered it to his wife. Yolanda declined.

She drained the wine in her glass. "But at what cost, John? What have we had to sacrifice for all this?"
"Let's not dwell on that tonight, darling," John said. "It's going to be different from now on."

"Will it though? Thirty years. Thirty-odd years I gave up for you and that business. I feel like we've spent all this time working for something that we'll only get to enjoy for a few more years. Was it worth it?"

John refilled their glasses again. "I'm going to make it up to you. I told you I had a surprise for you. Give me a minute."

He got up and went inside the house. Soon afterwards music could be heard from the speakers outside. It was a song from the eighties – *Careless Whisper*.

John returned to the table with something in his hand.

He smiled at his wife. "Does this song take you back?"

"It makes me feel old," Yolanda said.

"This was what we chose for our first dance at the wedding. I was dead against it – I recall you had quite a crush on the bloke who sang it."

"George Michael," Yolanda elaborated. "I don't think there were many young women who didn't have a crush on him back then."

John handed her the envelope he was holding.

"What's this?" she asked.

"Open it."

Yolanda took a long drink of wine and ripped open the envelope.

"Tickets?"

"Yes," John confirmed. "In a week's time, you and I will be embarking on the trip of a lifetime. From Southampton to the Caribbean. Twenty-four days at sea. What do you think?"

The song ended and started again. John had put it on repeat.

"Well?" he said.

"I don't know what to say," Yolanda said.

"Would you like to dance, Mrs Stewart?" John said and held out his hand.

"I would like that very much, Mr Stewart."

George Michael was singing about never dancing again.

John led his wife to the garden and pulled her in closer. They swayed in time to the music for a while and Yolanda suddenly froze.
"What's wrong?" John asked.
"I hate boats," Yolanda whispered in his ear.
John broke the embrace. He stared at his wife. "Are you OK? You look a bit pale."
"You know I hate boats," she said. "And you want me to spend more than three weeks on one."
"You've always wanted to go on a cruise."
"Since when?"
"Since forever."

Yolanda sighed deeply and returned to the table. She carved a chunk out of a piece of the blue cheese and stuffed it in her mouth. John came and sat down opposite her.
"It's you who was always talking about cruising in the Caribbean," Yolanda said.
Crumbs of cheese flew out of her mouth as she spoke.
"You, John," she added. "Always fucking you. Always what *you* want."
"I can cancel the trip," John said. "I can still get most of the money back."
"You do that. Fucking Caribbean. I can't think of anything worse."
She helped herself to some more cheese. This time she didn't even bother cutting it with the knife.

She said something else, but John couldn't make out the words through the cheese she was gobbling down. The song started for the third time and Yolanda got to her feet.
"I think you ought to go and lie down for a bit," John said.
"I think you ought to keep your opinions to yourself," Yolanda countered.
"I've had almost forty years of your opinions. And this wasn't the song from

our wedding – it was *Hold Me Now* by *The Thompson Twins*. You couldn't even get that right."

She stood up and picked up the bottle of wine. She looked at the label – *Chateau La Folie*, and took a long swig straight from the bottle.

John got to his feet. He took a couple of steps towards his wife and stopped when she raised the bottle in the air.

"What's got into you?" John said.

"I don't love you anymore. I don't even like you."

Yolanda tossed the bottle over her head. It landed with a dull thud on the grass. She started to laugh – this was clearly highly amusing for her.

"I'll fetch you some water," John offered.

He turned to go and as he did he felt a white-hot pain in the back of his neck. Something gave in his throat and the gasp he tried to make wouldn't come out. He put a hand to his neck and felt something hard and sharp protruding just below his trachea. The pungent reek of the blue cheese on the tip of the cheese knife entered his nostrils and John wondered if his senses were playing tricks on him.

Yolanda Stewart yanked out the knife and a spurt of blood followed it. She watched as her husband fell forwards. His legs didn't buckle, and he fell straight onto his face. Yolanda sat back down. She helped herself to a poppyseed cracker and used the bloodied cheese knife to smear it with a decent amount of brie. George Michael was still lamenting the fact that he was never going to dance again. John Stewart was in the same predicament.

CHAPTER TWENTY FOUR

O'Reilly looked at the woman lying in the bed next to him and he felt utterly content. Victoria was on her back with her mouth slightly open. Her chest was rising and falling slowly, and he could hear her soft breaths. He got out of bed as quietly as possible and picked up his phone. The screen told him it was just after seven. He would let his wife sleep a while longer.

He went downstairs to the kitchen and turned on the kettle to make some tea. Two of the cats were waiting at the back door to be let out. Juliet and Shadow wanted to go out and explore. The two ladies were early risers. Bram, the lazy ginger moggy O'Reilly had inherited, was not. O'Reilly suspected he was probably still fast asleep on one of the chairs in the living room. He opened the back door and left it open. It was still early but it was already very warm. Juliet and Shadow padded outside.

O'Reilly made his tea and picked up his phone. For the first time since he could remember there were no new notifications. Nobody had called him or sent him a message and he liked it. He would be able to ease into the day at his own pace, and that was something he rarely got to enjoy these days.

Bram finally put in an appearance. The ginger free-loader headed straight for his food bowl and made a sound O'Reilly didn't think a cat was capable of making when he realised the food he'd scoffed the previous evening hadn't been replenished.
"In a minute," O'Reilly told him. "Go outside for a bit – it's a grand day." Bram repeated the curious sound and went outside to join Juliet and Shadow.

Victoria came downstairs half an hour later. O'Reilly was already on his third cup of tea for the day. He kissed her on the cheek and asked if she wanted some coffee.
"I'd love some," she said.

"I fed the rabble," O'Reilly told her. "I'm a bit worried about Bram – he keeps making weird noises."

"He's always made weird noises," Victoria said.

"I haven't heard these ones before. If I didn't know any better, I would think I was being subjected to feline expletives."

Victoria started to laugh. "You have a vivid imagination, Liam. What time do you have to be at work?"

"Half-eight," O'Reilly said. "I thought I might get back behind the wheel again."

"Can you remember how?"

"I'm sure it'll come back to me," O'Reilly said. "What about you? What time are you planning on heading to the shop?"

"I've got the morning off. I have an appointment with the doctor, remember."

"Of course," O'Reilly said. "It slipped my mind. Do you want me to come with you?"

"You have work to do. It's just a routine checkup. I'll be fine."

"Let me know how it goes."

"Of course," Victoria said. "Is that coffee going to take long?"

"What?" O'Reilly said. "Ah, right – I'll get right onto it."

Thirty minutes later O'Reilly unlocked his car, got inside and closed the door. It seemed like an age ago since he'd last sat where he was now. He tried to remember exactly when it was that he last drove a car, and he realised it was a good few months ago. He wondered if it would even start. It was possible that the battery would be dead.

After the third turn of the key in the ignition the engine spluttered to life and stayed alive. O'Reilly checked to see if the mirrors were where they were the last time he drove and pulled away from the kerb. The fuel gauge told him he still had half a tank of petrol.

The drive across the island passed without incident and O'Reilly pulled into the car park of the Island Police HQ twenty minutes later. The clock on the dashboard told him there was ten minutes to go before the scheduled morning briefing. After grabbing a fourth cup of tea for the morning he headed straight for the briefing room.

DS Skinner and DC Owen were already seated. O'Reilly wished them good morning and put his tea down on the table.

"It appears I'm still capable of driving."

"You drove here?" DS Skinner said.

"It was about time I got back behind the wheel," O'Reilly said. "Everything was exactly as I remembered. Have we had any new developments overnight?"

"Nothing I'm aware of, sir," DS Skinner said.

"Me neither," DC Owen said. "Although I got to thinking about the wine at the warehouse. Don't you think it's strange that a few hours after the owner of the warehouse tells us the *Chateau La Folie* isn't due to be shipped for a week or so, we find out the shipment has already left?"

"The manager reckons Jacob Hunt doesn't play much of a part in the operational side of the business," O'Reilly said. "I get the impression he leaves that up to the people on his payroll and he reaps the profits. It's not unusual."

"I didn't get that impression of Mr Hunt, sir. He seemed to know exactly what was going on in the business."

"What difference does it make?" O'Reilly said. "The majority of the wine is off the island."

"Where did it go?" DS Skinner said.

"Bahrain and China."

"I wonder how long it takes to get there," DC Owen said.

"What does it matter, Katie?" O'Reilly said. "It's not our problem anymore."
"What if something similar happens there?" DC Owen said. "What if people in Bahrain and China drink the wine and start killing each other?"
"The police in those countries will deal with it. It is not the problem of the Island Police anymore. Has anyone seen Andy this morning?"

CHAPTER TWENTY FIVE

DC Stone turned up half an hour later. The rat-eyed DC was very red in the face, and he explained that his car had refused to start.
"It's probably the battery terminals," he said and sat down. "It's happened before."
"You could have informed us that you were going to be late," DI O'Reilly said.
"I did, sir," DC Stone said. "I sent you a message."
O'Reilly frowned and looked at the screen of his phone.
"So you did," he said. "No harm done. Let's make a start."
He went on to recap on what had happened on the island since the mania at the Gottlieb annual summer soiree.

"I've never seen anything like this before," he said. "We have three bodies, and we have three very unlikely murderers. A drunkard who killed his friend for no apparent reason – an old German lady who murdered her husband, and a schoolgirl who beat her best friend to death with a wine bottle. None of them remember anything about the murders, and none of them had any reason to want their victims dead. All three incidents share a common denominator – a brand of wine I'd never heard of before."
"*Chateau La Folie*," DS Skinner said.

"DI Peters and his team have completed the tests on the wine sold to the hotel in Albecq," O'Reilly carried on. "And there were no traces of the drug in any of the bottles."
"The doctor DI Peters introduced us to said something about the rapid breakdown of the drug," DC Stone put forward. "Perhaps the narcotic had already been broken down."
"Impossible, Andy," DS Skinner said. "The drug can only be broken down by the enzymes produced by the liver. It would remain intact in a bottle of

wine."

"Why was there no sign of that narcotic in any of the bottles Forensics analysed?" O'Reilly asked. "I'm baffled."

"What about the two cases sold to the boutique wine shop?" DC Stone said.

"DI Peters hasn't got round to those yet," O'Reilly said. "He got a bit behind yesterday, but we do know that the bottle found by Fort Hommet had traces of the drug in it, as did what was left of the bottle that killed the young girl yesterday. Both of those bottles came from the wine shop, so I'd expect the rest of the stock to contain the drug too."

"What are we going to base the focus of the investigation on?" DC Owen said. "Do we concentrate on the people who carried out the attacks or are we going to focus on how the wine became contaminated in the first place?"

"That's the million-dollar question, Katie," O'Reilly said. "We've had a spate of random acts of violence in a very short space of time. The people who carried out the attacks are not your typical homicidal maniac types, and none of them can remember anything. That leads me to believe that neither the victims nor the people who killed them are actually relevant. That wine is the key to this and that's what we'll hone in on. The wine was brought in from France in April. It means that, theoretically we have a three-month window from the wine arriving on the island and the victims unknowingly ingesting the drug."

"Where do we even begin, sir?" DC Stone said. "We don't know if someone spiked the wine at the warehouse or the places it was sold on to."

"Then we look harder," O'Reilly said.

"The boutique wine shop in St Georges hasn't reported any break-ins," DS Skinner said. "The same goes for the hotel in Albecq."

"I don't think that's where the wine was tampered with," DC Owen said.

"That wine was only sold to them last week. I believe we need to look more closely at the warehouse."

"There's something else I'm finding hard to understand," DC Stone said. "All but one of the guests at the Gottlieb party went mental at the same time."

"Eloquently put, Andy," O'Reilly said. "But go on."

"It looks like the entire case that was brought to the party was spiked. Why is it that only a few random bottles from the other cases were found to contain traces of the drug?"

"And why was nobody killed at the Gottlieb party?" DC Owen wondered. "The odds don't make sense. All twelve bottles at the party were laced and there were no fatalities, but we've got two separate instances where people died due to single bottles being injected with that drug. The numbers don't add up."

"Are you suggesting that this isn't as simple as we think?" O'Reilly said. "Are you implying that there really is method in the madness?"

"I'm just looking at the facts, sir. I can't believe the people who died were all victims of being in the wrong place at the wrong time. One victim – you could accept, but three is beyond belief."

"I'm slightly confused, sir," DC Stone said.

"You're not the only one," O'Reilly said.

"Do we follow the cases of wine to see where they could have been contaminated," DC Stone said. "Or do we look for a link between the victims?"

"We do both, Andy," O'Reilly decided. "And we also need to find out if anything connects the people who killed them. We've spoken to all of them apart from the young girl who decided to butcher her best friend yesterday. Katie and me can handle that. Will, I want you to have another word with the enigmatic drunk. I think you'll find Mike Trunk rather entertaining. And

Andy, I want you to see if you can get anything more out of the old German lady. When we're finished with that, I want to dig deeper into the lives of the people they chose to send to the big wide beyond. We may get a break and find something that ties them together – we may not, but we have to try."

CHAPTER TWENTY SIX

Belinda Cole wasn't alone when O'Reilly and DC Owen went inside the interview room. An elderly man was sitting next to her at the table. Belinda had been discharged from the hospital precisely an hour before she was picked up at home and told her presence was required at Island Police HQ. Her lawyer had got there surprisingly quickly. He introduced himself as Harry Ingram and informed O'Reilly that Belinda had been advised to answer all of their questions.

After turning on the recording device and going through the motions for the tape, O'Reilly looked closely at the teenager sitting opposite him. Belinda Cole looked deathly pale, and her puffy eyes told him that she hadn't slept much since she was admitted to hospital. She was a pretty, slightly chubby girl with freckles on her cheeks and nose. She really was nothing like the cold-blooded murderers O'Reilly had come across in the past.

"Belinda," he said. "How are you feeling?"
"Am I going to go to prison?" she asked.
"Let's not get ahead of ourselves here." It was Harry Ingram.
"Can you talk us through what you remember about yesterday?" O'Reilly said. "You and Joanne took a walk in the woods, is that right?"
"It was Joanne's idea," Belinda said. "She wanted to show me the view from the top of the cliff there."
"That part of the woods is off limits to the public, isn't it?" DC Owen said.
Harry glared at her. "Is that really relevant?"
"We're just trying to get a clear picture of what happened, Mr Ingram," O'Reilly said. "Go on, Belinda."
"Joanne brought along a bottle of wine," the teenage girl said. "She thought we could have a drink looking out to sea."
"Do you know where Joanne got the wine?" DC Owen said.

"I didn't ask. She's eighteen, so it isn't against the law, is it?"

"No, it isn't," O'Reilly confirmed. "You're not yet eighteen, are you?"

"It's my birthday in two days' time," Belinda said. "Am I going to spend my eighteenth in prison?"

"Not if I can help it," Harry said.

He placed a hand on her shoulder and Belinda quickly shook it off.

"How long have you and Joanne been friends?" O'Reilly said.

"Since we were little kids," Belinda said. "We lived on the same road on the golf estate in Perelle. We both went to the same school. Oh my God, what did I do to her?"

She rubbed her eyes even though there were no tears in them.

"What happened when you reached the clifftop?" O'Reilly said.

"I can't remember," Belinda said.

"Tell us what you *can* remember."

"We had a bit of wine. I think I drank more of it than Joanne did."

"You said it was Joanne who brought along the wine," DC Owen said. "Are you saying she didn't drink much?"

"She knows I like wine," Belinda said. "She was always the thoughtful one. Why did I kill her?"

"Can you explain why you think it was you who killed her?" O'Reilly asked.

"Because when I woke up, she was on the ground, and she was dead." Belinda looked right into O'Reilly's eyes when she said this. Her gaze was disconcerting, and the experienced Irish detective had to look away.

"Was it me?" Belinda said. "Was it definitely me who killed her?"

"We believe it was," O'Reilly said.

"Why? Why would I do that?"

"That's what we're trying to understand. The gap in your story is making that difficult for us."

"My client has already explained to you," Harry said. "That she has no recollection of the attack. I don't know what else you want her to tell you."

"A young girl is dead, Mr Ingram," O'Reilly said. "It's looking like your client was the one who killed her, and we need to know what happened."

"I'll tell you what I think happened, shall I?" Harry said. "I think what happened to my client is the same thing that has happened to a number of other innocent individuals on this island recently."

"I'll stop you there, if I may," O'Reilly said. "We're not here to listen to your wild speculations."

"Speculations?" Harry repeated. "This is a small island, Inspector."

"Detective Inspector," O'Reilly corrected. "There's quite a difference."

"Detective Inspector," Harry humoured him. "This is a small island, and there's not much that goes on that doesn't get out eventually. I've heard the rumours. There was something in the wine my client consumed that caused her to behave irrationally. Correct me if I'm wrong."

"I'm not going to comment either way," O'Reilly told him. "I've never held much stock in rumours."

"Where there's smoke, there's fire."

"We're getting off track," O'Reilly said. "Belinda, you claim not to remember anything about the attack on Joanne. There's one thing I'm finding hard to understand. The evidence at the scene suggests that Miss Hawkins was repeatedly beaten with the wine bottle found next to her. The bottle broke during the attack. The other half of the bottle was found quite a distance away from her body. Can you shed any light on that?"

"I can't remember," Belinda said. "How many times do I have to tell you? I can't remember."

"Can you think of any reason why you would want to get rid of half of the murder weapon?" DC Owen asked.

"Perhaps something in your subconscious mind prompted you to act," O'Reilly suggested. "You realised what you'd done, and you panicked."

"That's preposterous," Harry said. "My client has already explained that she has no recollection of the event, and you're talking about subconscious actions. I suggest you either charge her with something or let her go home. Don't you think she's been through enough?"

Belinda raised her hands and covered her face. "I can't do this."

"What can't you do, Belinda?" DC Owen said.

"Is there something you want to tell us?" O'Reilly asked.

Belinda removed her hands from her face. "I killed my best friend, and I can't remember any of it. If I knew why I did it, I would tell you. I don't remember. I don't remember hitting her, and I don't remember dropping the broken bottle off the cliff."

"I suggest we finish there," Harry said.

"I couldn't agree more," O'Reilly said. "I think we've got enough."

He stated the time for the tape and turned off the recording device.

CHAPTER TWENTY SEVEN

"She knows more than she's letting on," O'Reilly said to DC Owen. They were standing by the front desk. Despite Belinda Cole's lawyer's protests, the teenage girl had been remanded in custody. Harry Ingram had threatened to make life very unpleasant for O'Reilly to which the Irishman had replied:

Do your worst.

Belinda had sounded some warning bells with her revelation about dropping the broken wine bottle off the cliff. O'Reilly had mentioned that half of the bottle had been found some distance away from the other half, but he'd left out the detail about where it ended up. His suspicions were instantly aroused. She claimed to have no recollection of the murder, yet she remembered disposing of half of the murder weapon. It didn't add up, and O'Reilly decided they had more than enough to charge the young woman. Belinda Cole was definitely going to celebrate her eighteenth birthday behind bars.

"Where does the murder of Joanne Hawkins tie in with the others?" DC Owen said.

O'Reilly didn't get the chance to reply. PC London interrupted his thoughts.

"Sir," she said. "You need to hear this. I've just had a call come in. A man has phoned to tell us that his sister has killed her husband."

"Did he sound genuine?" O'Reilly said.

"He did," PC London confirmed. "His sister said she'd killed her husband, and she can't remember doing it."

The drive up to St Sampson took much longer than it usually did. The roads were clogged with tourists ticking things off on their *things to do in Guernsey* lists. According to the Guernsey Tourist Board, the population on the island more than doubled in July and August, and O'Reilly was now seeing this first hand.

The woman O'Reilly and DC Owen were on their way to see was a sixty-two-year-old called Yolanda Stewart. A couple of uniformed officers had been sent to check out her brother's story and it was confirmed when they found the dead man, face-down in the back garden. It wasn't yet clear how he had perished, but one thing was certain – the man was definitely deceased.

"Do you think it's connected to the others?" DC Owen said.
They'd just passed the Chateau de Marais Nature Reserve.
"It has to be, Katie," O'Reilly said. "A woman kills her husband and has no recollection of the event. I bet you when we get there, Mrs Stewart will be a frail old lady who has never had a homicidal urge in her life."

The house was grand, even by Guernsey standards. The double-storey property stood on four acres of prime real estate. Even from the road O'Reilly could see the harbour and the blue of the sea beyond. The house looked out onto the main shipping channel in and out of the island and a brace of passenger ferries could be seen far out to sea.

"Looks like DI Peters is already here," DC Owen said when they got out of the car.
The car belonging to the Head of Forensics was parked further up the street.
"For what it's worth," O'Reilly said. "I don't know what Forensics expect to get here. The interview with Belinda Cole is bothering me."
"Her demeanour was all wrong. It was as if she was trying a little too hard to appear to be in shock, if that makes any sense."
"It makes perfect sense, Katie. If I didn't know any better, I would say Miss Cole was putting on an act. And not a very convincing one."
"Do you think she killed her friend on purpose?"

"I don't know what to think," O'Reilly said. "All I know is there was something fake about her – something I can't quite fathom."
"It's going to be hard to make the charge against her stick," DC Owen pointed out. "What with the other murders. Her lawyer is going to milk that for all it's worth."
"We'll cross that bridge when we come to it," O'Reilly said. "We've got this bridge to get over first."

PC Woodbine was manning the front door, preventing anyone from going inside the house. The giant officer greeted O'Reilly and DC Owen and let them through.
"Where's Mrs Stewart?" O'Reilly asked him.
"She's inside, sir," PC Woodbine said. "Her brother is here."
"Does she need medical attention?"
"I didn't ask."
O'Reilly shook his head and made his way inside the house.

PC Hill was standing outside a door to the left of a wide hallway. He spotted O'Reilly and DC Owen and walked over to them.
"Afternoon, sir. Mrs Stewart is in the living room with her brother. "
"How's she doing?" O'Reilly asked.
"She seems OK," PC Hill said. "I asked her if she needed to go to hospital, but she said she'd rather stay here. Her brother is keeping her calm."
"We'll speak to her in a minute. Where's the husband?"
"Outside in the back garden. The sliding doors that lead out to the garden are in the extension next to the kitchen."
"Thanks, Greg," O'Reilly said.

The view from the back was truly spectacular. The property had been built on an elevated stand, and from the deck outside the kitchen there was an unobstructed view of the harbour and the open sea beyond. It was a clear day and O'Reilly could make out the clifftops of the island of Herm in the distance. He shivered. He'd spent some time on Herm recently and it hadn't been particularly pleasant. He'd made a vow never to set foot on the sinister chunk of rock ever again.

DS Henry Earle walked over. DI Peters' forensic technician didn't look well at all. He observed O'Reilly through weary eyes and shook his head.

"Is it that bad?" O'Reilly said.

"I've seen worse," DS Earle said. "So I don't know why it's affecting me so badly. It could have something to do with the way he was killed and what happened afterwards."

"Go on," O'Reilly said.

"It looks like he died due to a single wound to his neck. She used a cheese knife. It entered the back of his neck, passed through the trachea and exited out of his throat. Death will have been quick."

"What's bothering you so much about it?" DC Owen asked.

"We found the knife on the table next to a cheeseboard," DS Earle said. "And it looks like the wife helped herself to a bit of brie shortly afterwards. There's blood on the cheeseboard and in the brie itself."

"That's disgusting," DC Owen said. "Are you sure that's what she did?"

"It looks like it."

O'Reilly turned to look at the blanket on the lawn and the body concealed within.

"How long do you think he's been dead?" he asked.

"We'll know more after the postmortem," DS Earle said. "But I'd say he's been here all night. Liver mortis has already set in. He's got some mottling on his hands and face, and his eyes have already got the milky sheen on the lenses."

"It was warm last night," O'Reilly said. "That will have expedited the process. Did you find anything that might be able to help us figure out what happened here?"

"On the contrary, sir."

"I don't think I like the sound of that."

"There was an empty wine bottle in the kitchen," DS Earle said. "You'll never guess what brand it was."

"*Chateau La Folie*?" O'Reilly speculated anyway.

"Correct. And this bit, you're definitely not going to like. The bottle was not only empty – it had been rinsed out with water."

"Damn it. No chance of testing it then?"

"None whatsoever, sir."

"Why the hell would she wash the bottle?" O'Reilly said. "A woman kills her husband – she helps herself to a bit of cheese afterwards and then does a bit of cleaning up. I thought I'd seen all the madness I was going to see on this island in the past week, but it appears that I was very much mistaken."

CHAPTER TWENTY EIGHT

That was an understatement. The madness on the island was far from over. When O'Reilly went back inside the house in St Sampson he was told in no uncertain terms that Yolanda Stewart wouldn't be talking to the police any time soon. Yolanda's brother, James happened to be a lawyer, and he'd advised his sister not to say anything until he told her otherwise. O'Reilly wasn't particularly fazed by this – it wasn't anything he hadn't faced before, but when he explained to James that they would be arresting Yolanda, the protective brother in James had shown his face. He insisted that his sister receive the medical attention she needed. Yolanda Stewart was subsequently taken to hospital and O'Reilly knew he wouldn't be able to question her today.

That wasn't the end of it. Frieda Klein and Mike Trunk seemed to lose the power of speech at roughly the same time. O'Reilly didn't know why the German tourist and the eccentric drunk had decided on a sudden vow of silence, but both of them refused to say a word and there wasn't much the Irish detective could do about it. It was baffling, but he was powerless to change it.

"This is where we stand."

O'Reilly looked at the faces of the people seated in the briefing room. All of them looked like they were feeling the pressure. DS Skinner's eyes were half closed and it appeared as though it was a real effort to keep them open. DC Stone didn't look much better. The shifty-eyed detective didn't even try to disguise the yawns he had no control over. DC Owen appeared to be faring slightly better, but she too seemed more fatigued that usual. O'Reilly knew that it was up to him to try and perk them up a bit, but he was running out of ideas.

"We have a slight problem with Frieda Klein, Mike Trunk and Yolanda Stewart. All three of them have suddenly forgotten how to talk."

"That's definitely suspicious," DC Stone said.

"It is, Andy," O'Reilly agreed. "Three people who have committed murder in the past few days have gone mute on us. But as I've often said before there are plenty of ways to skin a cat. If they don't want to talk to us, we'll have to find another way to get what we want."

"How are we going to do that?" DC Stone asked.

"By talking to people who are happier to speak to us. I think it's time for a new approach. Everything about the recent events has been irrational. The madness on display has clouded our judgement and we need to start afresh."

DC Stone didn't even try to hide the groan he let forth.

"I appreciate your frustration, Andy," O'Reilly said. "We're all frustrated, but that's why we need to change tack. Up until now we've looked at the perpetrators of the murders as victims. We've been blinkered by the methods at play, and we haven't really considered the possibility that all of this was actually well planned."

"Are you serious, sir?" DS Skinner said.

"Deadly. What if there is more to this than we've thought about? Four people are dead, and all of them died at the hands of someone close to them."

"With respect, sir," DS Skinner said. "The majority of murders are carried out by someone who knows the victim."

"Granted," O'Reilly said. "But not all murders are committed by people who have no memory of the event and who subsequently lose the ability to speak. What do we know about these people? Pretty much feck all, and that won't do."

His phone started to ring. The screen told him it was his daughter, and he let it go to voicemail. Soon afterwards there was a beep to tell him that Assumpta had left a message. He would listen to it later.

"I appreciate that it feels like we've still got a long uphill slog ahead of us," he said. "But we always get there in the end. Let's go through the sequence of events once more. On Saturday afternoon, all hell broke loose at a party attended by some of the wealthiest residents of the island. Spontaneous violence was followed by mass amnesia. All but one of the guests experienced the same effects and we now know why."

"The only person who didn't drink the wine was spared from the psychosis it caused," DC Stone said.

"Precisely," O'Reilly said. "None of the other guests remember a thing about that afternoon and that was due to whatever drug that *Chateau La Folie* was contaminated with. Luckily, nobody was killed at the party."

"Later that night a drunk killed his friend," DC Owen said. "Fortunately, the attack was caught on camera, and that's why Mike Trunk gave himself up."

"And I can't be the only one who smells something iffy about that," O'Reilly said. "I don't buy the sudden guilt thing. Why did Mr Trunk give himself up?"

"The CCTV footage was pretty damning, sir," DC Stone said. "It wouldn't have taken us long to find the man."

"Something isn't right about it," O'Reilly said. "Why hand himself in if he's planning on telling us he can't remember anything about the attack?"

"It might all boil down to the man's conscience, sir," DS Skinner said.

"Perhaps," O'Reilly said. "If it was an isolated incident, but then we have the old German lady. Frieda Klein also has no memory of killing her husband, yet she confessed to the people on the beach."

"It is very odd," DC Owen said.

"And then we have the young woman who killed her best friend up by Bluebell Woods. Belinda Cole is not yet eighteen. She claims that an innocent stroll up to the cliff ended with her butchering her friend, and she too cannot remember any of it. Miss Cole isn't telling us everything."

"She slipped up," DC Owen said. "She broke down and said she couldn't remember killing Joanne Hawkins and she can't remember dumping half the bottle over the edge of the cliff. The DI never mentioned that. How is it that she has no recollection of killing Joanne, but she recalls dumping the murder weapon?"

"And why would she get rid of the bottle if she wasn't planning on carrying out the murder in the first place?" DC Stone said.

"We don't yet know what went on up in St Sampson," O'Reilly carried on. "Yolanda Stewart was taken to hospital on the recommendation of her brother. He's a lawyer and we're not going to be able to talk to her any time soon. Her husband died due to a single wound to his neck. An empty bottle of *Chateau La Folie* was recovered from the scene but unfortunately, Mrs Stewart felt the need to rinse it out."

"Why would she do that?" DC Stone wondered.

"Why indeed? It looks like Mrs Stewart killed her husband and sat down to enjoy a cheese platter."

"She used the knife that she killed her husband with," DC Owen added. "There was still blood on the knife and in the brie on the board."

"I feel sick," DC Stone said.

"You're not the only one, Andy," O'Reilly said.

His phone started to ring once more. The screen told him it was his daughter again, and O'Reilly knew it had to be important. Assumpta rarely called him when she knew he was at work. The ringtone went quiet.

O'Reilly got to his feet.

"I need to make a phone call. I shouldn't be long."

He left the briefing room and called Assumpta back. She answered immediately.

"Sorry to bother you at work."

"Is something wrong?" O'Reilly asked her.

"It's Bram," she said. "Victoria found him outside the back door. He wasn't moving, and he was making strange noises."

"He was doing it earlier," O'Reilly said. "Is he alright?"

"Victoria had a doctor's appointment so she asked if I could come and take him to the vet. I'm here now, and it's not looking good."

O'Reilly didn't know what to say. He and Bram had had a love-hate relationship from the onset, but he'd grown quite fond of the ginger brute. "The vet thinks Bram's abdomen is distended, and that's why he's experiencing discomfort."

"Can he fix it?" O'Reilly asked.

"He wants to do some tests first," Assumpta said. "He needs to get to the bottom of what's causing it. He's going to keep him in for at least a couple of nights, and he asked me to tell you it's not going to be cheap."

"What?"

"It could be a costly exercise."

"I don't give a flying fuck how much it costs, Summi," O'Reilly said.

"I'm just telling you what he told me."

"I'm sorry. I didn't mean to shout at you. I'll pay whatever it costs."

"I'll forward you the vet's details," Assumpta said. "I'm sure Bram will be fine. He'll be back annoying the devil out of you in no time."

They said their goodbyes and O'Reilly remained where he was in the corridor. He felt numb. Bram hadn't been in his life for very long – he hadn't been invited, but O'Reilly realised he couldn't imagine life without the annoying ginger squatter. No, life would definitely not be the same without Bram in it. The beep of the phone brought him out of his reverie. Assumpta had sent the details of the vet. O'Reilly saved it to his phone and headed back to the briefing room.

CHAPTER TWENTY NINE

The veterinary practice was a stone's throw from Victoria's house in Vazon. O'Reilly hadn't been there before. He'd returned to the briefing room with every intention of carrying on with the investigation, but his mind wasn't on it anymore. He couldn't concentrate on the case while Bram was in a cage at the vets. He needed to speak to someone to find out what was wrong with his cat.

"I've gone soft," he said to himself when he went inside the practice. A man on his way out cast him a curious glance as he passed.
O'Reilly walked up to the reception desk. A young woman was talking to someone on the phone. She was telling the person on the other end of the line that the guinea pig that had been brought in the day before hadn't made it. O'Reilly sighed. He imagined that somewhere on the island was a child about to have their heart broken.

The receptionist ended the call and smiled at O'Reilly. "Can I help you, sir?"
"The name's O'Reilly," he said. "My daughter brought a ginger cat in earlier."
"Ah, yes," the woman said. "Bram. He's quite a character."
"He is that," O'Reilly agreed. "Is he going to be OK?"
"Give me a minute. I'll see if Mr French is available. Please take a seat."

O'Reilly sat down on one of the chairs in the reception area. He picked up a magazine from the table and put it down again when he realised that it was a travel magazine, and the main feature was about things to see on the island of Herm. O'Reilly had seen more than enough of the chunk of land across the bay from Guernsey to last a lifetime, and he wasn't keen to revisit the place on the pages of a travel magazine.

A woman came in with a small black dog in her arms. She sat down next to O'Reilly. The dog crept over to him and made himself comfortable on his lap.

"Bruno," the woman said. "That's terribly rude."

O'Reilly scratched the dog's head. "It's OK. What are you in for, little fella?"

"I'm having him neutered," the woman explained.

You poor bastard, O'Reilly thought.

"It's for his own good," the woman added. "We live in an apartment complex, and he won't stop sniffing around the ladies there."

The receptionist appeared with a young man and O'Reilly was glad. The conversation with the owner of the unfortunate black dog was making him feel uncomfortable. The man introduced himself as Alvin French and asked O'Reilly to come through to his office.

"Please take a seat," Alvin said, and sat down behind the desk.

O'Reilly sat opposite him. "What's wrong with my cat?"

"How long have you got?"

"Excuse me?"

"I'm joking. It took three of us just to get him into his cage. He's a stubborn one."

"He lacks social skills," O'Reilly said. "Is he going to be OK?"

"I think so," Alvin said. "I still want to do some more tests to rule out anything serious, but it looks like Bram's discomfort is due to distension of his abdomen. It's relatively common in cats. Their abdominal muscles are relatively weak, and distension can occur."

"What causes it?"

"I'll have to carry out some further tests, but it looks to me like your ginger friend has a buildup of fluid in his abdominal cavity. I can drain it, and put him on a course of anti-inflammatories together with some antibiotics and he should make a full recovery. I'd like to keep him in for at least two nights though."

"That's fine," O'Reilly said. "He's a pain in the neck, but I've grown quite fond of him. How much do I owe you?"

"We'll worry about that when we've got Bram back on his feet," Alvin said. "I'm afraid I have to get ready for surgery now."

O'Reilly thought about the small black dog, and he crossed his legs without even realising he was doing it.

"I'll keep you up to date," Alvin said.

He held out his hand.

O'Reilly shook it. "Thank you. And I don't care how much it costs. I just want that ginger bugger back home."

"I understand," Alvin said. "We'll have him back to normal in no time."

O'Reilly left the vets and headed back to his car. He took out his phone and sent a short message to Assumpta telling her that Bram was probably going to be OK. Then he brought up Victoria's number and tapped call.

"Liam," she answered it. "I was just about to call you."

"Bram is going to be staying at the vets for a couple of nights at least."

"Oh," Victoria said. "That isn't why I was going to phone. I've got the all clear from the doctor."

O'Reilly felt terrible. The visit to the vet had made him forget all about Victoria's doctor's appointment.

"I'm so sorry," he said. "What did the doc say?"

"I'm in remission, Liam," Victoria said.

It was a word O'Reilly had been waiting to hear for some time, and right now it was the most beautiful word he'd ever heard.

"Liam," Victoria said. "Are you still there?"

"I'm still here. That's the best news ever."

"The bloodwork tests couldn't detect any trace of the cancer," Victoria said.

"You beat it."

"We beat it," Victoria said. "I couldn't have done this without you, Liam. Now, tell me about Bram."

"The vet thinks he's got a buildup of fluid in his abdomen. He wants to carry out some tests, but he doesn't think it's serious. Bram will be enjoying the hospitality of Vazon Veterinary Centre for a couple of nights."

Victoria laughed. "He's going to love that."

"Perhaps he'll appreciate the life he has with us more when he comes home."

"I very much doubt that. I'll let you get back to work."

"This is the best news," O'Reilly said. "We'll have to go out and celebrate later. I quite fancy another one of those seafood platters."

"We'll do that. I love you, Liam."

"I love you too."

O'Reilly ended the call and walked over to his car. Something was happening inside him. He opened the car and got in. He closed the door and glanced at his reflection in the rearview mirror. The image was blurred. The tears that were pouring from his eyes were making it impossible to see himself in the mirror.

CHAPTER THIRTY

In O'Reilly's absence the team had been looking more closely into the lives of the men and women who had suddenly turned homicidal in the past few days. DC Stone had managed to track down one of John and Yolanda Stewart's children. Kenneth Stewart had taken the news of his father's death remarkably well when DC Stone had called him and told him what had happened, and he'd agreed to talk to the rat-faced detective at his home in St Peter Port.

Kenneth lived in a three-bedroom apartment one street back from the esplanade. The apartment was double storey and from the top floor it offered views of the beach and Belle Greve Bay. Kenneth opened the door and looked DC Stone up and down.
"Can I help you?"
DC Stone showed him his ID. "DC Stone. We spoke on the phone."
"I see," Kenneth said. "You're not exactly what I was expecting."
DC Stone didn't know how to react to this. Kenneth invited him in and led him to a spacious sitting room.

"I'm very sorry about your father," DC Stone said.
"I must admit, it did come as a bit of a shock," Kenneth said. "You said my mother confessed to killing him."
"I'm afraid so."
"Jesus," Kenneth said. "I didn't think she had it in her."
"I'm not following you."
"I apologise. It still hasn't sunk in. What exactly happened?"
"We're still putting together the pieces at this stage," DC Stone said. "We haven't been able to speak to your mother. Her brother has advised her not to say anything until she's been checked over. We're hoping to talk to her tomorrow."

"That sounds like something Uncle James would do. Would you like something to drink?"

"No thank you."

A young girl entered the room. DC Stone guessed her age to be around four or five.

"Not now, Sadie," Kenneth said. "I'm busy."

"But Kenny won't let me watch my programme," the girl said.

"I said not now."

Kenneth fixed her with an icy stare, and it did the trick. She ran out of the room without saying anything further.

"Sorry about that," Kenneth said.

"Was that your daughter?" DC Stone said.

Kenneth nodded. "I was blessed with twins. Sadie and Kenneth Junior – Kenny. They live with me during the school holidays and the odd weekends."

DC Stone didn't comment on this.

"I'm divorced," Kenneth elaborated. "My ex got the kids and most of my money. Are you married?"

"I'm not."

"Stay that way. Marriage is a mug's game. What's going to happen to my mother?"

"It's difficult to say," DC Stone said. "Until we know exactly what happened, we can't say for certain how the incident will be handled."

"I'm not quite following you," Kenneth said. "Did she kill my father or not?"

"We believe she did, but we also have reason to believe that she didn't intend to kill him. It's possible she was drugged, and the narcotic caused her to behave irrationally."

"Is this connected to what happened at the Gottlieb function?"

"Are you friends with the Gottliebs?" DC Stone asked.

"We're aware of one another, yes."

"You have a brother, don't you?" DC Stone said.

"For what it's worth," Kenneth said.

"What do you mean by that?"

"I haven't seen Lloyd for almost ten years."

"Did you have a falling out?"

"Not really," Kenneth said. "Lloyd couldn't wait to get the hell off the island and he isn't in a hurry to return."

"Where is he now?"

"God knows. The last I heard he was somewhere in America. California, I think. Does he know about Mother and Father?"

"We haven't been able to get hold of him. Do you have any contact details for him? He needs to be informed."

"He'll be back," Kenneth said. "When he hears about the old lady, he'll be back. He wouldn't want to miss out on the opportunity of getting his grubby hands on the money."

"What money?"

"With my father out of the picture," Kenneth said. "It would be Mother who inherits the estate, wouldn't it?"

"I imagine so," DC Stone confirmed.

"But if she's convicted of killing the old bastard," Kenneth said. "I doubt she'll be entitled to a cent. Isn't that how it works?"

"I'm not sure. Was your father well off?"

"Are you kidding me?" Kenneth said. "Have you seen the house in St Sampson? The last valuation was somewhere in the region of twenty million. And he's recently sold his business. I heard he netted a cool twenty-five bar for that. So, yes – you could say my old man was well off."

DC Stone wasn't quite sure how to interpret Kenneth Stewart's reaction to the death of his father. It was possible his mother would be spending her remaining years behind bars, but Kenneth didn't seem particularly fazed about losing both parents in one fell swoop.

"Do you know if your parents were acquainted with someone called Mike Trunk?" DC Stone asked.

"The name doesn't ring a bell," Kenneth said.

"What about Otto and Frieda Klein?"

"I've never heard those names before. Although I didn't really mix in the same circles as my mother and father."

"What circles might those be?" DC Stone said.

"My father was a multi-millionaire, detective. OK, I benefited – my brother and I were educated in the best schools on the island, and we were forced to endure the vacations in the Caribbean and Aspen, but when I left for university, I put all that bullshit behind me."

"What do you do?"

"Engineering," Kenneth said. "My specialty is the mining sector. It takes me all over the world. That's probably why I'm no longer married. I have a conference call I need to prepare for."

"I won't keep you any longer," DC Stone said. "I really am sorry about your father."

"Don't be," Kenneth said. "If you'd known him, you wouldn't be sorry at all."

CHAPTER THIRTY ONE

By five that afternoon a picture of the four unconventional killers was starting to take shape. DC Owen had managed to get hold of a family member of Frieda Klein's in Germany, and it soon became clear that Frau Klein was no stranger to money. According to Frieda's cousin, she'd married Otto when she was seventeen. He was sixteen years her senior, and he was the sole heir to a fortune borne of oil. The cousin also told DC Owen that Frieda had never had to work a day in her life.

DS Skinner had come up trumps too. Belinda Cole was due to inherit a substantial amount of money in a few days' time. Her grandfather had set up the trust in her name and it would come to fruition on the day of her eighteenth birthday. Belinda was soon to become a very rich young woman.

"Miss Cole is going to be the holder of an unenviable record," DS Skinner told the team in the briefing room. "In two days, she will be the richest person we've ever held in custody."
"How much are we talking about?" DC Stone asked.
"Sixteen million," DS Skinner said. "Give or take a few pounds."
"Then she'll be the second richest person ever held in police custody on the island," DC Stone said.
"What are you talking about?" O'Reilly said.
"I did some digging, sir," DC Stone said. "When I got back from Kenneth Stewart's place. Mike Trunk isn't what he appears to be. He might come across as a hobo and a drunk, but he's worth more than the GDP of a small African nation. Twenty-two million to be precise."
"Are you sure?" DC Owen said.
"Positive. His financial records were easy to come by. Apparently, Mr Trunk made a killing in his prime as a finance expert. I also spoke to John Stewart's son. It's quite clear there was no love lost between him and his

father. When I told him I was sorry about John, he told me not to be. He said if I'd known him, I wouldn't be sorry at all."

"The plot thickens," DC Skinner said.

"This plot is thicker than my grandmother's potato soup," O'Reilly said. "God rest her soul. And to give you an idea about that – we used to have to eat it with a knife and fork. We're getting somewhere."

They were prevented from discussing it further when PC London came into the room.

"What is it, Kim?" O'Reilly asked.

"Sorry to interrupt, sir," she said. "But we've had a report of a break-in at a warehouse close to the port."

O'Reilly was confused. "And?"

"I thought you'd want to know about it," PC London said. "It's the warehouse owned by Jacob Hunt."

* * *

O'Reilly didn't know if the break-in at the warehouse that stocked the wine that caused the guests at the Gottlieb party to go berserk was relevant to the investigation, but something inside him was telling him it needed checking out. In essence, the warehouse was where the recent madness on the island had started, and that made it very relevant indeed.

The distribution hub was much busier than it had been when O'Reilly and DC Owen were there yesterday. Forklift trucks were buzzing back and forth between the loading bays. All but one of the bays had a container parked in front, waiting to be filled.

It had been Billy Foot who had discovered the break-in. The acne-scarred forklift truck driver had realised that something was wrong when he'd arrived at work for his late-afternoon shift. One of the doors that led inside to the warehouse was ajar and the lock had been forced. His first phone call had been to Melissa Paul, and the manager of the warehouse had arrived shortly afterwards. After a brief inspection it was clear that none of the wine had been stolen, but one of the offices had been ransacked and all of the electronic equipment was gone.

O'Reilly had requested DI Peters' presence at the warehouse. Usually, a break-in wouldn't warrant such a Forensics presence, but in light of recent events O'Reilly decided it was necessary now. DI Peters and DC Glenda Jackson were still busy at work in the wrecked office so Melissa Paul suggested they speak in the staff canteen.

"I see you're busy right now," O'Reilly said.
"Tuesday is our busiest day," Melissa explained. "We have stock coming in and out most of the night."
"It seems a bit late to start a shift," DC Owen said.
"We'll be operating through the night. That's the nature of the business."
"Has Mr Hunt been informed of the break-in?" O'Reilly asked.
"I left him a message."
"And he hasn't got back to you?"
"Not yet," Melissa said. "Can I ask why you're here? I'm sure you don't come out for every break-in on the island."
O'Reilly skirted the question. "Do you know what was taken?"
"It looks like it was mostly electronic equipment," Melissa said. "All the computers and laptops. It was probably an opportunist thing."
"When do you think the break-in happened?" DC Owen said.
"We closed down the warehouse yesterday at eight in the evening," Melissa said. "And we opened again this afternoon at four. That's when Billy realised that someone had been inside."
"Do you have CCTV in the warehouse?" DC Owen said.
"We have cameras outside looking onto the loading bays," Melissa said. "And there are a couple inside the warehouse itself."
"Can we take a look at the footage?" O'Reilly said.

"I would show it to you, if the devices the footage is stored on were still here."

"Are you saying the footage was lost with the computers?" DC Owen said.

"I'm afraid so."

"What about Cloud storage?" DC Owen said. "Surely you've got it backed up somewhere else. You should be able to log into the account from any device."

"I wouldn't know about that," Melissa said.

"Could you point us in the direction of someone who might know?" O'Reilly said.

"Why are you so interested in a break-in?"

"Please," O'Reilly said. "Could you find someone who can help us with that CCTV footage?"

Melissa left the room and returned with Billy Foot. O'Reilly thought the forklift truck driver smelled even more ripe today. The stench coming from him was a blend of BO and something sour. He grinned at DC Owen and his face flushed so deeply it accentuated the acne scars on his nose and chin.

"What can I help you with?" he asked.

"We're led to believe you know a bit about the CCTV system here," O'Reilly said.

"There isn't much to it," Billy said.

"We need to retrieve the footage from the past twenty-four-hours. Can you help us with that?"

"I doubt it."

"My colleague mentioned something about a cloud. Does that mean anything to you?"

"Cloud storage," Billy said. "Of course."

"So the footage is saved somewhere other than the IT devices in the office?" DC Owen said.

"I doubt it."

O'Reilly was starting to get annoyed. They were wasting time they couldn't afford to waste.

"Do you know what operating system the CCTV works through?" DC Owen said.

"As far as I know," Billy said. "Everything captured on the cameras is fed directly to the hard drive storage and nowhere else. Unless we find the stuff that was stolen, we're not going to be able to access the footage."

"Why the hell didn't Mr Hunt insist on this cloud thing?" O'Reilly said. "What's the point of having cameras if any Tom, Dick or Harry can just nick the drive where the footage is stored."

"Cloud storage costs extra," Billy said.

"Brilliant."

DI Peters came into the room in the nick of time. O'Reilly was very close to throttling the foul-smelling forklift operator.

"I want to show you something," the Head of Forensics said.

O'Reilly and DC Owen got up and followed him out.

"The CCTV footage is a dead end," O'Reilly said as they walked. "Apparently the footage went up in smoke when the devices it was stored on were lifted."

"It's not backed up on a Cloud," DC Owen added.

"Makes sense," DI Peters said.

"How does it make sense?" O'Reilly wondered.

"I think this was an inside job. You'll see what I mean in a minute."

He led them through the warehouse and stopped next to one of the doors that led outside. The metal door was covered with fingerprint powder.

"Did you pull any prints?" O'Reilly said.

"Plenty," DI Peters said. "But that's not what I want to show you."

He pointed to the section of the doorframe opposite the locking mechanism. The metal frame had been badly damaged, and the door was bent inwards.

"Looks like the work of a crowbar," O'Reilly said.

"Probably," DI Peters said. "Although in this instance the brute force was totally unnecessary."

"What are you saying?" DC Owen said.

"Look at the locking mechanism." DI Peters pointed to it.

"I'm no locksmith," O'Reilly admitted.

"It's a simple two-point locking system," DI Peters explained. "The deadbolt is locked straight into the door jamb, and the cylinder below it keeps the handle in place. It's an effective security measure."

"But they still managed to break in."

"They didn't break in," DI Peters said. "You jimmy a door with a crowbar and it doesn't look like this. It takes a lot of effort, and the resulting damage is more substantial than what we can see here. This door was already unlocked when it was subjected to the crowbar. Somebody unlocked it with a key and went at it with the crowbar to make it look like it was broken open. This was definitely an inside job."

CHAPTER THIRTY TWO

O'Reilly held the bottle of *Scapegoat* to his lips and took a drink. When he put down the bottle, he realised he'd downed most of it in one long sip. Victoria started to laugh. "Looks like you needed that."

"You're not wrong there," O'Reilly said. "What a day."

It was getting late by the time they'd finished at Jacob Hunt's warehouse, and he'd decided to call it a day. He would bring up the curious break-in first thing in the morning. Everyone on the team was dog-tired and it wouldn't be productive to carry on any longer today. He'd promised Victoria a meal out to celebrate the good news about her cancer and they were now back at the Red Snapper. O'Reilly was keen to see if he could polish off another seafood platter for two.

He raised the beer in the air. "Here's to my wife the superhero."

"I'm hardly a superhero, Liam," Victoria said.

She obliged anyway by raising her glass of water.

"In my eyes you are," O'Reilly insisted. "You beat it. You beat that bastard, and I'm the happiest man in the world right now."

"We beat it," Victoria said. "I couldn't have done it without you."

"Are you sure you don't want something a bit stronger than mineral water?"

"Maybe another time. I'm feeling good right now, and I don't want to do anything to mess that up."

A waiter approached the table and asked them if they were ready to order. O'Reilly asked him for another few minutes.

"You can bring us another round of drinks though," he added.

"Is there any news about Bram?" Victoria said.

"Nothing yet," O'Reilly said. "No news is good news, I reckon. He'll be fine. He's probably trashed the place by now."

"You're worried about him, aren't you?"

"Maybe a little bit," O'Reilly admitted. "I've got used to having him around. I'm sure he'll be fine."

The waiter returned with the drinks.

"Have you decided what you're going to eat?" O'Reilly asked Victoria.

"I feel like the cod and chips," she said.

"And a seafood platter for two," O'Reilly informed the waiter.

The young man eyed him quizzically.

"I have an exceptional appetite," O'Reilly told him.

The waiter raised an eyebrow and left them alone.

"I was thinking of taking a bike trip this weekend," Victoria said. "Are you keen?"

"On the Kawasaki?" O'Reilly said.

"Unless you've bought another bike without me knowing about it."

"Not likely. Where were you thinking of going?"

"There's a circular route Tommy and I used to do," Victoria said. "It starts in Vazon, we stop in L'Ancresse and head south to Jerbourg. Then we hit the coast road all the way to Pleinmont and finish up back in Vazon. It's a spectacular ride."

"Are you sure you're up to it?"

"It's just what the doctor ordered. I can handle it."

"I don't doubt that you can handle it," O'Reilly said. "I'm more worried about you handling having a portly Irishman on the back of the bike."

"I'm sure I'll manage."

"I don't know if I'll be able to get the time off. This investigation is making my brain hurt."

"Do you want to talk about it?"

"I don't know what you've read in the papers," O'Reilly said.

"I've seen snippets. Something about perfectly ordinary people committing murder for no reason. The latest Herald headline was something about madness on the island."

"For once, Fred Viking is not far off the mark," O'Reilly said. "We've had four separate incidents. Four individuals suddenly developed homicidal urges. None of the perpetrators are acquainted with any of the others, but I know for a fact that the murders are connected. Even though there is nothing that connects them apart from the fact that the killers are all filthy rich."

"Welcome to Guernsey," Victoria said.

"There is far too much money on this island."

The food arrived and the discussion was cut short. O'Reilly looked at the mountain of seafood on the plate and wondered if this was going to be the time when the platter would beat him. He dipped a prawn in some garlic sauce, took a bite and decided he was probably going to be able to finish it after all. The prawn really was delicious.

His phone started to ring when he was halfway through the seafood platter. The number was one he didn't recognise so he rejected the call.

"Who was it?" Victoria asked.

"I have no idea," O'Reilly said. "But it was probably something to do with work, and I'm busy right now. Tell me some more about this bike ride."

"You'll love it," Victoria said. "We'll set off at the crack of dawn and hit the roads before the traffic starts to build up."

"You're not planning on burning rubber, are you?"

"It's not that kind of ride. It's a leisurely cruise around the island. OK, I might be tempted to open her up a bit on the corners on the coast road, but that's what the Kawasaki is designed for. We can stop for lunch somewhere nice. It'll be a good way for you to see the island."

"I've seen plenty of the island," O'Reilly said. "And all I'm seeing at the moment is ridiculous amounts of money. I've never understood why people get so obsessed with money. From what I've seen, most of the rich people I've met are miserable."

"Is this where we engage in a deep, meaningful philosophical debate?"
"You can take the Irishman out of Ireland, and all that. But no. I'm not in the mood for a maudlin discussion on the moralistic failures of certain members of society."
"Way too deep, Liam," Victoria warned.
"I'll shut up," O'Reilly said. "I need to concentrate on getting through the rest of that anyway."
He nodded to the plate in front of him. All that was left were a few mussels, a couple of scallops and a solitary prawn.

His phone started to ring again. It was the same unknown number.
"Perhaps you ought to answer it," Victoria said.
O'Reilly sighed and did as she suggested.

It was nothing to do with work, and as O'Reilly listened to the man on the other end, he wished it was. Alvin French was the bearer of bad news. O'Reilly found it hard to decipher most of what the vet was telling him, but he did understand the general gist of it – Bram's condition was much more serious than initially suspected, and O'Reilly was warned to prepare himself for the worst.

CHAPTER THIRTY THREE

O'Reilly woke from a restless sleep and rubbed his eyes. The phone call from the veterinary practice had dampened the mood of the evening, and O'Reilly had asked for the bill soon after he ended the call. He wasn't able to finish the seafood platter for two. The news Alvin French had given him was grim. Bram had tested positive for something known as FIP. Feline Infectious Peritonitis was a viral disease in cats caused by certain strains of feline coronavirus.

O'Reilly had arrived home from the Red Snapper, booted up his laptop and made a cup of tea. He needed to know more about a virus he'd never heard of. He needed to know what Bram was going through. The research he did was hard going and it didn't exactly inspire confidence in Bram's chances.

According to the website he looked through, he learned that FIP comes in two different forms – an effusive or *wet* form, or a non-effusive or *dry* form, and Bram had been diagnosed with the former. The symptoms of this type of FIP appear rapidly and can include a buildup of fluid in the abdominal cavity. In certain cases this buildup can be excessive and it can result in the cat being unable to breathe properly.

There was a bit of good news on the pages that O'Reilly pored through. Until recently, FIP was considered untreatable and it was almost always fatal, but due to recent developments in veterinary medicine there were now medications available to treat the virus. Alvin French had mentioned some of these and the vet had promised to get Bram on a course of treatment straight away. Everything rested on whether the ginger moggie had been diagnosed in time. Once the virus took hold, it became more difficult to stop it from affecting the vital organs and O'Reilly hoped and prayed that this wasn't going to happen to Bram.

It had been after two in the morning when he finally closed down his laptop and headed up to bed, but his brain still couldn't switch off. He tossed and turned as he tried to process the information, and he'd only managed to drop off thirty minutes before the alarm on his phone told him it was time to get up.

O'Reilly made some tea and swiped the screen of his phone. He called the number for Alvin French but it went straight to voicemail. The young vet probably wasn't up yet. O'Reilly left a brief message asking him to call back when it was convenient.

The house felt strange without Bram in it. Even though the ginger beast usually only showed his face when there was something in it for him, O'Reilly missed knowing he was around somewhere. Juliet and Shadow were acting strangely too, and if O'Reilly didn't know any better, he would swear they'd sensed that there was something wrong with their friend.

"Are you alright?"

The voice in the doorway made O'Reilly jump. He hadn't heard Victoria moving around upstairs.

"Not really," he said. "I miss the fat little bugger."

"Bram will be alright," Victoria said. "He's a tough critter. He'll pull through this."

"The vet isn't answering his phone."

"It's seven-thirty in the morning, Liam," Victoria reminded him.

"I suppose so."

O'Reilly got up and walked over to his wife. He kissed her on the cheek and sighed.

"Right, I suppose I should be getting ready for work. I'll let you know if there's any news about Bram."

* * *

The drive across the island to work passed in a blur and when O'Reilly parked in the car park of the Island Police HQ he realised he couldn't remember any of it. He got out of the car and slammed the door.

"It's a damn moggy for Christ's sake."

He went inside the station and headed straight for his office. After making some tea he checked his phone to see if he'd received any recent messages. The screen told him he hadn't. He debated whether to phone the vet again but decided against it. There was a lot of work to get through today and he needed his mind to be completely focused on the investigation. Bram was in the best hands he could possibly be in.

DC Stone was alone in the briefing room when O'Reilly went in. He was scribbling something on the whiteboard at the back of the room.

"You're here early, Andy," he said.

"I couldn't sleep, sir."

"That makes two of us. What are you up to?"

"Something occurred to me when I was sitting in the kitchen at 3am this morning."

"What the devil were you doing in the kitchen at that time?" O'Reilly asked.

"Drinking coffee."

"And what was it that occurred to you?"

"What if this is about money, sir?" DC Stone said.

"You've lost me there."

DC Stone tapped the whiteboard. "The combined wealth of the four murderers is somewhere in the region of a hundred and fifty million pounds."

"That is a substantial amount of money," O'Reilly agreed. "But how does it tie in with the recent murders?"

"Hear me out," DC Stone said. "Frieda Klein isn't independently wealthy. It's her husband with the cash, but she'll probably inherit the lot, won't she?"

"Go on."

"It's the same with Yolanda Stewart. It's her husband who made the money, but now he's dead Yolanda will cash in. What if these men were killed for their money?"

"It's a half-decent theory," O'Reilly said. "But when you bring Mike Trunk and Belinda Cole into the equation it doesn't fit. The drunk and the teenage girl have no reason to kill anyone to get rich – they're rich already without any outside help."

"I'm just running out of ideas, sir," DC Stone said. "It's getting to me."

"This isn't about money, Andy," O'Reilly said. "You do not confess to a murder if you plan to benefit financially from the person you've killed."

"Unless you're convinced you're going to get away with it, sir."

O'Reilly looked at the man who had been in a relationship with his daughter for months as though he was observing him for the first time.

"Are you alright, sir?" DC Stone asked.

"I'm just grand, Andy," O'Reilly replied. "I believe you could be onto something there."

CHAPTER THIRTY FOUR

The first thing on the agenda at the morning briefing was the *break-in* at Jacob Hunt's warehouse. DI Peters was convinced it was an inside job – someone who had a key to the outer door had tried to make it look like a break-in and they hadn't done a very good job of it, and this is what O'Reilly decided to discuss first.

"If Jim Peters suspects this was designed to look like someone had broken in," he said. "I'm inclined to take his word for it. The metal door was damaged, but the locking system was in the open position. Someone used a key to get inside that warehouse."

"Do we know who has a key for that door?" DS Skinner said.

"According to Melissa Paul, only she, Billy Foot and Jacob Hunt are in possession of the keys. Melissa is the manager, so it's logical that she'll have a key. Ditto with Jacob – it's his warehouse, but I can't understand why the stinky forklift truck driver would have a key."

"Stinky forklift driver?" DC Stone repeated.

"You'll understand when you meet him, Andy. We'll be bringing in Mr Foot and Mrs Paul during the course of the morning."

"Shouldn't we be focusing on the murder investigation?" DS Skinner said.

"This is part of that investigation," O'Reilly told him. "Someone went to a lot of trouble to make sure we didn't get hold of the CCTV footage from the warehouse, and that makes me wonder if there is something on it that they really didn't want us to see."

"The footage from the cameras isn't backed up onto a Cloud," DC Owen said.

"I thought all CCTV was sent directly to Cloud storage these days," DS Skinner said.

"Only if you pay a subscription," DC Owen said. "And apparently Jacob Hunt didn't. Everything those cameras caught disappeared with the computer equipment stolen from the office."

"How much was taken?" DS Skinner said.

"All the electronic devices were missing," O'Reilly said.

"Including the external hard drives and all the peripherals," DC Owen said.

"That means they were probably in a vehicle," DS Skinner said.

"It's safe to assume they were," O'Reilly said.

"What about CCTV in nearby businesses? The warehouse that distributes the wine is in a part of the island where there are other similar buildings close by. We might get lucky with the cameras from one of those."

"It's worth a try." O'Reilly didn't sound very convinced. "I'll put some uniforms on it. Andy."

"Sir?" DC Stone said.

"You wanted to discuss a theory you'd come up with."

"This might sound a bit farfetched," DC Stone began.

"Farfetched is better than nothing," DS Skinner said.

"I thought hard about the murders last night," DC Stone said. "I did come up with a theory about it being about money, but that doesn't apply to half of them. But there was something that jumped out at me. None of the people who carried out the murders claim to have any memory of it. I don't buy that. We have four separate murders carried out by four people who don't know each other, and all four of them can't remember doing what they did."

"I thought we'd already covered that," DS Skinner said. "The drug in the wine caused the blackouts."

"What if it didn't? The only bottles of wine that tested positive for the mystery narcotic were the ones retrieved from the Gottlieb function, the one Belinda Cole drank from, and the bottle found at Fort Hommet. Nobody was killed at the Gottlieb thing, which means the only incidences of contaminated wine resulting in murder came from the bottles the drunk used to kill his friend and the wine Belinda drank before she murdered Joanne Hawkins. There is no proof that the same drug was in the bottles found at the other murder scenes."

"We assumed there would be," DC Owen said. "The behaviour of the people who carried out the murders was so similar that we automatically assumed it, didn't we?"

"What if that was the whole point?" DC Stone said. "What if that's how it was meant to look? I warned you it was a farfetched theory."

"I'm not sure I understand what you're implying, Andy," DS Skinner said. "Are you suggesting that four people who have never met each other all decided to commit murder in a way that would probably guarantee that they would get away with it? That's preposterous. And it's also impossible to pull off."

"Do you have any better theories?" O'Reilly said.

"No, sir," DS Skinner admitted. "But surely no theories are better than one so ridiculous it borders on madness."

"Madness is what we're dealing with, Will," O'Reilly said. "When you're dealing with madness, logical thinking falls out of the window."

"What's the plan of action for the day?" DC Owen changed the topic of conversation.

"An endless string of interviews," O'Reilly said. "We'll see if we can remind some unlikely murderers how to talk. Their sudden muteness yesterday makes me antsy, and I hate it when that happens. We'll also be questioning the people who have keys to Jacob Hunt's warehouse, including the big man himself."

His phone started to ring, and the name on the screen caused him to shoot up in his chair.

"Is everything OK, sir?" DC Owen said.

"I need to take this."

O'Reilly left the briefing room without offering any further information.

It was Alvin French. O'Reilly's finger was shaking as it hovered over the screen.

He managed to tap it to answer the call.

"O'Reilly." His voice was shaky too.

"Can you talk?" the vet asked.

"I can talk."

"I've got good news and bad news."

"Go on," O'Reilly urged.

"The good news is that Bram made it through the night. That's always a good sign where FIP is concerned. I've drained the fluids from his abdomen, and I've got him on a course of antivirals. The drugs are relatively new, but they've proven to be effective. I'm afraid it's a case of wait and see."

"OK," O'Reilly said. "Can I ask you to be honest?"

"Of course."

"What do you reckon his chances are?"

"It's too early to tell."

"You must have some idea," O'Reilly said. "Honest opinion."

"Fifty-fifty. I'm sorry I can't give you better news."

"Fifty-fifty is good enough for me," O'Reilly told him. "I'm sure some of my Irish luck has rubbed off on the free-loading bastard since he moved in with me."

"I'll keep you up to date."

O'Reilly thanked him and ended the call.

"Fifty, fifty," he said to himself.

There was still hope.

O'Reilly looked up and saw that PC Woodbine was walking in his direction. The giant PC had to duck underneath the doorframe by the reception area.

"Sir," he said. "I've got a woman by the front desk I think you need to speak to."

"Who is she?" O'Reilly asked.

"Her name is Connie Woodman, sir. She's come to report her husband missing."

"What the devil has that got to do with me?"

"Because she hasn't seen her husband since Saturday, and she referred to him as *Woody*."

CHAPTER THIRTY FIVE

O'Reilly studied the woman sitting in one of the chairs in the reception area and wondered if she was now a widow. Surely it was too much of a coincidence for a man known as Woody to have last been seen the night a man of the same name was butchered by Fort Hommet? He also wondered whether she had seen the footage posted by the Island Herald of the attack up by the fort, and if she had why had it taken her so long to come in? He guessed her age to be somewhere in the mid to late thirties region. She was a petite woman with short black hair, and the expression on her face was difficult to read. O'Reilly didn't think she could have seen the footage of her husband's murder – she seemed far too calm for that.

"Mrs Woodman," he said to her. "Could you follow me please."
"Who are you?" she asked.
"DI O'Reilly. We can talk in my office. Have you been offered anything to drink?"
"I don't want anything to drink. Do you know something about Woody?"
"Please follow me."

He closed the door of his office and asked Mrs Woodman to take a seat.
"You know something, don't you?" she said as she sat down.
"When did you last see your husband?" O'Reilly asked.
"Saturday."
"What time was this?"
"About five in the afternoon. I told the PC behind the desk all of this."
"Can I ask you why it's taken you so long to report him missing?"
"It's been three days," Connie said, rather vaguely.
"Could you explain what you mean by that?"
"It's the deal. He's not usually gone for more than two, but we agreed that

he would always report back before three days had passed."
O'Reilly was confused. He told Connie Woodman as much.
 "This isn't the first time Woody has gone walkabout," she explained. "God, it isn't even the fiftieth. He's been hitting the road, on and off since we got married. I got used to it after a while, and he always comes back."
"And you allow him to wander off?" O'Reilly said.
"There's not much I can do about it."
"Do you know why he feels the need to take these *excursions*?" O'Reilly didn't know what else to call them.
 "He's a free spirit," Connie said. "And he needs his own space more than most people do. I don't mind – we all need to be alone, don't we?"
O'Reilly didn't comment on this.
"OK," he said. "You say you last saw Woody on Saturday afternoon. Where was this?"
"At the hotel. The Grand on La Grange."
"Are you here on holiday?"
"It wouldn't have been my first choice," Connie said. "But when Woody won the competition, we could hardly say no, could we?"
"You won a holiday to Guernsey?"
"Woody did. He can't even remember entering the damn thing, but he was probably drunk, so I didn't question it."
"Does your husband drink a lot?"
"More than most. I don't mind – we all need an outlet, don't we?"
O'Reilly couldn't quite figure this strange woman out. He'd never come across such a tolerant wife before.
 "What did you do during your husband's absence?" he asked.
"I stayed in the hotel mostly," Connie said. "I'm not much of a tourist, and it's not every day you get to stay in a fancy hotel, all expenses paid. Do you know anything about where Woody could be?"

"I'm not sure. So, you remained in the hotel. How did you occupy your time? Did you perhaps log onto social media?"

"No way," Connie said. "I hate all that nonsense. I read my Kindle mostly. Are you going to do something about finding my husband – I miss him."

"I'll put the word out. Did he mention anything about where he might be going?"

"No," Connie said. "And I didn't ask. I appreciate that you must think our relationship is a rather odd one, but it works for us. Woody is always the sweetest, kindest man when he returns from his travels."

"You call him Woody," O'Reilly said.

"Everyone calls him that."

"What's his first name?"

"Warren."

"Warren Woodman?"

"That's correct."

"Could you describe your husband?" O'Reilly said.

"I can do better than that," Connie said.

She reached inside her handbag and pulled out a purse. When she slipped the photograph from its slot and showed it to O'Reilly, he gasped.

"What is it?" Connie said.

There was no doubt that the man in the photograph was the same man Mike Trunk had beaten to death next to Fort Hommet.

"What aren't you telling me?" Connie said. "Has something happened to Woody?"

"I'm afraid it has," O'Reilly told her.

"No. You're lying."

"A man matching your husband's description was killed on Saturday night, Mrs Woodman."

"You're a liar," Connie said.

"I'm afraid I'm telling the truth. The attack was caught on CCTV, and it was definitely your husband in the footage. I'm very sorry."

"That can't be true. This is Guernsey for fucks sake."

"Is there someone I can call for you?" O'Reilly said. "Do you know anyone on the island?"

"I," She said. "No, I don't know anyone here. Where is he? Can I see him?"

"I'm not sure that's a good idea. I really am very sorry."

"What happened?" Connie said. "You said he was attacked. What happened to him?"

"We're not quite sure yet."

Connie didn't say anything further. Her eyes focused on something behind him. O'Reilly turned and he realised she was staring at a photograph of Bram on the wall behind the desk. He turned back to see that Connie Woodman had stood up.

"Do you need a lift somewhere?" O'Reilly asked.

"I need to lie down."

"I'll arrange for someone to take you back to your hotel."

"Who would do such a thing? Woody never hurt anybody."

Something occurred to O'Reilly. It was probably a bad idea to bring it up, but he decided to do it anyway.

"Mrs Woodman," he said. "Connie. Do you know a man by the name of Mike Trunk?"

Connie turned to face him. "What?"

"Mike Trunk," O'Reilly repeated. "Do you know anyone by that name?"

Connie's facial features changed. There was an expression of utter confusion there now.

"Why are you asking me about Michael?"

"Do you know Mike Trunk?" O'Reilly said.

"Of course I know him," Connie said. "I was married to the man for almost a year."

CHAPTER THIRTY SIX

"We were married very young."

O'Reilly had managed to persuade Connie Woodman to sit down again. Her revelation about Mike Trunk was important – of that he was certain, and he needed to know more. He'd made them both a cup of tea and he was waiting to see what she had to say.

"We met at university in Bristol," Connie continued. "Michael was studying Economics, and I was doing a Humanities degree. When I saw him during Fresher's Week I was smitten. Michael wasn't at all like the other students – he was so sure of himself, and he didn't care what anybody thought of him. I fell head over heels. We got married six months into the first year. I was eighteen and he was a year older."

"What happened?" O'Reilly said. "You said you were only married for a year."

"Eleven months," Connie corrected. "It was a dumb idea. I mean, who gets married in their first year of university? We drifted apart, and I'd met Woody by then."

"Warren Woodman was at university with you?" O'Reilly said.

"God, no. Woody wasn't university material. He was working at a local pub. We got chatting one night, and we connected. He knew I was married, and he was nothing but a gentleman about it."

"What do you mean?"

"He refused to start up any kind of relationship until things were definitely over between me and Michael. The divorce was quick, and me and Woody could be together."

"How did Mr Trunk take it?" O'Reilly asked. "That must have been hard on him."

"I don't think it was. The divorce was amicable."

She stopped there. She was staring at the photograph of Bram again.

"Is that your cat?"

"It is," O'Reilly said. "He walked into my apartment one day, and he's never left. He's not very well."

"What's wrong with him?"

"I'm sure he'll be OK."

"Why did you ask me about Michael?" Connie said.

"His name came up in a case we're currently investigating," O'Reilly said. He didn't want to tell her any more than that.

"Did Woody know Mr Trunk?" he asked.

"Of course," Connie replied. "He knew him from the pub Michael worked in."

"Did they get on? Before the divorce, I mean?"

"They got on even afterwards," Connie said. "Like I said, we married far too young, and Michael was probably relieved when we broke up. It was a long time ago. Why are you investigating Michael?"

"I can't go into that. Do you know if your husband has been in touch with Mr Trunk recently?"

"I doubt it," Connie said. "I haven't seen Michael since a few months after the divorce. There's no reason Woody would need to contact him, and if he had, he would have told me. Did he have something to do with what happened to my husband?"

"I really can't go into it."

"He did, didn't he?" Connie shot to her feet. "Where is he? Is he here?"

"Please sit down, Mrs Woodman," O'Reilly said. "Drink your tea. You've had a terrible shock."

He wasn't expecting what happened next.

"Fuck you," Connie screamed. "Fuck you."

Then she was gone. O'Reilly could hear her screams all the way down the corridor. He got up and went after her. The only person by the front desk was a wide-eyed PC Woodbine.

"Where did she go?" O'Reilly asked him.

"I don't know, sir," the man mountain said. "She screamed at me, and she left the building. What is her problem? What a psycho."

"Her problem is this," O'Reilly said. "The woman has just found out that her husband is dead. She came to the island on holiday with him, and she's going to return home alone. That's her problem."

He left PC Woodbine to consider this and made his way to the briefing room.

"Sorry about that," O'Reilly told the team.

"Is everything alright, sir?" DC Owen said.

"We've had a development," O'Reilly said.

He didn't want to discuss the phone call with the vet. Instead, he told them about Connie Woodman.

"We've got an ID for the man who was killed up by Fort Hommet," he said. "His name is Warren Woodman, and he was on holiday here with his wife. She came in to report him missing."

"Why did she wait so long?" DS Skinner wondered. "He was killed on Saturday. That's more than three days ago."

"Apparently, Mr and Mrs Woodman have a peculiar arrangement. Mr Woodman often goes walkabout for days and his wife tolerates it. That's not the only development. It appears that Mrs Woodman was once married to Mike Trunk?"

"You're joking?" It was DC Stone.

"I'm not in a joking mood, Andy," O'Reilly said. "Warren Woodman's wife was once married to the man who killed him. It was a long time ago, but I believe it's significant."

"It has to be," DC Owen agreed. "I don't know how, but it has to be important."

"We've now got a bit of extra ammunition to use against Mr Trunk when we interview him again," O'Reilly said. "We'll use it to our advantage."

"When we first spoke to Mike Trunk," DC Owen said. "He told us he didn't really know this Woody character. He said he'd seen him around on the odd occasion, but that was all."

"How is that even possible?" DC Stone said. "You said he was here on holiday. He doesn't even live in Guernsey."

"They knew each other a long time ago," O'Reilly said. "Woody was one of the reasons Connie and Mike Trunk got divorced."

"Do you think he could have killed him because of it?" DS Skinner asked.

"It's possible, even though it was a long time ago. It's something to consider. This is the plan of action. Katie, I want you to accompany me in the interview with Mike Trunk. Will, you and Andy can have another stab at Belinda Cole. Tread carefully with that one. She's young, but she's devious. After that, we'll tackle Frieda Klein and Yolanda Stewart. Every one of them knows what this is all about, and one of them is bound to slip up somewhere along the line."

"What about the people from the wine warehouse?" DC Stone said.

"They're on the list, Andy," O'Reilly told him. "And we'll get to them in due course. We're getting closer – I can feel it in my belly."

CHAPTER THIRTY SEVEN

Mike Trunk didn't seem remotely perturbed about his predicament. He looked like a man for whom a stay in a holding cell was something he was accustomed to. He was sitting up straight in a chair in one of the interview rooms. A fierce looking woman was sitting by his side. She'd introduced herself as Davina Plough and she was Mr Trunk's legal representative. O'Reilly was instantly suspicious. When Mike came to confess to the murder by Fort Hommet he was alone, and in O'Reilly's opinion the presence of a lawyer today could only mean one thing – Mike was rattled.

"Mr Trunk," O'Reilly said after getting the formalities out of the way for the tape. "I trust you're being treated well?"
"I can't complain," Mike said. "It's better than sleeping in an abandoned beach hut."
"I wanted to ask you about that," O'Reilly said. "When I first met you, I seemed to have got the wrong impression. I assumed from your appearance that you were a man a bit down on his luck."
Mike shrugged his shoulders. "I get that a lot."
"What I can't understand is why a man of your means chooses to live the life you do."
"I'm not sure I'm following you."
"You're following me perfectly well, Mike," O'Reilly said. "You're an extremely wealthy man."
Another shrug of the shoulders. "Money isn't everything."
"Can I ask you where you're going with this?" Davina asked.
"I'm trying to ascertain why a man with more than twenty million in the bank chooses to sleep on the streets," O'Reilly told her.
"My client's lifestyle choices have no bearing on why he was arrested."
"If you say so," O'Reilly said. "Mike, could you explain why you live like you

do?"

"I told you," Mike said. "Money isn't everything."

"I'd like to recap, if I may," O'Reilly said. "When we first spoke to you, you told us you'd killed your friend Woody. You claimed to have no memory of the event, but you saw footage of the murder on the Island Herald's site and felt compelled to come here and confess. Is that correct?"

"It was the right thing to do," Mike said.

"So you said. Has anything else about that night come back to you?"

"I still don't recall killing him."

"What about the events that led up to the murder?" DC Owen said.

"It talks," Mike scoffed.

DC Owen ignored him. "Well? Can you tell us what you do remember about that night?"

"I'm experiencing a weird feeling of déjà vu here."

"There's nothing wrong with your memory now then?" O'Reilly said.

"There really is no need to be obtuse," Davina said.

"It's a terrible habit of mine. Mike, could you please humour us."

"I met up with Woody," Mike said. "He'd brought along a few bottles of wine, and we drank it. End of story."

"Except that's not the end of the story, is it?" DC Owen said. "There are still quite a few pages of this story left. Where did Woody get the wine?"

"I told you," Mike said. "He nicked it."

"Did he say where he stole it from?" O'Reilly asked.

"He didn't say, and I didn't press him about it. We drank the wine, Woody suggested a trek up to the fort and the rest, as they say is history."

"You seem to be taking this remarkably well," O'Reilly said.

"How else am I supposed to take it?" Mike said. "The CCTV footage leaves little doubt about what happened. I killed him. The fact that I don't remember it is irrelevant, isn't it?"

"Is it?" DC Owen said. "Aren't you curious about why you committed murder?"

"There must have been something wrong with the wine."

"Now we're getting somewhere," O'Reilly said. "Why would you think that?"

"Because I've been drinking copious amounts of the stuff for years, and nothing like that has ever happened before."

"What do you think was wrong with the wine?" DC Owen said.

"You tell me."

"My client has been more than cooperative with you," Davina Plough said. "He's told you what he can remember, and he was the one who came to you in the first place. I'm sure you're aware that time is running out for you. I suggest you either charge Mr Trunk or you release him."

"We've still got a good few hours," O'Reilly said. "According to the statutes set out in the law. Mr Trunk, do you want me to tell you what I think happened?"

"I'm all ears," Mike said.

"I think it was you who provided the wine. You plied Woody with the stuff and persuaded him to go with you up to Fort Hommet. You weren't aware of the CCTV camera there. You got him where you wanted him, and you bashed his brains in with the wine bottle. Then you dragged him down onto the rocks. Does that sound about right?"

"I saw the CCTV footage," Mike said.

"I know you did, and that's why you came to confess. You panicked, didn't you? You knew it was only a matter of time before we came for you, and you thought you'd get in first. You thought you would confess to the murder and claim to have no recollection of it. You can't think of any reason why you would want to kill Woody, and you thought you'd come here and tell us you needed to do the right thing."

"It's the truth," Mike said.

"I don't believe you."

"That's irrelevant."

"How so?"

"What you believe and what a jury of our peers believes are two different things," Mike elaborated. "There was something in that wine that made me act like I did, wasn't there?"

"What makes you think that?" DC Owen said.

"Because I'm not an idiot. I may be an occasional drunk, but I'm not stupid. Something in that wine caused me to flip. You know it, and I know it."

"Are you still going along with the story that you had no intention of killing your friend Woody?" O'Reilly said.

"Why would I want to kill him?" Mike said. "I hardly knew the bloke."

"Where did you meet him?" DC Owen said.

"I'd seen him around."

"When was this?" O'Reilly asked.

"How am I supposed to remember that?"

"OK," O'Reilly said. "You didn't know Woody very well."

"Correct."

"And you knew him only as Woody?"

"He didn't give me any more than that."

"Does the name Warren Woodman ring any bells?"

It was a subtle change but both O'Reilly and DC Owen noticed it. There was a definite spark of recognition in Mike Trunk's eyes.

"I knew a Warren Woodman once," he admitted.

"When was this?" O'Reilly asked.

"A very long time ago."

"What about Connie?" DC Owen said.

"Connie?"

"She once went by the name of Connie Trunk I believe," O'Reilly said.

"Oh, that Connie."

"Now she's Connie Woodman," DC Owen said.

"But you knew that didn't you?" O'Reilly said. "Just as you knew the man you bludgeoned to death was Warren Woodman."

"You're kidding me?"

"I only joke with people I like," O'Reilly said. "Connie Woodman came to see me earlier."

"That's nice. How is she?"

"She's not too well. She would quite like to know why her ex-husband butchered her current husband."

CHAPTER THIRTY EIGHT

Mike Trunk didn't take any further part in the interview and O'Reilly had no option but to bring it to its conclusion. The drunk millionaire was charged with the murder of Warren Woodman, and now the hard slog began. O'Reilly was determined to disprove Mike's version of events. He knew that a *diminished responsibility* plea was on the cards, and he needed something concrete to contradict that claim.

It transpired that Mike had no reason to sleep rough on the island. After a quick look through the records, they found a property listed in his name. The modest two-bedroom apartment was in one of the complexes in St Peter Port and O'Reilly was now armed with a warrant to go through it with a fine-toothed comb. Belinda Cole, Yolanda Stewart and Frieda Klein were all still refusing to talk. The three women weren't budging, and O'Reilly didn't think it would be productive to get them to change their minds without something damning to throw at them. Warrants had been procured to search the Stewart household and the place of residence of Belinda Cole. The German woman was on holiday and the hotel room she'd been staying in would also be thoroughly scrutinised.

O'Reilly didn't think it was necessary to suit up and boot up before he went inside Mike Trunk's apartment. After all, this wasn't considered to be a crime scene and when he bumped into DI Peters and saw that the Head of Forensics was *sans* SOC suit, he knew that DI Peters was on the same page as him.

"What are we looking for?" DI Peters asked him.

"Anything that might lead us to the truth about why Mike Trunk felt the need to kill the man who took his wife from him twenty years ago," O'Reilly said. "Correspondence between the two men – stuff like that. We've got his phone in evidence but there might be a laptop here we can go through."

"You really believe he set out to kill Warren Woodman that night, don't you?"

"I do," O'Reilly confirmed. "We've just interviewed the man again, and he sounded some very loud alarm bells. He knows we know he killed Mr Woodman in cold blood, and he knows we know he remembers every second of it. Hopefully something here can help us prove it. Do you know if anything has been found at the Stewart residence or at Belinda Cole's house?"

"Not yet. You'll be the first to know if anything turns up."

O'Reilly went into the kitchen. He didn't know what he was expecting, but it definitely wasn't this. He would have thought a man with Mike Trunk's means would have expensive appliances and fancy worktops, but there wasn't much inside this kitchen apart from an old toaster, a cheap kettle and a three-plate gas hob. A small fridge stood against one of the walls. O'Reilly walked up to it and opened it wide. Inside was half a pint of milk and a block of cheese that had globs of blue mould around the edges.

He checked the cupboards but there wasn't much inside them either. Two cups, a few plates and half a bottle of cheap gin was all he found. There was a chest of drawers attached to the worktop in the centre of the room. The first drawer contained a cutlery set and a selection of knives. The second was empty as was the third. In the bottom drawer was a number of envelopes bound in an elastic band. O'Reilly took them out.

He unwound the elastic band and flicked through the correspondence. It was mostly utility bills and bank statements. O'Reilly found the most recent bank statement and had a quick read through it. It was for a savings account and Mike Trunk's current balance was just short of six million pounds. Another bank statement told the Irishman that the drunkard had another four million in his current account. There were very few transactions on the account and none of them seemed suspicious. O'Reilly wondered where Mike held the rest of his fortune. After looking through the rest of the correspondence he realised there was nothing here that helped them in any way.

DI Peters came into the kitchen.

"I found a laptop. It's password protected, but I expected it to be. I'll take it back with me and let the tech team have a go at it. If there's anything incriminating on it, we should know in a day or two. Did you find anything in here?"

"There isn't much here," O'Reilly said. "You wouldn't think this bloke was a multimillionaire."

"Is this the only property he owns?"

"It's the only one we could find that's registered in his name," O'Reilly said. "It's possible he has others – you know how it goes with the well-heeled, but this is the only place we know about."

His phone started to ring. The screen told him it was DC Owen.

"Katie," he answered it. "Please tell me you have good news."

"That depends," she said. "It could be nothing, but Belinda Cole has a calendar on the wall in her bedroom. Most of it is blank, but on Monday's date a large *M* was written in capitals and underlined."

"That was the day she killed Joanne Hawkins," O'Reilly remembered.

"That's right. On its own it doesn't mean much, but I got hold of Andy and you'll never guess what was written on the desk calendar in Yolanda Stewart's home office?"

"*M*?" O'Reilly guessed anyway.

"Same thing. The capital letter was circled. And it was also written on Monday's date. Yolanda killed her husband on Monday evening."

"That's very interesting, Katie. It has to mean something."

"Did you find a calendar at Mike Trunk's place?"

"I wasn't looking for one," O'Reilly said. "I'll see what I can find. Thanks,

Katie."

He ended the call and told DI Peters about the mystery letter *M*.

"I can't see a calendar anywhere in here," DI Peters said.

O'Reilly looked around the kitchen, and he couldn't find one either.

"What do you think it means?" DI Peters asked.

"I have no idea," O'Reilly said. "But it's suspicious that both women wrote the letter *M* on the dates they committed murder. I'm going to take a look in the other rooms."

He left the kitchen and checked the rooms, one by one. The first room was obviously a spare bedroom. The bed was made, and it looked like it hadn't been slept in for a while. There wasn't much inside the room apart from the bed and a chest of drawers against the wall. The next room was the bathroom. O'Reilly didn't expect to find a calendar in there, so he cast the room a quick glance and left.

Another room looked like it passed as a study. A desk stood against the far wall. There was a thick layer of dust on it, and when O'Reilly looked closely, he saw the outline of dust where the laptop used to be. A wooden pen holder and a rusty metal ruler stood on top of one of the two speakers at the back of the desk.

The desktop calendar was on the other speaker. O'Reilly picked it up and he spotted it straight away. On Saturday's date, someone had written the letter *M* in red ink.

CHAPTER THIRTY NINE

"We've had a number of developments," O'Reilly said. "The letter *M* was written on calendars belonging to three of the murderers. The dates correspond to the days Belinda Cole, Mike Trunk and Yolanda Stewart decided to commit murder."

"That's interesting," DS Skinner said.

"It certainly is," O'Reilly agreed. "We couldn't find a letter *M* anywhere in the hotel room Frieda Klein was staying at, but the others have to be significant."

"Are we going to question them about it?" DC Stone asked.

"We would, if they were playing ball, Andy. None of them are talking, and that makes me think this is part of some bigger plan."

"What other developments do we have?" DS Skinner said.

"PC London escorted Warren Woodman's wife back to her hotel," O'Reilly said. "Kim had the presence of mind to enquire about the holiday Mrs Woodman told us her husband had won. Nobody at the hotel knew anything about a competition. The hotel room was booked a month ago. One week in the presidential suite with all expenses paid."

"Who booked it?" DC Owen said.

"That's going to take a bit longer to check," O'Reilly said. "But my gut is telling me it was Mike Trunk. I think he lured this Woody character to the island, with the promise of a luxury holiday."

"If that's the case then his *diminished responsibility* defence goes out of the window," DS Skinner said.

"It certainly does. If we can tie the booking to Mr Trunk it proves premeditation."

"It should be easy to find out," DC Stone said. "Surely we just need to follow the trail of money."

"Often it's not that simple, Andy," O'Reilly said. "When you have access to the amount of money that Mr Trunk has access to, it's easy to cover your tracks."

"Offshore credit card transactions are difficult to trace," DC Owen said. "Mike Trunk might have money stashed away somewhere we won't be able to find it."

"Why now?" DC Stone said. "If we're assuming the drunkard lured Warren Woodman to the island, planning to kill him – why now? It's been twenty years since Warren stole Mike's wife. That's a long time to plan a revenge."

"And how does it tie in with the other murders?" DC Skinner wondered. "We have four people who don't know one another, and they've all committed murder after drinking so-called contaminated wine."

"Something has to link those people together," O'Reilly decided. "We know they're not acquainted, so that leads me to believe that there is something else that connects them."

"A person we haven't yet considered?" DC Owen suggested.

"Possibly. We'll know more when the tech team have gone through their electronic devices. With any luck we'll find correspondence that leads us somewhere. In the meantime, does anyone have anything else to bring up for discussion?"

It took a while for someone on the team to speak up. In the end it was DC Owen who was the first to break the silence.

"I think Mike Trunk was aware of the CCTV camera by Fort Hommet?"

"What are you thinking, Katie?" O'Reilly said.

"He knew all about the camera and that's why he chose that particular place to carry out the murder. It's the only way his amnesia story would work."

"You're right," O'Reilly said. "And Fred *the Ed* just happened to give him a helping hand along the way. That was a stroke of luck for him. But you're absolutely right. Mike kills Warren Woodman in front of the camera, and it all but guarantees that he will be apprehended. I also believe he modified his plan when he saw the footage on the Herald's site. He was planning on waiting for us to come to him, but the airing of the murder gave him a better idea. He comes in to confess because he claims it's the right thing to do, and he sticks to his amnesia story. It's an elaborate plan, but it's one he thinks he can pull off. All he needs to do is feign memory loss."

"Traces of narcotic were found in the bottle by Fort Hommet," DC Stone reminded him. "How do we explain that?"

"I don't know, Andy," O'Reilly said. "But I do know that, apart from the one at Bluebell Woods none of the other bottles of wine were spiked. Any other thoughts?"

"Motive," DS Skinner said. "If we believe the murders were premediated, what about the motivation behind them. The only motive we've considered is Mike Trunk's resentment for Warren Woodman and that's a sketchy motive at best. Connie Woodman left him twenty years ago."

"And what would drive a seventeen-year-old girl to kill her best friend?" DC Stone said. "Or an elderly German woman to kill her husband of forty years?"

"Or a sixty-odd year old to butcher her husband?" DC Owen added.

"Money and jealousy," O'Reilly said. "Age-old motives for murder. Frieda Klein and Yolanda Stewart would benefit financially from the deaths of their husbands, but only if they're acquitted."

"It still doesn't explain what drove Belinda Cole to kill her friend," DS Skinner pointed out. "Where does that one fit into the equation?"

"I really don't know," O'Reilly said. "This investigation is baffling the hell out of me, and I'm tempted to wash my hands of it."

"You can't be serious, sir?" DC Owen said.

"I'm deadly serious, Katie. I'm this close to letting it be – leaving it in the hands of the gods, if you like. All four of them are behind bars, and perhaps it's time to leave it up to the judicial system to determine their fate. I'm done with it. I'm sick to the back teeth of it if you want to know the truth."

With that, O'Reilly got to his feet, picked up his mobile phone and left the briefing room.

CHAPTER FORTY

"What's got into the DI?" DC Stone asked.

"I wasn't expecting that," DC Owen said. "I've never known O'Reilly to react like that. He must have something on his mind."

"His cat isn't doing too great. Assumpta had to take him to the vet and it's not looking good. Perhaps he's worried about that. I don't think he's been sleeping well."

"I'm not just going to give up," DC Owen decided. "I don't have it in me to admit defeat, and I didn't think O'Reilly did either."

"I'm all ears if you have any ideas."

"Something ties those people together. We find out what that is and we get closer to putting this behind us. We need to dig deeper into the lives of those unlikely killers. Right now, we know hardly anything about any of them."

DS Skinner agreed. They were in danger of running out of steam – O'Reilly's outburst hadn't helped, and they needed to try and keep some momentum going. DC Owen suggested that she and DC Stone should find out more about Belinda Cole. The seventeen-year-old's actions were baffling. They still couldn't understand what had driven a teenage girl to commit murder.

After a brief conversation with Belinda's brother, they learned that she was in a relationship with an older man. Henry Graham was twenty-one and he'd recently graduated from university in London. He was staying at his parents' house in St Martin. DC Owen decided to catch him unawares. In her experience the element of surprise often worked in their favour.

Henry was a tall man with unusual green eyes. When he stood on the doorstep, they observed the two island detectives with a blend of suspicion and curiosity.

"Can I help you?"

He had a hint of an accent.

DC Owen showed him her ID. DC Stone did the same.

"Island Police?" Henry said. "This will be about Belinda."

"Can we come inside?" DC Owen asked him.

"Would it be possible to talk out here? My mother and father are home, and I don't want to give them any more excuses to lecture me."

DC Owen didn't ask him to elaborate. She suggested that they took a walk, and Henry was quick to oblige. He glanced behind him and closed the door with a barely audible click.

They walked for a while and Henry sat down on one of the benches looking out to Moulin Huet Bay. The beach was packed with holidaymakers and there were a number of sailing boats bobbing around in the breeze.

"How long have you known Belinda?" DC Owen asked.

"Years," Henry said. "I was in the same year as her brother at school."

"I believe you and she were in a relationship," DC Stone said.

"I suppose so."

"What do you mean by that?" DC Owen said.

"We hooked up during the Christmas break last year. Belinda knew I would be heading back to London for the final semester, so it wasn't anything serious."

"Were you or were you not together?" DC Stone said.

"It's complicated. She wanted me to travel the world with her. She'll be coming into some money soon, and she expects me to go along with her for the ride."

"But you're not happy with that?" DC Owen said.

"I didn't slog my guts out for the last three years at Uni to waste it. I have my future to think about."

"What are you studying?" DC Stone said.

"Geology. I've just found out I've got a place on a research team in Argentina. It's all I've ever wanted to do."

"Was Belinda aware of this?"

"I thought she was. Look, I don't know anything about what happened to Joanne."

"Did you know Joanne Hawkins?" DC Owen said.

Henry nodded.

"Could you give us a bit more than that?" DC Stone said.

"We got on well. She understood my love of geology. Not many girls get it."

"Was Belinda one of the ones who didn't *get it*?" DC Owen said.

Another nod.

He gazed out to sea. The sunlight caught in his eyes and DC Owen found herself staring at them. They really were unbelievably green.

"Joanne was dedicated," Henry said. "She was about to leave the island to study medicine. She would have done well too."

"Can you think of any reason why Belinda would want to hurt Joanne?"

"No. I don't understand what happened. They said it was something to do with drugs."

"We don't know that," DC Stone said.

"That's what they're saying in the papers. The wine they were drinking had been spiked with something."

"Have you ever known Belinda to be violent in the past?" DC Owen said. The silence that followed told her he was mulling this over.

"Henry," DC Owen urged. "Is there something you'd like to share with us?"

"There was an incident when I was back for the Christmas break," he said. "Belinda was pretty drunk, and I bumped into an old schoolfriend I hadn't seen for years and we got chatting. Belinda didn't appreciate it."

"What did she do?" DC Stone said.

"She cornered the woman in the Ladies, and she assaulted her. Nothing serious – I think it was more of a threat to get her to back off."

"Is Belinda a jealous woman?" DC Owen said.

"She can be."

A sudden gust of wind caused an empty crisp packet to take to the air. Soon afterwards, one of the boats out in the bay was flattened. DC Owen watched as the main sail came into view again as the boat slowly righted itself.

"I'm going to ask you this again," she said. "Can you think of any reason why Belinda would want to hurt Joanne?"

The nod was barely noticeable.

"Henry."

"It's my fault, isn't it?"

"What makes you think that?" DC Stone said.

"I was only trying to get her to back off."

"What happened?" DC Owen asked.

"Joanne and I were getting close," Henry said. "We both knew the score – she would be starting her medical degree in the autumn, and I was hoping to be travelling to Argentina, but we spent a bit of time together."

"Did Belinda know about this?"

"I made sure she did."

"Why?" DC Stone said. "Why would you do that?"

"I told you," Henry said. "I only wanted her to back off. It happened about a month ago. I knew she was always at the tennis club in La Rocques on Saturdays, and I knew she would walk to the café on the beach afterwards. God, what have I done?"

"Talk to us, Henry," DC Owen said. "What happened?"

"I parked the car on the esplanade," he said. "Joanne was with me. She had no idea why we were there. Belinda saw us."

"What did she see?" DC Stone said.

"Use your imagination. Fuck, this is all my fault, isn't it?"
"Are you telling us you parked the car where you knew Belinda would be to make her jealous?" DC Owen said.
"You didn't see her," Henry said. "I thought she would see me and Joanne and walk away, but that look in her eyes."

    He rubbed his face with both hands and breathed out deeply.

"I've never seen such fire," he said. "I'll never forget that look. There was fire in her eyes. Real fire. This is all my fault."

CHAPTER FORTY ONE

"How are they treating you?"

O'Reilly looked at the sorry figure of the cat on the blanket inside the cage. Bram was lying on his side and his eyes were barely open.

"I trust the food is up to your high standards."

He was well aware that Bram hadn't eaten anything since he'd been brought in, but he wasn't sure what else to talk about.

Alvin French had informed him that there had been no change in Bram's condition. The young vet had explained that this was a good sign. The antivirals he'd prescribed were doing their job, and the virus hadn't been able to inflict any further damage. Once again, it was a case of wait and see. Alvin had done everything he could for Bram and now it was up to him to fight it. O'Reilly didn't think Bram had it in him to give up.

"You're stronger than me, cat."

He wasn't sure if Bram was listening.

"You need to get better," he carried on, regardless. "As far as I'm aware, you still have at least half a dozen of your nine lives left."

Bram stretched out his front legs and yawned.

"Am I boring you?"

Alvin French appeared in the doorway.

"Can I offer you something to drink?"

"A cup of tea would be grand if it's not too much trouble," O'Reilly said.

"No trouble at all. You're very fond of him, aren't you?"

"I didn't think I was," O'Reilly admitted. "Our relationship is a strange one."

"I'll sort out that cup of tea."

He left and returned soon afterwards with some tea and a cup of coffee for himself.

"Tell me about this strange relationship."

"I'm sure you have more important things to do," O'Reilly said. "You don't want to be stuck listening to a morose Irishman."

"I don't, as it happens. I mean I don't have more important things to do. It's pretty quiet today."

O'Reilly told him all about Bram. He told him how the ginger beast had ambled into his apartment one day and stayed put. He didn't know where Bram had come from, but he'd clearly taken a shine to the Irish detective, and not once had he shown any indication that he would be hitting the road again.

He related the story of how Juliet had come to live with him too. Hers was a similar tale to Bram's. O'Reilly wasn't sure how she ended up on his doorstep, but she too had refused to budge when she realised how good life was in the O'Reilly household.

"I've never been much of a cat person," O'Reilly said. "We always had dogs when I was a kid, and I have no idea why I seem to attract the mangy beasts."

"Cats are exceptional judges of character," Alvin said. "Their senses are infinitely more acute than ours. You should take it as a compliment."

His phone started to ring in his pocket. He took it out and looked at the screen.

"Looks like I spoke too soon. A dog has been hit by a car, and I'd better get ready for her. Talk to him – talk to Bram. You're welcome to stay as long as you like."

"Thanks," O'Reilly said. "I appreciate it."

"What do you feel like talking about, cat?" he said when Alvin had gone. Bram's eyes opened wider.

"Looks like it's up to me then. Perhaps you can help me for a change. Tell me what you think about this. We've got four dead bodies. All four were killed by someone they knew and the people who committed the murders are probably the most unlikely killers I've ever come across. Are you keeping up – am I going too fast for you?"

"No?" O'Reilly said. "Good, because I'm not finished yet. If that wasn't bizarre enough for you, what if I told you that none of the murderers can remember a thing about the deed itself. Or that's what they're claiming. You couldn't make it up, could you?"

He stopped there and drank some of his tea. He looked at Bram and if he didn't know any better, he would swear his ginger friend looked more at ease. His top lip was curled up, revealing his front teeth. O'Reilly thought he could be smiling.

"The thing is this," he carried on. "I don't know how to carry on. I've reached a stage I never wanted to reach, and I'm not sure how to get past it. All four killers are banged up, but I've got a terrible feeling that they're all going to get away with it. They're all filthy rich and there's a good chance they'll pay their way out of jail. I'm all ears if you have any suggestions."
Bram stretched his legs again, and O'Reilly sighed. His mobile phone started to ring, and Bram's eyes opened wider.
"You recognise that ringtone, don't you?" O'Reilly said.
He let the call go to voicemail.

"OK," he said. "I'll make you a deal. It's a one-time offer – never to be repeated, and if you tell anyone about it, I'll deny it. Understood?"
O'Reilly was sure that Bram was purring. He looked closely at his throat and there it was – a subtle quiver below his chin.
"Here's the deal," he said. "You have to make it through this. I know you can do that, but here's a little incentive for you to sweeten the deal. I'm dangling a carrot here and I don't often do that. You're going to pull through, and you're going to come home with me. Juliet and Shadow miss you. I do too. If you get better, I'll make sure your life from now on is the one you seem to

feel you're entitled to. I don't know much about cats, but I get the impression that a sense of entitlement comes with the species. Anyway, you'll enjoy better food, and you can sleep on the bed when you feel the need. How does that sound?"

Bram seemed wide awake now. His green eyes were focused on O'Reilly's.

"What?" the Irishman said. "You want more than that? Alright, I'll try to treat you with a bit more respect, how about that? Come on, you're killing me now. Do we have a deal or not?"

Bram closed his eyes in reply. O'Reilly didn't think there was any point in carrying on the discussion. The terms of the deal were clear, and the ball was now in Bram's court.

"I'll be back," O'Reilly said. "You think hard about what I said."

He finished his tea and checked his phone to see who had called him. It was DC Owen. O'Reilly left Bram in peace and made his way to the reception area. He thanked the man behind the desk and went outside. He tapped the screen of his phone and listened to the message DC Owen had left him.

CHAPTER FORTY TWO

"Why did I have to come to the station?" Billy Foot said.

The young forklift operator seemed agitated. The skin on his cheeks had flared up again, accentuating his acne scars. The reek of him had filled the interview room and DC Stone was tempted to open the door.

"I told you everything I know at the warehouse," Billy added. "I'm going to get into trouble if I don't go back to work."

"We'll try not to take up too much of your time," DC Owen said.

"We're already running behind. The break-in has put us behind schedule, and Mr Hunt isn't going to be impressed."

"It can't be helped," DC Owen said. "You were the one who reported the break-in, is that correct?"

"I was the first one to arrive for the afternoon shift," Billy said.

"I believe you have keys to the warehouse," DC Stone said.

"That's right."

"Why is that?" DC Owen said. "Forgive me if I'm talking out of turn, but why would a forklift truck driver be given keys? Surely only the warehouse manager and the owner of the business would be trusted with keys to the building."

Billy's face flushed a deeper shade of red. "I'm a bit more than a forklift driver. I've been working there longer than most of the employees. I've been there longer than Mrs Paul even."

"I apologise. I wasn't aware of that. Mr Hunt must trust you then."

"Of course."

"How old are you, Billy?" DC Stone said. "You said you've been working at the warehouse for quite a while, but you don't look like you're long out of school."

Billy glared at him. "I'm twenty-five. How old are you?"

DC Stone didn't reply to that. "Can you talk us through what happened yesterday? What time did you get to work?"

"Just before four."

"And you were the first to arrive for the afternoon shift?" DC Owen said.

"I usually get there before everyone else."

"What did you do when you arrived?" DC Owen said.

"I set about opening up," Billy said.

"Is that your usual routine?" DC Stone said.

"Sometimes Mrs Paul is already there when I arrive, but yesterday I got there before her."

"Talk us through the process." DC Owen said.

"Process?"

"When you open up," DC Stone said. "Where do you start?"

"The door on the side," Billy said. "The one that had been damaged."

"Why do you start there?" DC Owen said.

"Because that's one of only two ways to get inside the warehouse. The loading bays can only be unlocked from the inside. And the main staff entrance is easier to open from the inside too. Why are you asking me all these questions?"

The stench inside the room was getting oppressive. DC Stone couldn't take it any longer. He got up and opened the door wide.

"It's getting hot in here," he explained and sat back down.

"What did you do when you realised there had been a break-in?" DC Owen asked.

"I phoned Mrs Paul," Billy said.

"You didn't think to phone the police first?" DC Stone said.

"It wasn't my call to make. Mrs Paul is the manager there – she doesn't live far from the warehouse, and she got there quickly. I called the police when she arrived and told me to."

"Have you had any break-ins before?" DC Owen said.

"Not that I can remember."

"Why do you think the only things that were taken were the computer equipment in the office?"

"I suppose it's easy to sell."

"I'm finding this hard to understand," DC Owen said. "Someone broke into the warehouse and all they took were a few bits of computer equipment. The office is nowhere near the side door. It was quite a risky thing to do for a few hundred pounds' worth of stuff. Don't you think?"

"I don't know what to think," Billy said. "Is this going to take much longer?"

"Were you the one who locked up on Monday evening?" DC Owen said.

"What?"

"Could you answer the question," DC Stone said. "Was it you who locked up after the shift on Monday?"

"I don't think so."

"Could you think harder?" DC Owen said.

"No," Billy said. "It wasn't me. Mrs Paul stayed later than I did. She must have locked up."

"Has there ever been an occasion where you've arrived for work to find the warehouse hasn't been locked?" DC Stone said.

"Never," Billy said.

"And you, Melissa Paul and Jacob Hunt are the only people with keys?" DC Owen said.

"I've already told you that."

"We're just trying to figure out why the side door was unlocked," DC Stone said.

"It wasn't unlocked," Billy argued.

"It was," DC Owen told him. "It was unlocked and someone tried to make it look like the door had been forced. Unfortunately, they didn't do a very good job of it. There are only two possible explanations for that – either whoever was responsible for locking up on Monday was negligent, and the person who broke in wasn't aware of it, or someone unlocked the door with a key before the break-in and went at it with a crow bar to make it look like it had been broken open. Which scenario do you believe is most likely?"

"I don't know what you want me to say," Billy said. "I thought it had been forced open."

"So you keep saying," DC Stone said.

Billy looked right at him and for a moment DC Stone was worried he was going to start crying.

    He didn't.

"I haven't done anything wrong," he said. "Why are you accusing me of something I didn't do?"

"We're just trying to establish all the facts," DC Owen said. "I think we can conclude there. We appreciate you coming in."

CHAPTER FORTY THREE

DC Owen found O'Reilly inside his office. He was looking at something on the screen of his laptop.

"Is everything alright, sir?"

O'Reilly looked up at her. "I just needed some time out, Katie. I'm back now."

"That's good to hear."

"What have I missed?"

"Andy and I have just had the pleasure of the forklift operator from Jacob Hunt's warehouse," DC Owen told him. "Andy almost choked on the smell. He used half a can of air freshener afterwards, and it still didn't help."

"He is a bit ripe. What could he tell you?"

"I think he was just in the wrong place at the wrong time. He said it was Melissa Paul who locked up on Monday, and apparently, she's never forgotten to secure the warehouse before. That means whoever broke in was in possession of a key."

"Have you spoken to the manager?"

"The DS is with her now," DC Owen said.

"What about Jacob Hunt?" O'Reilly said. "What does he have to say on the matter?"

"We've been unable to locate him. He's not answering his phone, and he's not at home."

"Interesting. What do you think happened? What is your gut telling you?"

"The logical assumption to make would be either Jacob Hunt or Melissa Paul was responsible for the break-in," DC Owen said. "They wanted to make it look like the hard drives containing the CCTV footage were stolen."

"That wasn't what I asked," O'Reilly said. "I don't want logical assumptions – what are your instincts telling you?"

"I don't think Jacob or Melissa are involved, sir."

"Neither do I," O'Reilly agreed. "Both of them would have had ample opportunity to erase the CCTV footage, and we'd be none the wiser. What we need to ask ourselves is this – what the devil was on the footage that caused someone to go to all this trouble to get rid of it?"

"Someone tampered with the bottles of *Chateau La Folie* inside the warehouse," DC Owen said. "And they were caught doing so on camera."

"That's my feeling too. We find those hard drives we find out who is behind all of this."

"Is that what we're going to focus on?"

"No," O'Reilly said. "Those drives could have been destroyed for all we know. That's what I would have done. I would have got rid of them. What we need to do is keep applying pressure to the four people in custody. That's how we're going to put this one to bed. One of them is bound to crack, and my Irish intuition is still telling me it's going to be the seventeen-year-old rich kid."

"About that, sir," DC Owen said. "Andy and I spoke to her ex-boyfriend, if you can call him that. His name is Henry Graham, and it looks like he was the catalyst for Belinda's irrational behaviour. Henry and Joanne Hawkins were seeing each other behind Belinda's back. Henry wanted Belinda to back off, so he came up with the bright idea to try and make her jealous. He made sure she saw him and Joanne getting cosy in his car. He didn't expect her to react like she did."

"And you believe that's why Belinda killed Joanne?" O'Reilly said.

"Apparently, Belinda has a history of violence."

"Jealousy, revenge and financial gain," O'Reilly said out of the blue.

"Sir?"

"Classic motives for murder, Katie. All we're missing is hatred, and we've got a full house."

"Belinda Cole let the green-eyed monster get the better of her," DC Owen said. "It's possible Mike Trunk still resented Warren Woodman for taking his wife, so he exacted his revenge, and Frieda Klein stands to gain substantially from her husband's death. What about Yolanda Stewart? What is her motivation?"

"Andy mentioned something the son told him," O'Reilly said. "When Andy expressed his sympathies for John Stewart's murder, the son said there was no need. He said if he'd known the man, he wouldn't be sorry at all. It's possible that Yolanda despised her husband enough to want him out of her life. Find out if John Stewart had any pre-nuptial contracts in place. The same goes for Frieda Klein's husband. It's not uncommon with the well-fed of society. Perhaps the only way these women could be rid of their husbands and come out on top was to end their lives."

"But they would need to get away with it in the process," DC Owen pointed out.

O'Reilly didn't comment on this. His eyes drifted to the screen of his laptop again.

"What are you looking at?" DC Owen said.

"Something to consider, Katie," O'Reilly said.

He turned the laptop round so she could see the screen.

"*The perfect murder*," she read.

"I've just been doing a bit of research," O'Reilly said. "God help me if my search history is ever scrutinised. A detective inspector looking for ways to get away with murder could be frowned upon by certain people."

DC Owen laughed. "I'm sure that's not going to happen, sir."

"In this day and age," O'Reilly said. "It ought to be impossible to carry out the perfect murder. Forensic science has advanced to such an extent that anyone who thinks they can kill someone and get away with it will be sadly disappointed. There will always be something they'll overlook in the process. Combine that with the number of CCTV cameras in place nowadays and the technology the police now have at their disposal, committing murder and not getting caught should be a thing of the past."

"Are you suggesting these people set out to commit the perfect murder?" DC Owen said.

"Something like that," O'Reilly confirmed.

"Four people?" DC Owen said. "None of whom are acquainted with any of the others? It's not possible."

"I understand your misgivings, but I'm starting to wonder if these unlikely killers had a bit of help. I think they had some assistance along the way, and I also believe that assistance didn't come cheap."

CHAPTER FORTY FOUR

By five that afternoon the team had made a number of breakthroughs and O'Reilly's earlier maudlin frame of mind was long forgotten. Bram's predicament was still occupying a place in the back of his mind, but O'Reilly had decided that the ginger moggie was going to be just fine. He knew the chat they'd had earlier would have done the trick. Bram would be back to his old self in no time.

"We're getting somewhere," O'Reilly told the rest of the team. "Before we begin the briefing I'd like to apologise for my behaviour earlier."
"Is everything alright, sir?" DC Stone asked.
"I've said everything I'm going to say on the subject, Andy. We have more pressing matters to attend to. Our esteemed guests are still refusing to cooperate, and we'll have to carry on without their input. What do we know about Otto Klein's and John Stewart's pre-nuptial arrangements?"
"Two phone calls was all it took to get the information on the Germans," DS Skinner said. "Otto and Frieda were married in 1979 and there was a prenuptial contract in place."
"I thought there might be," O'Reilly said. "Did you manage to get any details?"
"Otto's father made a substantial amount of money investing in oil," DS Skinner said. "Otto, as the only child was the sole heir, but Otto Senior put some conditions in place. The pre-nup was one of them. In the event of a divorce, Frieda would walk away with what she entered into the marriage with – next to nothing."
"The details of John and Yolanda Stewart's marriage were trickier to get hold of," DC Stone said. "John's lawyer refused to even discuss it without a warrant ordering him to do so, but there are plenty of ways to skin a cat."
"That's my line, Andy," O'Reilly said. "But go on."

"I got hold of the younger son. His name is Kenneth, and when I spoke to him yesterday, he was very open about the relationship between his mother and father so I thought I'd give it a try. Nothing ventured, nothing gained as it were."

"Just spit it out," O'Reilly said.

"Sorry, sir," DC Stone said. "When I asked if he knew whether his father had some kind of prenuptial contract in place Kenneth's exact words were – I'd bet my life on it. That bastard wouldn't enter into any kind of deal without making sure his own interests were covered. Those were his exact words."

"So you said. And there we have two very plausible reasons to commit murder."

"Belinda Cole's boyfriend believes she killed Joanne Hawkins out of jealousy," DC Owen said. "He made sure Belinda saw him and Joanne together and he thinks that's what pushed her over the edge."

"And then we have our drunk multimillionaire," O'Reilly said. "Warren Woodman took Mike Trunk's wife from him. It was twenty years ago, but stranger things have happened."

"I'm still struggling to understand how it all fits together," DS Skinner admitted.

"These people didn't act alone, Will," O'Reilly said. "They had a bit of help – a bit of costly help. We haven't found any suspicious transactions in any of their financial documents, but we will. You mark my words. These so-called perfect murders won't have come cheap."

"Are you suggesting they paid for the services of some kind of hitman?" DS Skinner said. "Because all four of them were the ones to carry out the murders, and you're overlooking the fact that at least one of them doesn't have access to large sums of money."

"No," O'Reilly said. "This wasn't the work of a hitman. I believe the murders were orchestrated. The killers were given instructions about how to carry them out, and as for the money aspect – I believe payment will be due on completion. After the fact, which in this case is when these four murdering, rich bastards get away with murder and get their filthy hands on the cash. I could be wrong."

"With respect, sir," DS Skinner said. "I think you are. There is nothing pointing in that direction. Nothing at all."

"On the contrary," O'Reilly said. "Look at the facts. We've got a mild-mannered, highly educated sot. We have an elderly German lady who hasn't had to work a day in her life, and we've got a sixty-two-year-old lady who should be enjoying her retirement. Then there's a young woman not long out of school – questionable killers, every one of them. All of them have, or soon will have access to virtually unlimited funds, and all of them have a motive for the crime. That's the clincher for me – motivation. What more do you need?"

"Proof, sir," DS Skinner said, matter-of-factly. "We know they carried out the murders but there is no proof that they had any kind of help when they did so."

O'Reilly sighed and then he started to laugh. He rubbed his hands together and looked at each and every one of the police officers sitting around the table.

"Who fancies a drink?"

Nobody on the team replied.

"I really feel like a drink," he added.

"Assumpta has offered to go through a story I'm writing, sir," DC Stone said. "It's for my creative writing course."

"That's fine, Andy," O'Reilly said. "It's fine."

"I'm playing squash," DS Skinner said. "I can cancel if you want me to."

"Don't," O'Reilly said. "Katie?"

"I'm really not in the mood, sir," DC Owen said.

"Brutally honest as ever. Never mind."

"My dad will be in The Boathouse if you want some company," DC Owen said.

"I'll bear that in mind," O'Reilly said. "Tomorrow is another day. Tomorrow we will find our proof. *You persist in your incredulity. My words have not convinced you, and I see you require proofs.*"

O'Reilly had never before seen three more baffled looking detectives.

"It's from The Count of Monte Cristo," he explained. "Google it, Andy. Tomorrow we will have our proof. Get yourselves off home."

CHAPTER FORTY FIVE

O'Reilly had never felt more unpopular in his life, and that was saying something. His company had never been particularly sought after and it had never bothered him before. At school he'd had very few friends – when he joined the ranks of the Gardai that number dwindled further still, but here on the island he thought he could always count on someone to call on when he felt like a bit of company, but that was not the case this evening. Even his wife had turned him down when he asked if she felt like grabbing a few drinks and a bite to eat. Victoria told him she was tired – they'd eaten out a lot recently and she felt like a quiet night in. She didn't mind if he wanted to go out on his own though, and that's precisely what O'Reilly did.

He was glad to see a familiar face when he went inside The Boathouse. Tony Owen was sitting at one of the tables by the huge window. He was sipping a beer and gazing out onto the marina below. O'Reilly had grown to like DC Owen's father. The ex-DI was a man who called a spade a spade and he was someone O'Reilly didn't mind spending time with. He got a *Scapegoat* from the bar and walked over to Tony's table.

"Do you mind if I join you?"

Tony looked up in surprise. "Liam. I was miles away there. Take a seat."

O'Reilly obliged. He took a sip of his beer and let out a contented sigh.

"I needed that. Katie said you might be here."

"I'm getting to be one of those retired men who develop habits and routines," Tony said. "It's Wednesday ergo, I'll be at The Boathouse."

"Routine is vastly underrated," O'Reilly said. "There's nothing wrong with a bit of routine in life."

"Although I did have an ulterior motive for coming here. There's a yacht in the marina that's up for sale, and I'm thinking of putting in an offer. I've been busy giving her a once over. She's the one with the black mast. Two boats down from the vessel some idiot decided to paint pink."

O'Reilly followed his finger.

"She looks very nice to me. The one with the black mast, I mean."

"Westerly 24," Tony elaborated. "Centre cockpit and bags of space. She's slow as hell, but she's reliable."

"You've just described me to a tee," O'Reilly said.

Tony laughed. "Don't put yourself down. What brings you here tonight?"

"You know how it goes?"

"One of those days?"

"One of those weeks," O'Reilly said. "Did you ever get the feeling when you were in the job that the people on your team weren't on the same page as you?"

Another laugh. "Only on a daily basis. It's why they pay us a bit more. What's on your mind?"

"How long have you got?"

"I'm in no rush to be anywhere. I'll get us another round in, and you can tell me what's bothering you."

Three beers later and O'Reilly thought he'd covered everything. The buzz of the beer and the emptiness in his stomach was telling him he ought to eat something. He got the attention of a waiter and ordered two fish and chips. Tony had objected – apparently his wife was cooking something at home, but O'Reilly had been very insistent.

"Probably for the best," Tony said. "My wife's cooking hasn't got any better. Do you really believe these people were following instructions?"

"It might sound a bit fantastic," O'Reilly admitted. "But it's the only theory I've got. None of these people have shown as much as an inkling of a homicidal urge in their lives. And now they've suddenly decided to start killing. We've had four dead bodies in as many days."

"That is strange," Tony admitted. "And you believe they've paid a lot of money for this?"

"Whoever orchestrated it went to a lot of trouble. They won't have done it for nothing."

"I thought I'd seen everything. I've met John Stewart."

"Nobody has a nice word to say about the man," O'Reilly said. "When did you have the pleasure of his company?"

"It was definitely not a pleasure. It was a while ago, but I remember it well. I was still in uniform, and we pulled a car over one night. It was some fancy sports model, and it was all over the road. When it finally managed to stop we saw there were two kids inside. They couldn't have been older than sixteen. The driver was John Stewart's son. Lloyd, I think his name was."

"I think I can guess the rest," O'Reilly said. "Rich kid threw his dad's name at you and expected that to be the end of it?"

"Close," Tony said. "We had no option but to arrest Lloyd. He was underage – no driving license, and he was drunk. His old man took umbrage to this, and he tried to throw his weight around. You know how it goes. *Do you know who I am*? That sort of crap."

"What happened?"

"The kid got off with a slap on the wrists. His dad was pals with the CO at the time, and we had no say in the matter. I wouldn't have cared – I knew the score, even back then, but John Stewart refused to leave it at that. He tried to go for a police harassment charge."

"He sounds like someone who is definitely better off six feet under the ground," O'Reilly said.

"He is," Tony confirmed. "Luckily for us there were limits to how far the CO was willing to overstep the line. The charge was thrown out, but John Stewart still pressed for an apology?"

"You didn't?"

"Of course I didn't," Tony said. "I don't care how much money someone has I have more self-respect than that."

The fish and chips arrived with another couple of beers. O'Reilly was glad – he hadn't eaten much all day, and the beer had gone straight to his head. He had to admit that it felt good to talk about the investigation with someone not on the team. He was well aware that he shouldn't be discussing it with anyone outside the Island Police, but as far as he was concerned, once a DI always a DI.

Tony finished first and O'Reilly realised it was the second time that week that someone had beaten him eating a meal. He wondered if he was losing his touch.

"That was delicious," Tony said. "But I really should be getting going."
He took out his wallet and removed a few notes.
"Put that away," O'Reilly said. "This is on me. Call it a consultation fee."
"I couldn't ask you to do that. I wasn't really much help."
"I insist," O'Reilly said. "It was grand to see you again."
"Likewise," Tony said. "I'll be here again if you feel like another chat, same time next week. The exciting life of a retired police detective."
"I'll bear that in mind."

O'Reilly ordered another *Scapegoat* and the ache in his bladder was telling him he needed to make some room before he drank any more. He left the table and made his way to the Gents. The bar was packed now. All of the stools were occupied, and one of them was taken up by someone O'Reilly recognised straight away. He barely knew the man but the bandages on his face and neck were something you couldn't really miss. The pain in his bladder was growing and it was informing him that if he didn't make it to the Gents now, he would find himself in an embarrassing predicament. He wasn't aware that the man with the bandaged face had spotted him too, and he didn't notice the drink that was in front of him.

O'Reilly left the Gents suitably relieved. He walked back to his table and stopped as he passed the bar area. The bandaged man had gone. O'Reilly approached the bar and caught the attention of one of the bar staff. She walked right over to him.

"The man who was in here just now," O'Reilly said. "The one with the bandages on his face – where did he go?"

"He left," the bartender said. "He downed his drink, slapped a twenty on the counter and left."

"Do you know him?"

"Of course. It's Mr Spring. Mark Spring."

"Is he a local?" O'Reilly asked.

"I suppose you could say that. He's been coming in for a few years."

"He's teetotal, isn't he?" O'Reilly remembered.

The bartender laughed. "If you say so."

"I met him last week," O'Reilly said. "And he told me he hasn't touched a drink for three years."

"He was talking shit. Mark likes a drink as much as the rest of us. Too much, sometimes. We've had to ask him politely to leave on more than one occasion."

CHAPTER FORTY SIX

O'Reilly had slept well. He'd arrived home and headed up to bed and the beer had helped him on his way. Victoria wasn't in the bed next to him when he woke, and he wondered if he'd overslept. His phone wasn't on the bedside table where it usually was so he couldn't check the time. He went to the bathroom and went downstairs. The clock on the wall told him it was just after seven.

"Morning," Victoria said.
She handed him a cup of tea.
"How's the head?"
"Grand," O'Reilly said.
"I just thought that from the noise that was coming out of your mouth when you came to bed, you'd knocked back quite a bit."
"Was I snoring?"
"Enough to scare the daylights out of two cats. Juliet and Shadow scarpered as soon as you started up the chainsaw."
"Sorry about that," O'Reilly said. "I got chatting to Katie's dad, and we might have a had a few beers. Is there any news on Bram?"
"Nothing," Victoria said.
O'Reilly sipped his tea. "I went to see him yesterday. Bram, I mean."
"You didn't mention anything."
"It was a spur of the moment thing. I don't know why, but I felt like I needed to see him. I might have made a deal with him, and you're probably not going to like it."
"What did you do, Liam?" Victoria said.
"I promised him that if he got better, life would improve for him when he came home."
"That cat's life can't get any better. Bram doesn't know he's born."

"I was desperate," O'Reilly explained. "I know he's only a cat, but I don't know what I would do if he didn't come home again. I'd better go up for a shower. I smell like a brewery."

* * *

O'Reilly's thoughts turned to Mark Spring on the drive across the island to the Island Police HQ. He wondered why Mark had told him he hadn't touched a drop of alcohol for three years and he also wondered if the lie was relevant to the current investigation. He couldn't think why it would be. Perhaps Mr Spring was in denial – it wasn't unheard of, and O'Reilly decided it was none of his business.

A bumper bash accident just north of Le Foulon added an extra ten minutes to the journey and O'Reilly made it to St Peter Port with minutes to spare before the scheduled morning briefing. He reckoned that the minor car accident was an omen. It was a sign telling him that there was no point in having a morning briefing. As far as he was concerned there was nothing new to discuss. They could speculate until the cows came home, but the only way they were going to get the answers they needed was to ask the right questions to the right people. He made up his mind. They were going to interrogate the four suspects again and they were going to do it aggressively. He informed the rest of the team of his decision.

"We're going to go for the jugular," he said.

He'd suggested a change of scenery to discuss the impending interviews, and the team were now seated in the canteen. O'Reilly had made the mistake of selecting what was advertised as tea from the machine in there. He took a small sip and winced. "What is this shite?"

"It's tea, sir," DC Stone stated the obvious.

"It tastes like it was brewed in the arse crack of a Scotsman," O'Reilly said and deposited the paper cup, tea and all into the nearest rubbish bin. "Where was I?"

"The jugular, sir," DC Stone reminded him.

"Right. Every one of those rich murderers has the answers we need, but we only need one of them to crack. I want to throw everything we know about them *at* them. I want us to get dirty if necessary. Their legal reps will try and shut us down every step of the way, but that's what they're paid to do. I don't give a damn about them. Let's quickly run through what we know about these depraved individuals."

It was a longer discussion than O'Reilly anticipated, but when they were finished, he was satisfied that they had enough dirt to dish out. He'd never been one to advocate a *gloves off* approach, but needs must and right now it was absolutely necessary. In his experience he knew that even the most hardened criminal had a breaking point. There was a limit to how much they could endure before they crumbled.

He was informed that it was going to take some time to round up the respective legal representation, so he went to his office and made a proper cup of tea. The swill from the canteen had an unpleasant aftertaste and it still lingered, even though he had only taken a small sip. He took out his phone and brought up the number for Alvin French. This time the vet answered straight away.

"Great minds think alike," Alvin said. "I was about to call you." O'Reilly couldn't read much into the tone of his voice whether he was about to get bad or good news. He remained silent and waited for Alvin to tell him. It was the latter. "You'll be glad to hear that Bram bit one of my assistants when he tried to force his medication down his throat this morning."

"I'm sorry about that," O'Reilly said.

"Don't be," Alvin said. "We wear protective clothing for a reason. Bram has perked up no end, and I see no reason why he shouldn't make a full recovery. He was extremely lucky – if he'd been brought in any later the outcome could have been much different."

"Thank you," O'Reilly said. "I can't thank you enough."

"I'd like to keep him in for a couple more days," Alvin said. "Just to be on the safe side, but you can probably expect to have him home by the weekend."

O'Reilly was only aware of the grin that had appeared on his face when he took a sip of tea and half of it ran down his chin. He didn't care. Bram was coming home. He recalled the pact he'd made with the ginger brute, and he realised he didn't care about what that entailed either.

CHAPTER FORTY SEVEN

O'Reilly made a rather unorthodox decision. He and DC Owen would conduct all four interviews consecutively. It was going to be a draining day for both of them, but O'Reilly believed it was the best way forward. He opted to tackle Frieda Klein first. In his opinion she was probably the least likely to crumble under pressure. They would take a perfunctory approach with her, and merely skirt the surface of what was behind the murder of her husband. It was possible that she would slip up somewhere down the line, but O'Reilly didn't expect her to. From what he'd seen of the elderly German lady he'd got the impression she was a cool customer.

Yolanda Stewart would be interviewed next. O'Reilly was interested in her relationship with her husband and he would focus mainly on that. Her youngest son had left the island a decade ago and he'd never returned. Mrs Stewart would be asked why she thought this was. The conversation with Tony Owen had given him a bit more background information about the dynamic in the Stewart family and O'Reilly was hoping to use this to his advantage.

The penultimate interview would be with Mike Trunk. The drunk millionaire was clearly a well-educated, intelligent man but O'Reilly knew that people like him often liked to show off. They had an inbuilt desire to demonstrate their superiority and sometimes it was that arrogance that was ultimately their downfall.

Belinda Cole would be questioned last. O'Reilly hoped that by then they would have enough information from the other three murderers to lure her into a trap. He also planned to rattle her with talk of the relationship between Joanne Hawkins and Belinda's boyfriend, Henry. It was going to be an exhausting day, and O'Reilly reckoned he would probably need at least two showers to wash the grime off him when it was over.

PC Woodbine informed him that Frieda Klein's lawyer had arrived. O'Reilly asked DC Owen if she was ready, and she answered in the affirmative.

"Ready as I'll ever be," she added.

Frieda Klein seemed nervous when she was ushered into one of the interview rooms and O'Reilly decided that this was a good sign. It was clear that the time she'd spent in the custody suite hadn't been to her liking. He introduced everyone for the record and looked across at the elderly German woman.

"How are you feeling?"

"Could we just get to the reason we're all here?"

It was Frieda's lawyer. He was a tiny man with big eyes. The hair on his head was clearly not his own. He'd adjusted the wig three times in the short space of time he'd been in the room. He'd introduced himself as Gareth Miller.

"We can do that," O'Reilly said. "I'd like to go back to Sunday afternoon if I may. Can you talk us through what you remember about that afternoon, Frieda? Is it OK if I call you Frieda?"

She shrugged her shoulders. "It's my name. I've already told you what I remember about Sunday afternoon."

"Could we do it once more? Sometimes, people tend to recall things they hadn't thought about before after some time has passed."

"Otto and I had lunch at a restaurant on the beach," Frieda said.

"That was the Cobo Beach Hotel?" DC Owen said.

"If you already know, why do you ask?"

"Carry on please," O'Reilly said.

"I had prawns and Otto opted for the veal."

"Did you have anything to drink with the meal?" O'Reilly asked.

"I had a bottle of wine."

"Could you tell us what wine it was?" DC Owen said.

"It was *Chateau La Folie*," Frieda said.

"That particular brand isn't on the wine list at the restaurant, is it?" O'Reilly said.

"You know it isn't."

"Yet you still ordered it. Are you in the habit of ordering items that are not on the menu?"

"Sometimes. Often, a restaurant will go the extra mile if you're willing to pay."

"And the Cobo Beach Hotel is one such restaurant?" DC Owen said.

"Apparently, so."

"I know we've gone over this," O'Reilly said. "But can you tell us why you wanted that particular wine?"

"Why do you drink a particular brand of beer? Because it's to your taste. What a ridiculous question."

"Sometimes we need to ask ridiculous questions," O'Reilly said. "Perhaps this one isn't so ridiculous. Did you actually order that brand of wine because it was an essential part of the plan?"

Frieda started to talk but O'Reilly held up his hand to stop her.

"I'm not finished," he said. "Please bear with me. You needed that specific wine, didn't you? It was specified in the instructions you were given. That wine was very important for the plan to work."

"I have no idea what you're talking about," Frieda said.

"I think you do. You and Otto had a pre-nup in place when you got married, is that correct?"

"How is that relevant?" Gareth Miller wondered.

"I'm trying to establish a motive for Mr Klein's murder," O'Reilly said.

"I thought we'd already established that Frau Klein has no recollection of the events surrounding her husband's death," Gareth said.

"We've established no such thing," O'Reilly said. "Frau Klein isn't telling us the truth. Isn't that right, Frieda? You recall everything about that afternoon."

"I don't remember killing my husband," Frieda said.

"So you keep saying," DC Owen said.

"Can we go back to the prenuptial contract?" O'Reilly said. "I believe that was Otto's father's idea. Smart move on his part."

Frieda's eyes darkened. "You know nothing of that."

"Enlighten me then."

"It has nothing to do with you."

"Can you explain the terms of the pre-nup?" DC Owen asked.

"I'd rather not," Frieda said.

"I'll help you then," O'Reilly said. "According to that contract, in the event of you and Otto getting divorced, you wouldn't be entitled to a cent of his fortune. That must sting a bit. In fact, the only way for you to get your hands on the money is if your husband exits the marriage in a body bag."

"That is totally uncalled for." It was Gareth Miller.

"I apologise," O'Reilly said.

He decided to try a change of tactic.

"Frau Klein," he said. "Frieda. I don't know how much you know about the law."

"I'll interrupt you there, if I may," Gareth said.

"Be my guest."

"The law on the Bailiwick of Guernsey happens to be the same as in Germany. In other words, my client is innocent until proven guilty and it is your job to do that."

"True," O'Reilly admitted. "But that wasn't what I was getting at. I don't know whose idea this was, Frieda. I don't know who orchestrated this elaborate plan, but whoever it was clearly doesn't know much about the law. Did you know that even if you get away with your *diminished responsibility* claptrap there is a distinct possibility that you will spend a good few years behind bars. Were you aware of that when you decided to do this?"

Frieda fixed her eyes on his. "I did not set out to kill my husband. I had no reason to kill him, and I have no recollection of it. I had no reason to want him dead."

"You had seventy-five-million reasons," DC Owen said.

"That is enough," Gareth said. "I will not tolerate much more of this."

"Let's wrap things up then," O'Reilly said. "I know you're lying to us, Frieda. You remember every second of the murder of your husband. You expect us to believe that you killed him because you were under the influence of some mystery narcotic. The fact that we could find no trace of that drug in the bottle you drank from means it's not looking good for you. The rock you used to bash his brains in had your fingerprints all over it – you confessed to a crowd of people, and your excuse about the tainted wine cannot be substantiated. You might want to reconsider your options. You are going to prison – it's up to you to decide whether it's worth carrying on with this pathetic charade of yours or not. Do you have anything you'd like to say?"

"No comment."

"I thought you might say that," O'Reilly said.

The interview was definitely over.

CHAPTER FORTY EIGHT

O'Reilly wasn't best pleased when he realised who Yolanda Stewart's legal representative was. It was her brother James, and O'Reilly knew the next hour or so was going to be unpleasant. The interview with Frieda Klein hadn't been a particularly productive one, but O'Reilly hadn't expected it to be. He was hoping to make more progress with Yolanda but there was a good chance that her brother was going to throw a spanner or two in the works.

"Yolanda," he said. "How are you feeling?"

"How do you think she's feeling, Detective Inspector?" James said. "She's been locked up for no reason. Her husband of thirty-five years is dead, and she's being treated like a common criminal."

"She murdered her husband," DC Owen reminded him.

"And she has no recollection of the event," James said. "She is a sixty-two-year-old woman, and she has been treated extremely badly."

"Could you do me a favour?" O'Reilly said.

"What?"

"Could you please decide whether you're here in your capacity as Yolanda's legal representative or if you're here as her brother, because if the latter is the case, you have no business in this interview room."

"I'm Yolanda's lawyer."

"I'm glad we've got that sorted out," O'Reilly said. "Can we make a start?"

He didn't spend much time on the details of the murder itself. The evidence at the scene suggested the aftermath of the act was rather grisly and he didn't think it would do any good to bring it up just yet. Instead, he asked Yolanda about her relationship with her husband.

"What sort of a question is that?" James asked.

"One I would very much like your client to answer," O'Reilly said. "You may have noticed I didn't refer to her as your sister. You aren't helping here. Yolanda, what was your relationship like with your husband?"

"It was fine," she said.

"Your youngest son left the island a long time ago, didn't he?" DC Owen said.

"What's that got to do with anything?"

"Why did he leave?" O'Reilly asked.

"A lot of youngsters leave Guernsey," Yolanda said. "There isn't much for young people on the island."

"But most of them come back from time to time," DC Owen said. "To visit family and friends. Lloyd hasn't set foot on the island in over a decade. Why is that?"

"He lives a long way away."

"Where is that?" O'Reilly said.

"Los Angeles."

"And he hasn't been back to see his family?"

"It's not a crime, is it?"

"No," O'Reilly confirmed. "Have you been over to Los Angeles to see him? I've always wanted to go."

"I haven't, no."

"Did you have a falling out?" DC Owen said.

"What on earth has this got to do with my sister... My client's arrest?" James said.

"I was just wondering if John Stewart was the reason his son has stayed away so long," O'Reilly said. "Yolanda, is that why Lloyd hasn't been back? Perhaps he'll come back now his father is dead."

James shot up from his chair. "You are treading a fine line here, Detective."

"Please sit down," DC Owen told him.

James obliged.

"Where did you buy the wine?" O'Reilly said. "The wine you drank the night you murdered your husband – where did you get it?"

"I bought it from the wine shop in St Georges," Yolanda said.

"Is it a favourite of yours?"

"I'd never tried it before."

"Why did you choose it then?" DC Owen said.

"It looked interesting. *Chateau La Folie.* I thought it sounded rather quirky."

"It's not cheap," O'Reilly said.

"Do you think my client really cares about that?" James said.

"Fair point," O'Reilly said. "What I'm really curious about is why we found the empty bottle next to the sink. It had been rinsed out, and that bit, I can't figure out. You drank some wine, you killed your husband, helped yourself to some cheese and rinsed out the empty wine bottle. Why did you do that?"

"I suppose I was running on autopilot," Yolanda said. "I was probably in shock."

"I've seen the effects of shock," O'Reilly told her. "I've never seen someone rinse out a wine bottle before."

"I always wash the bottles out."

"Why?" DC Owen said.

"For the recycling. The bin for the bottles waiting to be taken away to be recycled tends to smell if you don't rinse the bottles first."

"I don't believe you, Yolanda," O'Reilly said. "I'll tell you what I think happened. I think you rinsed out that bottle because there was nothing in the wine that caused you to act like you did. You knew we would want to test it, so you eliminated that risk by cleaning the bottle. That was part of the plan, wasn't it?"

"What plan?" Yolanda said.

"The plan you were told to follow. You bought that wine because that too was in the instructions. You drank the wine, and you killed your husband. How did that feel, by the way?"

"This is outrageous," James said.

"Murder usually is," O'Reilly informed him. "Did you plan to use the cheese knife all along, Yolanda? Was that also in the plan, or did you improvise that part?"

"You're a horrible, horrible man," Yolanda said.

"I've been called worse," O'Reilly said. "Well? Can you remember helping yourself to some cheese after you butchered your husband? Can you recall spreading a decent amount of brie onto a cracker using the same knife that was responsible for stopping his heart?"

"I shall be taking this further," James informed him. "This is 2019. This is Guernsey – it is not a Gestapo interrogation."

"Those Nazis did seem to get results though, didn't they?" O'Reilly said. "But I digress."

"I insist that you terminate this interview immediately," James said.

"In a minute," DC Owen told him.

"Let me explain to you what's going to happen, Mrs Stewart," O'Reilly said. "You have two choices. You can either tell us what really happened that night – perhaps it will ease your conscience a bit. Or, you can persist with this fictional version of yours and maybe you'll be able to sleep easy in your prison cell – maybe you won't. Either way, the outcome is going to be the same."

Yolanda's silence told him she had nothing more to say on the matter.

CHAPTER FORTY NINE

"Where's O'Reilly?" DI Peters asked DC Stone.

"Katie and the DI are conducting all four interviews," the rat-faced DC told him. "O'Reilly thought it might work in our favour."

"He could be right. I've finished with the analysis of the prints from the warehouse, and something doesn't add up."

"What did you find?"

"We took fingerprints from the manager and the forklift operator for comparison," DI Peters said. "The forklift driver's prints were on the side door. I expected them to be."

"He often opens up the warehouse," DC Stone said.

"But I also found his prints inside the office. His fingerprints were on the office door, and they were also on the desk where the computer equipment used to be."

"Can you tell how recent they are?"

"Not without conducting further, time-consuming tests," DI Peters said.

"I'll get hold of the manager," DC Stone said. "She should be able to tell me if Billy Foot ever had reason to go inside the office."

"We should have something back from the IT team later today," DI Peters said. "I've been informed that they've managed to get into the phones belonging to all four suspects, so hopefully we'll have something concrete then. Does O'Reilly have any new theories?"

"He does, sir," DC Stone confirmed. "He thinks all of this was carefully planned. All four of them have motives for the murders, and all of them have the means to pay someone to orchestrate it."

"That's a bit farfetched, isn't it?"

"A bit, but so is four strangers committing murder and claiming to have no recollection of it. The DI believes somebody is working behind the scenes to make sure these people get away with it."

"The perfect murder," DI Peters mused. "I'll believe it when I see it. Let me know what the warehouse manager has to say."

"Will do, sir," DC Stone said.

He decided to go outside for a cigarette before making the call to Melissa Paul. It had been a while since he'd smoked one and his body was telling him that it needed its nicotine fix. He greeted PC London behind the desk and went outside. The temperature had dropped and the clouds crowding together overhead suggested a summer rainstorm was on the cards. DC Stone was glad – he wasn't a big fan of the heat.

He lit a cigarette, inhaled and breathed out slowly as the nicotine did its job. He wondered if O'Reilly and DC Owen were making any progress in the interview rooms. He hoped so – this investigation had been the most taxing one he'd ever worked on, and he couldn't wait to put it behind him. He took another long drag on the cigarette as the first drops of rain started to fall.

* * *

Mike Trunk was accompanied by the same lawyer as last time. Davina Plough's facial expression told a story of its own. O'Reilly thought she looked like she would rather be anywhere else but in an interview room right now. He wondered why she was so displeased. Was it possible that she was concerned about her client's shaky story? O'Reilly hoped so.

"Mike," he said after he'd introduced everyone for the tape. "Is there anything you'd care to share with us?"

"It looks like rain," Mike said. "I can smell it, even in here."

"I was hoping for something more than a weather forecast. Things are not looking great for you, and you can save us all a whole lot of time and effort right now. I can see your lawyer doesn't really want to be here. Is that right, Mrs Plough?"

"It's Miss," Davina said.

"My apologies," O'Reilly said. "In hindsight, that ought to have been obvious. Mike, talk to us."

"I've told you everything," Mike said.

"That may be true," DC Owen said. "But a lot of what you've told us *isn't* true. When we first spoke to you, you claimed to have bumped into Warren Woodman on and off. That was a lie."

"My memory ain't what it used to be," Mike said. "Sue me."

"Mr Woodman doesn't even live on the island, Mike," O'Reilly reminded him. "Why would you tell us you'd seen him around? That was a stupid mistake to make. You should have known something like that would come out in the end."

"Like I said," Mike said. "My memory isn't great these days. Too much booze."

"How much did this cost you?" O'Reilly asked. "How much are you going to have to pay for the pleasure of getting away with murder?"

"I assure you I haven't forked out a cent," Mike said. "You're barking up the wrong tree here. You're welcome to check."

"Payment upon completion," DC Owen said. "Is that the deal?"

"I don't know anything about any deal."

"What does the letter *M* represent?" O'Reilly said.

"What?" Mike said.

"There was a desk calendar in your home office," DC Owen said. "The letter *M* was written on Saturday's date."

"That was the day you murdered your ex-wife's husband," O'Reilly reminded him. "What does the *M* represent?"

"I can't recall writing it."

"Perhaps it's *M* for murder," DC Owen suggested.

"Or *M* for Mike. I really don't know."

"How did you manage to steal the wine, Mike?" O'Reilly said.

"You really are all over the place today," Mike said. "Is this some new interrogation technique you're trying out?"

"Please just answer the question?" DC Owen said.

"I already told you," Mike said. "It was Woody who provided the wine."

"Another lie. Mr Woodman was not the kind of person to steal anything. You stole that wine, and you lured him to his death. There is something I'd like you to clear up, if you can."

"I'll do my best."

"When we tested the residue in the broken bottle we found traces of a new narcotic. We now know that this particular drug can cause violent episodes in anyone who ingests it. You claim to have never had a homicidal thought before, and that could be justified by the presence of the drug in the wine you consumed, but I don't think that's the case."

"I'm all ears."

"I'm starting to think that the drug was added after the fact," O'Reilly said. "That was part of the plan, wasn't it? It was how you were supposed to kill someone and get away with it. You had as much of that drug in your system as I do right now."

"Prove it," Mike said.

Davina Plough gave a subtle shake of her head.

O'Reilly noticed it. "Thank you, Mr Trunk. I've been doing this for a very long time and it's not the first time I've had to listen to those two words. *Prove it*. In my experience, they are the words of the guilty."

"As far as I'm aware," Mike said. "I've told you all I know, and I believe it's now up to you. I don't recall killing Woody, and I had no reason to want him dead. End of story."

"When was the last time you had any contact with Connie Woodman?" DC Owen asked.

"What has that got to do with any of this?" Davina said.

"Please answer the question, Mike," O'Reilly said.

"I haven't seen Connie in years," Mike said.

"Are you sure? You've already admitted that your memory isn't what it used to be. I've had word that we've managed to access your mobile phone and your laptop."

"Good for you."

"And our team are exceptional," O'Reilly added. "They can perform miracles with anything IT orientated."

"I haven't seen Connie in years," Mike said once more.

O'Reilly decided to wrap things up.

"Interview with Mike Trump, part 1 concluded."

He stated the time for the tape and turned off the recording device.

"Part 1?" Mike repeated.

"You don't need to concern yourself with that," O'Reilly told him.

"No," Mike said. "What does that mean?"

"It means that you've been charged with murder," DC Owen said. "And that in itself means we can and will question you as many times as we see fit. We have the authority to do that."

"Ask your lawyer if you don't believe us," O'Reilly said.

"You've got nothing," Mike said. "You really have sweet FA."

"OK," O'Reilly said. "In that case you've got nothing to worry about, have you? Katie could you arrange for someone to escort our guest to his quarters?"

CHAPTER FIFTY

O'Reilly decided to take a break before they tackled the interview with Belinda Cole. He was hungry, and he needed a moment to take his mind off the lies he'd had to listen to all morning. He asked DC Stone to go and fetch some food for everyone from the café on the esplanade, and the shifty-eyed detective was happy to oblige.

O'Reilly was taking the weight off his feet in his office when DI Peters knocked on the door and came inside with a young woman O'Reilly didn't know.

"Liam," he said. "I'd like to introduce you to Sarah O'Connell. Sarah has recently joined the tech team, and she's hit the ground running."

She was a tall, blond woman with intense blue eyes. She was carrying a flip file.

She held out a hand to O'Reilly. "I'm honoured, sir. I've read all about you, and I really can't wait to work alongside you."

O'Reilly recognised the accent immediately. It was unmistakably southern Irish.

He shook her hand. "Where are you from? Let me guess – Cork?"

Sarah blushed and giggled. "Close, sir. County Cork – Fermoy to be exact."

"You have my utmost sympathy."

"Sir?"

"Never mind. Is there something I can do for you?"

"It's more about what we can do for you," DI Peters said. "Sarah may have found something important."

"Take a seat," O'Reilly said.

"I don't know how much you know about social media," Sarah began.

"I don't use it," O'Reilly told her.

"I rarely do either," Sarah said. "But all four of your suspects do. They all have Facebook accounts, and all of them have used the Messenger service." She opened up the file she was holding.

"I've emailed everything to you," she said. "But I thought I might go through it with you in person. It was more of an excuse to get to meet you than anything else."

O'Reilly looked at her and waited for her to continue.

Sarah broke eye contact first. "So, these are printouts of some of the correspondence I came across in the course of my analysis."

"I may not know much about Facebook," O'Reilly said. "But I do know that the company is notoriously reluctant to divulge any of the info about its subscribers. I've known it to take months to get hold of anything."

"That's true," Sarah said. "But there are ways around that."

"I trust this is all above board."

"I wouldn't know about that. My expertise is in IT – I don't know much about the law. Let me explain how Facebook operates."

"Could you do me a favour?" O'Reilly asked. "Could you keep it simple?"

Sarah smiled at him. "I can do that. I was able to access two of the accounts relatively quickly."

She scanned the first piece of paper.

"Frieda Klein and Yolanda Stewart had virtually no security in place. It's relatively common in older subscribers. Their Facebook accounts were open to anybody with access to Frieda and Yolanda's phones."

"Does that mean anyone can get into their account?"

"With their phones, yes," Sarah confirmed. "Of course, it would be difficult without them. For example, I wouldn't be able to access their accounts from another device, but I digress. Whenever you post something on Facebook, it remains there perpetually. Even if it's deleted it can still be retrieved with a bit of knowhow. Unfortunately, that is not the case with Messenger."

"What did you find?" O'Reilly asked.

"I'm coming to that," Sarah said. "Both Frieda and Yolanda corresponded with the same person a little over a month ago. This is the thread of messages."

She handed O'Reilly four sheets of paper.

"Sweet Jesus," he said after taking a quick look at the first one. When he looked up, he realised Sarah was observing him with wide eyes.

"I apologise," he said. "This is remarkable."

"There's some bad news though," Sarah said. "Accessing the accounts of the suspects was relatively simple, but finding the identity of the person Frieda and Yolanda were in contact with will be extremely difficult, if not impossible."

"*M*," O'Reilly read from the page. "That's all it says."

"That's all I can tell you."

"This is enough to nail them," O'Reilly said. "This is all the proof we need. Everything is here. Dates, times, instructions. All of it. This is basically a how-to guide about committing the perfect murder. You said you couldn't access the accounts of the other two. What about Mike Trunk and Belinda Cole."

"What I actually said was that it was more difficult," Sarah said. "Their Facebook accounts were password protected. They had security measures in place that meant they were required to enter their passwords each time they logged in, even from a familiar device."

"How did you crack the passwords?"

"I didn't have to," Sarah told him. "Once you have a username and email address, you can bypass that, assuming you have their mobile phone in your possession that is."

"Go on."

"How many times have you forgotten a password?" Sarah said.

"It happens to me on a daily basis," DI Peters admitted.

"Me too," O'Reilly said.

"That's why Facebook has methods in place," Sarah said. "You click the option that tells them you've forgotten your password, and you're asked for the email address you use for Facebook and a password link is sent to it. Mike Trunk and Belinda Cole both had further security measures in place in the form of an OTP request, but I had their phones so that didn't pose a problem."

"OTP request?" O'Reilly repeated.

"One time pin," Sarah translated. "A code is sent to your phone to verify that it is a genuine password reset request. I got into their accounts in a flash. And this is what I found there."

four more sheets of paper were handed across the desk.

A cursory glance told O'Reilly that it was more of the same. The mystery *M* character was issuing instructions to Mike Trunk and Belinda Cole.

"This is extraordinary," O'Reilly said. "Truly extraordinary. How did you even come up with this?"

"Come up with what, sir?" Sarah said.

"Checking their social media," O'Reilly elaborated.

"Phone records are risky, sir. And they're relatively easy to come by. Whoever orchestrated this was under the impression that Facebook was a fortress that was impossible to breach, but it's not really. In my opinion, this was rather sloppy – I would have made sure I deleted every message ever sent. But then again I'm an IT specialist not a detective."

O'Reilly liked her. It wasn't simply a case of Irish solidarity – there was something about this unusual woman he felt instantly drawn to.

"This is the ammunition we've been looking for," he said.

"We still don't know who it is that's behind it," DI Peters reminded him. "We have no idea who's pulling the strings behind the scenes."

"Is there any way you can find out who it is?" O'Reilly asked Sarah.

"I did think of a sort of sting," she said. "A trap to get them to reveal themselves, but I don't think that would work. He or she will definitely be aware that these four people are in custody, and they will probably also know that access to their social media will be cut off. I'll keep working on it." She stood up and tapped the papers on the desk.

"I hope you can find everything you were looking for in there."

She grinned and O'Reilly was sure she'd performed a subtle curtesy. She left the room without closing the door.

"Which planet did she come from?" O'Reilly said when she'd gone.

"Same one as you, Liam," DI Peters replied. "Planet Ireland. I really must make a plan to visit the place one day."

"It rains a lot."

"A bit of rain never bothered me. This is the breakthrough we've been waiting for."

"I still don't get it," O'Reilly said. "All this careful planning, and they leave something as incriminating as this on a social media platform."

"Perhaps it really is as your countrywoman suggested," DI Peters said. "They thought Facebook was an impenetrable fortress and they became complacent. This is the proof you were looking for. I'd better get back to work."

O'Reilly stretched his arms and yawned. He looked down at the papers on his desk. Something didn't feel right about them – it had been too easy, and when that happened, he tended to smell a rat. There was a knock on the door and DC Stone came in with the food.

"Thanks, Andy," O'Reilly said. "Have you eaten yourself?"

"I ate my sandwich while I was walking back," DC Stone told him.

"Good, because I have a job for you. I want copies of that file printed out for everyone on the team."

"What's in the file?"

"Something that I find suspiciously convenient," O'Reilly said. "I want the rest of you to take a look through it to see if you agree with me."

CHAPTER FIFTY ONE

"This is incredible," DS Skinner remarked.
He'd just had a read through the printout of the instructions given to Mike Trunk. The alcoholic millionaire had been advised every step of the way. Warren Woodman would be lured to the island with a free holiday in one of the most exclusive hotels Guernsey had to offer. All Mike had to do was wait for further instructions.

They'd arrived on the Friday before the murder. Mike would find four bottles of the *tainted* wine in a disused beach hut in Cobo. The wine hadn't in fact been spiked with anything but the small capsule that accompanied the four bottles would make it look like it had. Warren Woodman was unaware that he was being watched the whole time, and Mike was instructed when to strike.

For the plan to work the murder would have to take place in front of the CCTV camera by Fort Hommet. That was important. Mike was even directed how to behave after the deed was done. He was then told to wait for the light of day, by which time he was assured that the Island Police would have cottoned on to the CCTV camera. The live posting of the murder on the Island Herald's online forum was a bit of serendipity, and Mike Trunk reckoned he was going to get away with it.

"That's why the wine we tested came up positive for the narcotic," DS Skinner said when he'd finished digesting the message thread containing the instructions on how to commit the perfect murder.
"Mike Trunk had some of the drug with him all along." DC Stone had also read the printout. "All he had to do was put it in the bottle after he'd killed Warren Woodman and we would think the wine was contaminated with it from the start. It's unbelievable."

"Frieda Klein was told to eat lunch at the beachfront place in Cobo Bay," DC Owen said. "She was instructed to order a bottle of *Chateau La Folie*, even though it wasn't on the wine list there. There were assurances in place that the wine would reach her table. How did they make sure of that?"

"With a bit of help," O'Reilly said. "This was extremely well organised, and we're looking at the involvement of more than one person."

"The German lady was then told to suggest a walk along the beach," DC Owen continued. "She would stop by the rocks and carry out the murder of her husband. She would feign confusion and tell whoever was around at the time that she thought she'd killed her husband. Whoever set this up reassured her that in light of the recent madness on the island, the police would link the murder to the death of Warren Woodman and the chaos that ensued at the Gottlieb function."

"There was no mention of Frau Klein adding the drug to the bottle in this instance," DS Skinner pointed out.

"It would be too risky," O'Reilly decided. "Whoever came up with this scheme has put contingency plans in place. That's why we didn't find any trace of the narcotic in any of the bottles at the hotel the wine came from. We just assumed that Frau Klein had ingested the stuff and the bottle she drank from couldn't be located."

"Yolanda Stewart's instructions weren't carried out as specified," DC Stone noticed. "She was meant to bash her husband's brains in with the empty wine bottle. Why did she use the cheese knife?"

"Only Mrs Stewart will be able to shed some light on that, Andy," O'Reilly said. "But I believe an awful lot of hatred came out that evening. By all accounts, John Stewart was a horrible man. It's possible that years of pent-up fury were released when Yolanda killed him."

"She was instructed to rinse out the bottle," DC Stone added.

"Her excuse about the recycling was a plausible one," O'Reilly said. "She washed out the bottle, so we had no idea whether the wine was tainted or not, and we assumed the worst again. That was a blunder on our part."

"Mrs Stewart waits for a while," DC Stone said. "Then she calls her brother claiming that she's killed her husband. Once again, she's told to feign amnesia. This is starting to make me feel ill."

"You're not the only one, Andy," O'Reilly said. "Then we have Belinda Cole. On her Facebook Messenger were instructions telling her how to get away with the murder of Joanne Hawkins. Belinda was told to buy a bottle of *Chateau La Folie* from the wine boutique in St Martin. She was then advised to suggest a party up by Bluebell Woods. Joanne was told that there would be other people there, so she wasn't in the least bit suspicious. Belinda waited until they were in an isolated spot, and she killed her friend."

"Forensics found traces of the drug in the residue in what was left of the bottle," DC Owen said. "Because a vial of the narcotic was left in the bushes outside Belinda's house."

"Miss Cole deviated from the plan too," O'Reilly said. "There was nothing in the instructions about throwing half the bottle off the cliff. Why did she do that?"

"Perhaps she really did lose her mind for a moment," DC Stone suggested. "Maybe the enormity of what she'd done dawned on her and she wasn't in complete control of her facilities."

"Faculties, Andy," O'Reilly corrected. "Your creative writing course isn't helping, is it?"

"You know what I meant."

"Where do we go from here, sir?" DC Owen said.

"Where indeed," O'Reilly said. "We have four of the most unlikely killers any of us have ever seen and now we know why. We have ample evidence to ensure that all of them spend a couple of decades behind bars, but I'm still not satisfied. I want the people behind this. This is a plot that involves a good few people, and I want them all to pay for it."

"How did these people even choose the potential murderers?" DC Owen wondered. "It's not like they could put an ad on social media. *How would you like to commit murder and get away with it? Guaranteed results*."
"I really don't know, Katie," O'Reilly said. "But you've raised a valid point."
"And what about the money?" DS Skinner said. "If we're working on the assumption that these people paid handsomely to get away with murder – where is the money? There was no mention of that in the social media threads, and we haven't found any suspicious transactions in any of the killers' bank statements."
"We still have a lot of work to do," O'Reilly said. "We've got all four of these sick individuals backed up against a brick wall, but I want the bastards pulling the strings behind the scenes. This was a series of extravagant murders, and that's why the instructions on social media are niggling away at my insides. In the words of our new IT whizz kid – that was rather sloppy."
"New IT whizz kid?" DC Stone said.
"You'll get to meet her sooner or later, Andy. But you do not go to all this trouble and leave such blatant evidence behind, and I want to know the reason for that."

CHAPTER FIFTY TWO

Belinda Cole looked like a different person to the one O'Reilly remembered from his last conversation with her. Today was her eighteenth birthday but O'Reilly thought she'd aged a lot more than that during her short stay in the holding cell. Her eyes were red and puffy, and O'Reilly wondered if she'd been crying. She was accompanied once again by Harry Ingram and the elderly lawyer had made it clear from the start that Belinda was ready to cooperate fully. O'Reilly suspected he was now more interested in his fee than the fate of his client. Today was a bitter-sweet day for Belinda Cole – a substantial amount of money was now in her bank account, but she wasn't going to be able to spend it for a very long time.

"Belinda," O'Reilly began. "We're going to do things a bit differently today. Mr Ingram has advised us that you're ready to talk but before you do that, I have to inform you that we don't actually need your version of events to secure a conviction anymore. Do you understand?"

Belinda gave a subtle nod of her head.

"For the tape please," DC Owen said.

"I understand."

Belinda's voice sounded different too, and it made O'Reilly slightly depressed. She spoke like a small child who had been caught stealing apples.

"Having said that," he said. "We would appreciate it if you could help us."

"My client will tell you everything you need to know," Harry said. "And I would ask you to take that into consideration."

"I'll reserve judgement on that until I've heard what she has to say," O'Reilly said. "Belinda, why did you kill Joanne Hawkins? You'd been friends for ten years."

"She stole my boyfriend," Belinda told him.

"You're eighteen," DC Owen said. "You were seventeen when you caught Henry Graham with Joanne. If every teenager went around killing someone who'd betrayed them there would be very few teenagers left."

"I loved him," Belinda said. "I still love him."

O'Reilly wasn't really interested in that. He wanted to know who was behind the planning of the murders.

"You had a bit of help," he said. "Can you tell us who organised all of this?"

"I don't know," Belinda said.

"I haven't got time for this. I was under the impression that you wanted to talk."

"I really don't know," Belinda insisted. "I never met these people."

"How did you even find them?" DC Owen said.

"I didn't."

"That makes no sense whatsoever," O'Reilly said.

"Someone contacted me."

"Do you have a name for us?"

"I don't know who it was," Belinda said. "I'm telling the truth."

"For once, I actually believe you. Go on."

"It was about a month ago. I was in a bad place for a while. Henry had broken up with me and I might have vented on social media a bit too much. I was devastated. I suddenly started getting these DMs from someone I didn't know."

"DMs?" O'Reilly said.

"Direct messages," DC Owen explained.

"What did these direct messages say?" O'Reilly said.

"I thought it was just some troll at first," Belinda said. "Someone winding me up about what I was posting. They were telling me to toughen up. *Don't get mad, get even* – that kind of thing."

"And that led up to you killing your best friend?" DC Owen said.

"Of course not. The messages stopped coming a few days after they'd started and then I got one more a couple of days after that. It told me that a gift had been left for me. I was given the location, and I went to check it out."

"What was this gift?" O'Reilly asked.

"It was a just an envelope with a piece of paper in it directing me to another location."

"Didn't you think that was suspicious?" DC Owen said.

"I was curious. The next envelope asked me if I wanted to commit murder and get away with it."

"Did you?" O'Reilly said. "Did you want to commit murder?"

"No way. But there was also a photograph in that envelope. It was Henry and Joanne. I'm sure you know what I mean. I thought that time I'd seen them in the back of Henry's car was a one-off, but it was clear they'd been going behind my back for ages. I wanted to kill her when I saw that photograph."

Something didn't make sense to O'Reilly. Why hadn't the IT team found the messages Belinda had just spoken of. He asked her about it.

"I was told to delete them," she said.

"You deleted the messages you received containing the instructions you were to follow," DC Owen said. "And we were still able to retrieve them."

"I didn't delete those ones," Belinda said. "I was told not to."

"Interesting," O'Reilly said. "I'm still finding it hard to believe you would kill your friend of ten years."

"You wouldn't understand."

"Help me to understand."

Belinda rubbed her eyes. The tears in them were real now.

"I don't know what happened to me," she said. "I started to become obsessed. The messages started again. Joanne and Henry were still carrying on behind my back. They were playing me for a fool."

"But they weren't," O'Reilly told her. "We spoke to Henry Graham, and it only happened twice."

"I had photographs to prove it."

"Do you still have them?" DC Owen said.

Belinda shook her head. "I was told to get rid of them. I burned them."

"Can you talk us through the events that led up to the murder itself?" O'Reilly said.

"I was told to buy the wine," Belinda said.

"*Chateau La Folie*?"

"That's right. Some kind of drug was to be added to the wine afterwards."

"That was left outside your house, wasn't it?" O'Reilly remembered.

"I was to tell Joanne that there was a party up by the cliff at Bluebell Woods, and that's where I would kill her. Afterwards I was told to pretend to be insane."

"We've read the message thread containing the instructions," O'Reilly said. "How did it make you feel? How did it feel to extinguish the life of a girl you'd known since primary school?"

"I felt nothing. I was indifferent. It was like I was on the outside watching it from somewhere else. It didn't make me feel anything."

"I must admit, I'm starting to feel a bit nauseous," O'Reilly said. "So I'll ask you one more question and we can wrap this up. How much did you pay for this? This was a highly organised operation, and it can't have been cheap. How much did it cost you for the privilege of getting away with murder?"

"Two million," Belinda said.

"There was no mention of the price anywhere in the instructions we read," DC Owen said.

"That came later," Belinda said.

"How?" O'Reilly said. "We could find no suspicious transactions in your bank accounts."

"That's because my grandfather's inheritance hadn't yet been paid over," Belinda said. "I was approached by a man shortly after I killed Joanne. He told me the price – he told me to wait until the smoke had cleared before I paid up, and he also told me what would happen if I didn't pay."

"And what was that?" O'Reilly said.

"The messages containing the instructions would be sent straight to you – to the police, and I would go to jail."

"What did this man look like?" O'Reilly asked, even though he already had a good idea what she was going to say.

"He was tall."

"And he had a camera around his neck?" O'Reilly guessed.

"That's right."

O'Reilly stood up. He needed some air. He asked DC Owen to conclude the interview and left the room without further explanation.

CHAPTER FIFTY THREE

"The plot behind this is much more intricate than we initially thought," O'Reilly said.

A few things had become clear in the interview with Belinda Cole, and he wanted to bring the team up to date. He'd also invited Sarah O'Connell to the briefing. He was hoping the young Irishwoman would be able to shed some light on some of the more technical aspects.

"There are more players than we assumed there were," he said. "Belinda Cole was approached by a man after she killed Joanne Cole. And I'm pretty sure I spoke to the bastard when I arrived on the scene. He told us his name was Steven Platt and he said he was on the island because his grandfather was a German soldier buried in the graveyards below Bluebell Woods. I've since learned that the details he gave us were incorrect, and nobody bothered to try to find him."

"We're starting to get a picture of how this was designed to work," DC Owen said. "Belinda was contacted and offered the chance to commit murder and get away with it."

"What I don't understand," O'Reilly said. "Is how the IT team managed to retrieve the message thread containing the instructions for the murders, but they failed to find the original messages – the ones that lured the would-be killers in the first place. I was hoping you might shed some light on that, Sarah."

"Easy," she said.

O'Reilly smiled at her. "I was hoping you might say that."

DC Stone was grinning a rather disturbing grin. Ever since he'd been introduced to the woman from County Cork, he hadn't been able to take his eyes off her. O'Reilly wondered if this was the start of something. Was it possible the rat-faced detective's future as a part of the O'Reilly family was on shaky grounds? He realised that he didn't feel the least bit guilty about considering this, and he also knew it wasn't really within the realms of possibility anyway. Sarah O'Connell was a pretty, intelligent woman and Andy Stone really was a remarkably unattractive man.

"The only reason we were able to retrieve the messages containing the list of instructions," Sarah said. "And we couldn't find any trace of the initial ones is the sender of the messages dictated it that way."

"Are you suggesting they wanted us to find the instructions?" DC Owen said.

"Yes. If you delete a message on your side after the recipient has read it, it will still be there for them. I believe the sender requested that the recipient delete the original messages but not the later ones containing the instructions."

"Belinda Cole did mention something about being told not to delete the later ones," DC Owen said.

"But you didn't find anything to corroborate this," DC Stone said to Sarah. She looked at him as if he was an idiot. "Of course we didn't. I believe that was the whole point, don't you see?"

DC Stone really wasn't off to a great start with Sarah O'Connell.

"The order about not deleting the messages containing the instructions could have been in the notes Belinda received," O'Reilly suggested.

"I think so too," DC Owen said.

"And she no longer has them," DS Skinner said. "She burned the lot."

"I still don't get it." It was DC Stone. "My brain isn't following this."

"It's looking like these unlikely murderers were well and truly shafted, Andy," O'Reilly said. "A seed is planted in their heads, and whoever is behind this makes damn sure that seed grows. The bait is taken and they're slowly reeled in. Once the murders are over and done with, the contingency plan comes into play. They have no choice but to pay up. If they don't the alternative is a guaranteed jail term."

"Is this sort of thing normal on the island?" Sarah O'Connell asked.

"I suppose it is," O'Reilly said. "You get used to it after a while. The question we need to ask is this – how do we catch the people responsible?"

It was a question posed to everyone on the team, but all eyes were now on the newcomer to the island.

It took Sarah a while to notice it.

"Are you asking me?" she said.

"Do you have any ideas?" O'Reilly said.

"Not right now. But I'm not accustomed to being put on the spot like this. Give me a few hours."

"We've yet to speak to the other three suspects," O'Reilly said when Sarah had gone. "But I imagine they're all going to tell us the same as Miss Cole did. Even though these people set out to kill, we need to consider them as victims in this if we're going to make any headway with the brains behind the whole thing."

"They paid to get away with murder, sir," DC Stone said.

"No, Andy," O'Reilly said. "Technically, they didn't. The people working behind the scenes haven't yet received a penny, and they're not going to. I believe that's going to irritate them a bit. This won't have been cheap to pull off. They will have needed quite a few people on the payroll and I doubt those people would have agreed to it without payment upfront. Someone is considerably out of pocket and I'm hoping that's going to cause them to make a mistake. Let's look at this again bringing what we now know into the equation. Feel free to throw a few ideas around. I don't care how crazy they might seem – madness seems to be the prevailing mood on the island right now. Anything goes."

"This all started with a party at the Gottlieb estate," DC Owen said. "All of the bottles of wine there tested positive for the mystery narcotic. Now we know Belinda Cole and Mike Trunk were given vials of the drug to add to the wine it probably means the Gottlieb madness was an integral part of the plan."

"Of course," O'Reilly said. "While it's true that nobody at the party was killed, whatever was in that wine made them all go berserk. How did that case of wine get contaminated?"

"Someone either spiked the wine at the warehouse," DC Stone said. "Or it happened at the party itself."

"Jacob Hunt donated the wine," O'Reilly said. "As per tradition. He had a case delivered to the function by one of his drivers, so it's possible that the driver was on the payroll of the people behind the recent madness on the island. Andy, can you see if you can find out who transported the case of wine to the Gottlieb estate."

"No problem, sir," DC Stone said and got to his feet.

He left the room and returned less than a minute later.

"That was quick," O'Reilly said.

"I'm an idiot, sir," DC Stone said.

"The thought has crossed my mind on the odd occasion, Andy."

"No, sir," DC Stone said. "With everything that's been going on, I forgot to update you on something DI Peters found at the warehouse. There were fingerprints in the office that didn't make sense. They were left by Billy Foot, the forklift driver. I got hold of the manager and she can't remember Billy ever setting foot inside the office. He had no reason to ever go in there."

"How did they get there, then?" DS Skinner said.

"What if Billy is the one who faked the break-in?" DC Stone said. "He knew the CCTV footage needed to be wiped, so he made it look like a break-in to get rid of the hard drives. And if that's the case, it's also reasonable to suggest that he's the one who laced the Gottlieb wine with the drug."

"Andy," O'Reilly said. "If you didn't have a face a myopic rhino would take offence to, I would kiss it right now."

"Thank you, sir."

"I want a car dispatched to the smelly forklift man's residence immediately," O'Reilly said.

"What do we tell him?" DC Stone said.

"The same as usual," O'Reilly said. "The bare minimum.

CHAPTER FIFTY FOUR

It took Billy Foot less than the time it took for the officers who transported him from his house in Fort George to the Island Police HQ to break down, and O'Reilly wondered if this was a new record. Billy was hardly what anyone would consider a criminal mastermind, and he'd wanted to confess everything on the short drive. Luckily it was PC London and PC Hill who had paid him a visit, and he was advised not to say anything until they arrived at Island Police HQ.

The computer equipment that had been stolen from the warehouse hadn't been destroyed, as O'Reilly had expected. It was found in Billy's bedroom underneath his bed, along with twenty-thousand pounds in cash. O'Reilly was informed that the stench in that room was something PC Kim London would never forget. PC Greg Hill also told the Irishman that he was half-expecting to discover a corpse along with the cash and the loot from the warehouse. The reek in the room was that bad.

Billy told them everything, and it didn't take very long. A stranger had approached him a month ago as he left the warehouse. He would be paid forty-thousand-pounds if he agreed to do what the man told him. He was given half of the money right then, together with a bottle full of clear liquid. Another bag contained a syringe with a thin needle and some red wax. Billy was told that when he'd followed the instructions to the letter, he would receive the other half of the money.

Billy injected the bottles of wine in the case set aside for the Gottlieb party, but he neglected to consider the CCTV cameras in the warehouse. That only occurred to him later. He wasn't a criminal genius but even he knew the police would want to look at the footage sooner or later, so he came up with the idea of the break-in. It might have worked if he hadn't been careless enough to leave his prints in the office where the hard drives were kept.

He told O'Reilly that he still hadn't received the balance of the money, but the Irishman had lost interest by then. He knew that Billy Foot was but a miniscule piece of the puzzle they were constructing, and what he'd gleaned from the foul-smelling forklift driver wasn't going to move them forward in the investigation. Billy couldn't describe the man who'd given him the initial twenty-thousand and O'Reilly knew that even if he hadn't been caught, he probably wouldn't have received another penny.

He was feeling frustrated and considering the progress they'd made in the past twenty-four-hours this wasn't really justified. Five of the participants in the recent madness that had played out on the island were definitely out of action, but they weren't the players O'Reilly was after. He wanted the people behind it all, and he didn't think that was going to happen today. That's why, at six that evening he decided to call it a day.

Victoria had sent him a message to ask him if it was OK that she'd invited Assumpta and DC Stone for a meal at their house in Vazon and O'Reilly got the impression it was happening regardless of what he thought about it. As he drove across the island, he reckoned it wasn't such a bad thing. Andy Stone aside, it had been a while since he'd had chance to catch up with his daughter and it would be nice to see her again.

Assumpta's car was already parked outside when he arrived, and O'Reilly wondered how long she'd been there. He parked behind her car and walked up the path towards the house. The paving was still wet from the recent downpour and rainwater was dripping from the leaves on the trees.

O'Reilly was met with a beer and a warm hug when he went inside the house. He kissed Victoria on the cheek before he took a long drink from the bottle of *Scapegoat*.

"That was quite a welcome," he said. "I feel like I ought to have walked in and shouted something like *Darling, I'm home*."

"Don't you dare," Victoria warned. "Assumpta is here already."

"So I see. Andy shouldn't be long. He just wanted to grab a quick shower. I'm going to do the same – it's been a pretty dirty day, and I need to wash that grime away."

Twenty minutes later O'Reilly was feeling more refreshed. He took another beer from the fridge and asked Victoria if she needed any help in the kitchen.

"Assumpta and I have it all organised," she told him. "Andy arrived while you were in the shower. You can go and keep him company in the living room."

"I'd rather not."

"Dad," Assumpta said. "You don't have to be a grump all your life."

"Do as you're told for once," Victoria added.

O'Reilly reluctantly obeyed. DC Stone was sitting on the sofa. He was flanked on either side by a cat. Juliet and Shadow were fast asleep and O'Reilly's thoughts turned to Bram. He was looking forward to seeing his ginger friend again.

"I was told to get out of the kitchen," he told DC Stone.

"So was I," DC Stone said. "Your cats have no manners."

"Those two are saints compared to my ginger squatter."

"How is he?"

"The vet reckons we'll have him back home soon," O'Reilly said. "What happened to you today?"

"Sir?"

"You're usually pretty sharp where modern technology is concerned, but your mind seemed to be elsewhere when we were discussing the ins and outs of Facebook Messenger. It wouldn't have anything to do with the new

IT woman, would it?"

The instant flush on DC Stone's face confirmed it.

O'Reilly raised an eyebrow. "Is there something you want to tell me?"

"Of course not," DC Stone said. "I love Assumpta more than anything in the world, but that accent does something to me. I can't explain it."

"Are you sure you don't want to get anything off your chest? The Irish accent does something to you, does it? Do I need to be concerned?"

"What?" DC Stone's face was now the colour of beetroot. "Urgh. Of course not."

"Glad to hear it."

Assumpta came in to tell them that the food was ready and the relief on DC Stone's face was so obvious that she cast him a curious glance before she went back to the kitchen.

CHAPTER FIFTY FIVE

O'Reilly had no sooner sat down to eat than his phone started to ring. He let it go to voicemail. Victoria had cooked a lasagne and O'Reilly tucked in. He was starving. DC Stone helped himself to half the amount O'Reilly had dished up.
"Have you lost your appetite, Andy?" O'Reilly asked him.
"I don't really eat much," DC Stone said.
   "How are things at work?" O'Reilly asked Assumpta.
"The madness murders are taking up all of our time," she said.
"Madness murders?"
"It's what everybody is calling them. I think it stems from the thing on the Herald's site, and we have no option but to go along with it. Are you any closer to cracking it?"
"We made great progress today," O'Reilly said. "We've got five of the players banged to rights, but we're still missing the ones who orchestrated the whole thing."
"What's it all about?"
"Off the record?"
Assumpta gave him the look that she'd perfected over the years. O'Reilly held up his hands in apology.
"Off the record then," he said. "It was all about money. Ironically, none of that money is going to exchange hands. And it's thanks mainly to a lovely lass from County Cork. Isn't that right, Andy?"
DC Stone almost spat out the mouthful of food he was chewing.
   "She's new to the IT team," O'Reilly spared him from commenting. "Lovely girl. She managed to trace a string of messages on social media, and that's all the proof we needed. All four of the murderers are up shit creek without a paddle, but I want more than that. I want to know who was

behind it. The girl from Fermoy has promised to see if she can come up with anything."

His phone rang once more. A glance at the screen told him he should probably answer it.

"Speak of the devil," he said. "Please excuse me."

He exited the room to take the call.

"Are you OK?" Assumpta asked DC Stone. "You look a bit red in the face."

"I'm just tired," he said. "It's been a draining week. This lasagne is really good."

"I had a bit of help," Victoria said.

She raised her glass of water and Assumpta toasted with her wine glass.

"Do you know who Liam is talking to?" Victoria said.

"It must be important if he's taking the call in the middle of a meal," Assumpta said. "Not much interrupts my dad when he's busy filling his belly."

O'Reilly came in and sat back down. "Sorry about that."

"Who was it?" DC Stone asked.

"Work?" Assumpta guessed.

"Right," O'Reilly confirmed. "It was the new IT woman. She thinks she's found something."

"What is it?" DC Stone said.

"She wants to show me."

"Do you want me to come with you?" DC Stone offered.

"She's going to come here," O'Reilly said. "I told her I would come out to her, but she said she didn't mind. That's OK, isn't it?"

This question was directed at Victoria.

"If it'll help you to wrap up the investigation," Victoria said. "I'm all for it. You haven't forgotten about the bike ride this weekend, have you?"

"I'm looking forward to it."

"Are you sure you're ready to get back on a bike?" Assumpta said.

"I'll be on the back," O'Reilly assured her. "No stress. And my lovely wife has promised to take it easy."

Victoria crossed her fingers and secretly showed them to Assumpta under the table.

"Don't scare him now," Assumpta said.

"What's for pudding?" O'Reilly asked.

"Are you serious?" DC Stone said.

He still hadn't finished the food on his plate.

"Deadly, Andy," O'Reilly said.

"I'll fetch the cheesecake," Victoria said.

"I'll give you a hand," Assumpta said.

"Are you sure it's a good idea for Sarah to come here?" DC Stone said in a voice not much louder than a whisper.

"Don't worry," O'Reilly said. "I'll speak to her alone in another room if you're so worried her accent is going to give you another funny turn."

"I didn't mean it like that. This is your home. This is Victoria's home, and perhaps it would be better to wait until tomorrow to discuss whatever it is she's found. At the station."

"Aren't you intrigued?"

"Of course I am," DC Stone said.

"Time is running out, Andy. The people behind this are going to get wind of the developments. They probably already know that the four killers are about to spill the beans and they're probably running scared. We need as much info as we can get, and we need it now. Who's to say the ones pulling the strings haven't already upped and left the island. I would if I was in their shoes."

"Who's shoes?" Victoria said.

She placed the cheesecake on the table and told O'Reilly to help himself. "Don't mind if I do," he said and cut himself a large slice. "We were just talking about the new information the IT woman has for us. It must be important if she's coming here in person with it."
The doorbell sounded.
"That'll be her now," O'Reilly said.
"I'll get it," Victoria offered.

"This cheesecake is delicious," O'Reilly said and took another mouthful.
"I don't know where you put it," DC Stone said.
"Grab a slice," Assumpta said. "While there's still some left."
They could hear muted voices. Victoria was inviting Sarah O'Connell in. The voices got louder as they got nearer to the dining room.
"Help yourself to some cheesecake," Victoria said in the doorway.

O'Reilly got to his feet. "Good to see you again."
Assumpta was sitting with her back to their visitor.
"Summi," O'Reilly said. "I'd like you to meet our lady from Fermoy."
She stood up, turned around and stopped dead. O'Reilly watched as the facial expressions of the two young women changed. They looked as though they were both in severe shock.
"Assumpta," Sarah spoke first.
"Sarah," O'Reilly's daughter said.

CHAPTER FIFTY SIX

A few miles south a man was packing some things in a hurry. He needed to get off the island, and he needed to do it now. He checked the side compartment of the holdall for the third time and got the same confirmation – his passport was in there. He'd packed a few changes of clothes and some basic toiletries. Whatever he forgot, he would have to buy when he got to wherever he was heading. He still hadn't made his mind up about where that would be.

He'd removed most of the bandages from his face so as not to arouse suspicion, but it really hadn't made much difference. The eyepatch would make him stick out like a sore thumb. There wasn't much he was going to be able to do about that. It would be dark soon, and he hoped that would work to his advantage.

He'd heard about the developments in the murder investigation, and he hadn't been particularly fazed that all of the killers had been charged and all of them were probably going to be spending the next twenty years in jail. There was nothing that could be traced back to him – he'd made damn sure of that.

At least he thought he had. The phone call had taken him by surprise. A woman with an Irish accent had called to ask him a few questions about an article he'd forgotten he'd written. It was a short piece about modern trends in finance. After the crisis in 2008 the financial world changed dramatically, and the man with the eyepatch had composed a piece for an online journal. He didn't know how many people had read it, but he didn't think many had. The Irish woman had asked if he wrote the piece entirely on his own. He replied in the affirmative and asked about the reason for the phone call. Her reply confused him at first. She told him she was simply following instructions. She told him to enjoy the rest of his evening.

A quick Google check of the number she'd phoned him on told him he needed to leave. He didn't know the relevance of the reference to the online article, but he did know that it wasn't the reason for the phone call. Why was someone called Sarah O'Connell phoning him about that? Why was a woman who worked for the Island Police interested in an article he'd forgotten all about? Sarah O'Connell had rattled him, and that wasn't supposed to happen.

* * *

"It was really just a stroke of luck," Sarah O'Connell said.
She was sitting with O'Reilly and DC Stone in the living room of Victoria's house. O'Reilly had been surprised at Sarah's and Assumpta's reaction when they saw each other, and he'd asked them if they knew each other.
"We met at university," was Assumpta's reply.
"It's a long story," Sarah said at exactly the same time.
O'Reilly wasn't in the mood for a long story. He wanted to see what the woman from Fermoy had to tell him.

"Often that's all it boils down to," he said. "A bit of luck, and us Irish folk are blessed with more than most. What can you tell us?"
"When I was at Uni," Sarah said. "I did a computer science degree, but I was able to select a few modules to do on the side. One of those was Forensic Psychology, and I chose to do a thesis in forensic linguistics. It was a fascinating subject, and it's one I'm still very interested in."
"What is forensic linguistics?" DC Stone asked.
"To break it down into layman's terms," Sarah said. "Consider it the same as voice analysis. We all have a different voice. No two people's voices are identical. There will always be subtle differences in tone and timbre – accent and lilt, that kind of thing. The same thing applies to linguistic analysis. No two people write in the same way. Some may prefer the direct approach on paper, and others will be more descriptive. Take the Irish for example. We,

as a nation have an inbuilt talent for tale telling. It's in our blood, but I digress."

"I could listen to you speak all night," DC Stone said.

Sarah observed him suspiciously. O'Reilly did the same.

"During my time at university," she continued. "I decided to experiment, and I combined both of the disciplines. IT and forensic linguistics. I devised a program that would enable me to compare linguistic styles. Basically, it meant I could feed a piece of writing into the database and the program would compare it with other pieces in the database. I modified it over the years so I wouldn't have to physically enter every piece of writing I wanted to compare something with, and I added a search bot to speed things up a bit. In essence I can send this bot into cyberspace, and I can have a list of results back in minutes."

"How come I'm not aware of this program?" O'Reilly asked.

"Because I've only just told you about it. This is the first time I've actually put it into practice in a real-life investigation."

O'Reilly was fascinated. He'd heard about forensic linguistics, but he'd never been in the position to see it in action.

"You got a hit, didn't you?" he asked.

"I think I did," Sarah confirmed. "The analysis narrowed it down to sixteen possibles. I could discount thirteen of these on the spot – none of the names who came up live anywhere near Guernsey. One of the remaining people is dead, and another one resides in France."

"It's possible they could have orchestrated it from there," DC Stone said.

"That's what I thought," Sarah said. "But when I contacted the man, he told me he had no idea what I was talking about."

"I'm falling a bit behind here," O'Reilly said. "What did you actually send this bot into cyberspace with?"

"The thread of messages containing the instructions for the murders."
"And you got a hit?"
"I got more than that," Sarah said. "I got a name. An online article on the changes in the financial world after the crash in 2008 was so similar in linguistic style, I knew it had to be the one. I managed to get the author's details, and I phoned him. His reaction told me everything I need to know. His name is Mark Spring and he lives two and a half miles from here."

O'Reilly didn't react straight away. He was struggling to comprehend what Sarah Connell had just told him.
"Did you call it in?" he asked.
"I didn't think I had the authority to do that," Sarah said. "I wanted your opinion first."
"Fair point. Andy, you know what to do."
DC Stone was already making the call. If Mark Spring was still on the island, he would soon be apprehended.

CHAPTER FIFTY SEVEN

Mark Spring was panicking. He was on the road east towards St Sampson and he was finding it difficult to drive. He didn't consider that his impaired vision would affect his ability to drive. He couldn't see out of his left eye and that was causing some problems. He was driving far too quickly, and he eased his foot off the accelerator.

He knew it was only a matter of time before they came looking for him. He had a boat moored in the harbour in St Sampson. He planned to sail across to Herm and wait it out there for a couple of days. He would then head across to France. He didn't have a plan after that. He had enough cash to see him through for a while, but he should have had much more. The eight million that was supposed to have been transferred to his Cayman Island account wasn't going to materialise anymore, and he was furious.

He'd almost reached La Villocq when he spotted the flashing lights approaching. Three police cars were driving at speed, and Mark slowed down further. He remembered the eye patch and turned his head as they passed. In his rearview mirror he could see that they hadn't stopped or turned around. His heartbeat was throbbing in his ears, and he was starting to sweat. The palms of his hands were moist and sticky on the steering wheel.

Mark didn't see any more police cars during the journey east. He turned right by Vale Castle and made his way towards the marina. There were very few other vehicles on the road, and he was glad. He was going to make it. He had no idea what he was going to do when he got to France, but at least he would be a free man. He was going to get away – he could feel it.

He slowed as he neared the entrance to the marina, he flicked on the indicator and proceeded to make the right turn. If he had the luxury of sight in his left eye he would have seen the 4x4 in his peripheral vision, but the only thing that informed him about the black Landrover was the huge bang as it hit his car, side-on. The heavy 4x4 sent Mark's car skidding across the road. It spun a few times before colliding with a tree by the entrance to the marina. The air bags in Mark's car worked as they were supposed to work – they exploded on impact and now Mark was unable to move. He was dazed and he was confused, but he was still very much alive.

* * *

"He's gone," O'Reilly said.
He put down his phone and punched the coffee table hard.
"Easy there," Victoria said. "That table belonged to my parents."
"Sorry," O'Reilly said. "That was PC Hill. Mark Spring has done a runner. Uniform went to his place in Perelle and his fiancé said she'd come home to find a note. He said he was sorry, but he had to leave. That was it."
"Damn it," DC Stone said. "We were so close."
"We've got every officer on the island out looking for him," O'Reilly said.
"This is my fault, isn't it?" Sarah said. "I should have called it in as soon as I knew."
"We don't know how long he's been on the run," O'Reilly said. "The fiancé hasn't seen him since this morning. He could be anywhere by now."
"But me calling him didn't help, did it?" Sarah said. "It must have been me that prompted him to leave."
"It's nobody's fault," DC Stone said. "If he's still on the island, he'll be found. We have the details of his vehicle."
"According to Naomi Potter," O'Reilly said. "She's his fiancé – he keeps a boat in St Sampson. We've got someone checking it out now."

His phone started to ring again. He snatched it up and answered it. It was PC London. "We've found Mark Spring, sir."
"That was quick," O'Reilly said.

"He was involved in an accident just outside the gates of the marina. It looks like he got sideswiped by a 4x4."

"Is he alright?"

"He was taken away in an ambulance. His car had a load of airbags."

"Are you sure it's him?" O'Reilly asked.

"Positive, sir. It's the car registered to him, and how many people on the island do you know who wear an eyepatch?"

"Which hospital was he taken to?"

"The Princess Elizabeth. He's not going anywhere."

"We'll see what he has to tell us tomorrow," O'Reilly said. "Thanks, Kim."

"I'd better be going," Sarah said.

"You did good work there," O'Reilly told her. "Exceptional work."

Sarah nodded and got to her feet. O'Reilly watched her go. He could hear the sound of voices in the kitchen. Assumpta was finishing off washing the dishes. Her voice was clearer than Sarah's. O'Reilly was sure she told Sarah to leave it. Soon afterwards he heard the door open and close.

"That's that then," he said. "Tomorrow's another day. I'm going to see if Summi needs a hand in the kitchen."

He was curious. It was quite obvious that Assumpta and Sarah O'Connell were acquainted, and O'Reilly wanted to know more.

Assumpta had finished cleaning up in the kitchen and she was sitting at the table with a bottle of wine in front of her. O'Reilly watched her drain a glass in one go and then top it up again.

He sat down opposite her. "Are you going to tell me what's on your mind?"

"Could you close the door," she said.

O'Reilly obliged her. "What's going on, Summi? How do you and Sarah know each other?"

"I don't want to talk about it."

"OK. Are you alright?"

Assumpta didn't reply. She took another sip from the glass and sighed deeply. O'Reilly remained quiet too. The only sound in the kitchen was the ticking of the clock on the wall.

"We were lovers."

Assumpta looked O'Reilly in the eye when she made this revelation.

"I see," he said, even though he didn't really.

"It wasn't real," Assumpta added. "I don't think either of us knew what we were doing. We met at a pub in Dublin. I was in my final year and Sarah was a Fresher. We hit it off straight away, and one thing led to another. I don't expect you to understand."

"You might need to help me a bit," O'Reilly said.

"It only lasted a couple of weeks," Assumpta said. "It was the start of summer, and I think we just got caught up in a wave of excitement. If you were to analyse it, you'd probably say it was some kind of experimental phase we were both going through. I like men. I liked men back then and I like them now, so I don't really know why it happened. Are you mad?"

"Mad?" O'Reilly said. "A bit shocked, maybe – but nothing you do will ever make me mad. Of course, I'm not mad."

"I got a bit of a fright when I saw her earlier," Assumpta said.

"I got the impression that she did too," O'Reilly said.

"What's she doing here?"

"She's working for the Island Police," O'Reilly said. "She's new to the tech team, and she's proven herself already. Did you not stay in touch?"

"We parted amicably," Assumpta said. "I think we both realised that what we had wasn't real – it was a mistake, and it would have been difficult to remain friends afterwards. We used to cross paths every now and then – it's hard not to in a place as small as Dublin, but we never really reconnected. You're not going to tell Andy, are you?"

"It's not my place to do so," O'Reilly said.

"You seem to be taking this very well."

"How else am I supposed to take it?" O'Reilly said. "I'm not an old prude, and whatever you do, you're my daughter. You'll always be my baby girl, no matter what you do. After your Mammy died, I made a promise to always have your back, and I intend to keep that promise."

"I love you, dad."

"I love you too, Summi."

"You never judge people, do you?"

"It's not in my job description," O'Reilly said.

"You know what I mean. You've never once judged me on any of the decisions I've made."

"That's not strictly true. The jury is still out where Andy is concerned." Assumpta smiled for the first time in the conversation. "You're not kidding anyone, dad. I suppose we should be going."

"Make sure Andy drives," O'Reilly said. "You've knocked back quite a bit of that stuff."

He nodded to the bottle of wine.

"Yes, dad," Assumpta said and saluted. "Thank you."

"What for?"

"For just being you."

"Are you going to speak to Sarah? Perhaps you two should talk."

"We'll see," Assumpta said.

CHAPTER FIFTY EIGHT

According to the doctor O'Reilly spoke to, Mark Spring had been extremely lucky. The airbags in his car had not only saved his life – they'd prevented him from sustaining any serious injuries. He was suffering from whiplash, and he had a number of bruises on his chest and abdomen from the sudden impact of the airbag, but apart from that he'd escaped the accident relatively unscathed.

The man sitting up in the hospital bed didn't look particularly lucky and O'Reilly suspected he wasn't feeling especially blessed either. The car accident had truly scuppered his plans to elude arrest.

O'Reilly pulled up a chair next to the bed and sat down. DC Owen remained standing.

"How are you feeling?" O'Reilly asked.

"How does it look like I'm feeling?" Mark said.

"It hasn't been your week, has it? What were you thinking - driving half-blind?"

"Sir," DC Owen said. "We need to record this."

"So we do," O'Reilly remembered.

DC Owen had brought along a portable recording device which she switched on.

"Where were we?" O'Reilly said. "That's right – what were you thinking - driving half-blind?"

"I'm glad you're finding this amusing," Mark said.

"I'm not laughing. Four people are dead, and you were responsible for all of their deaths."

"Nonsense. The people who killed them wanted them dead. All I did was help them to get away with it."

"But they didn't get away with it, did they?" DC Owen said.

"It's lucky for them you agreed to payment on completion," O'Reilly said. "Do you want to talk to us about it?"

"It wasn't supposed to end like this," Mark said.

"That's what all apprehended killers say. Did you really think you were going to be able to pull something like this off? The whole concept is preposterous – absolute madness."

"That's precisely what it was supposed to be. I knew I shouldn't have trusted the teenager. It was her who messed this up."

"How did you even come up with an idea like this?" O'Reilly said.

"It was a flash of inspiration one night," Mark said. "I was watching a documentary about an undercover police officer posing as a hitman. A gun for hire, and somewhere in the programme it mentioned that almost all people who hire someone to kill are caught out. Something always goes wrong for them. I reckoned I could get away with it. I came up with a premise so ludicrous nobody would even consider it."

"Four perfect murders," DC Owen said.

"How did you choose them?" O'Reilly said. "How did you select your would-be killers?"

"Very carefully," Mark said. "My specialty is finance, but I happen to know a thing or two about IT too. I monitored a group of people for a while. I kept an eye on their social media – I scrutinised them from a distance, and I whittled the group down to three after a lot of time and careful consideration. It was no secret that John Stewart was a first-class bastard. I went to school with his son, Lloyd. John is the reason Lloyd got off the island as soon as he could and never came back. Yolanda was more than happy to accept my services. The same goes for Frieda Klein. That sweet old German lady is anything but."

"Why did Mike Trunk want Warren Woodman dead?" O'Reilly asked.

"They hadn't seen each other for twenty years. That one makes no sense."

"I thought it might spice things up a bit," Mark said. "Mike didn't have a clue who he would actually be killing."

"I'm not following you."

"You probably considered the motive in that one to be jealousy," Mark said. "Or something like that, but how could it be when Mike didn't recognise the man he was going to kill as the man who married his ex-wife two decades ago. Mike couldn't care less who he dispatched. He got a hard on just from the idea of committing the perfect murder. It's as simple as that."

"You said you whittled the list down to three," DC Owen said. "You're forgetting about Belinda Cole."

"That little bitch was my only mistake," Mark said.

"I can assure you," O'Reilly said. "You made more than one."

"I suppose I got greedy," Mark admitted. "Belinda was easy to manipulate. I suppose you could say I groomed her. I'm not particularly proud of it. What's going to happen to me?"

"You'll probably get off with a slap on the wrists," O'Reilly said. "After all, it wasn't you who killed those people, was it?"

"You're kidding me?"

"Of course I'm kidding you, you idiot. Conspiracy to commit murder will probably be the main one. Accessory to murder and as many other charges I can come up with. You'll be lucky to see the outside of a prison again."

"How did the Irish woman track me down?" Mark said. "I left nothing behind that could be traced back to me."

"That's the problem with killers these days," O'Reilly said. "They think they're smarter than the people paid to catch them. There will always be something they overlook. There is no such thing as the perfect murder. And you tried to pull off four of them. That wasn't too bright."

"How?" Mark said. "You have to tell me how she found me. What is she – some kind of super sleuth?"

"Something like that. Who else did you have on your payroll?"

"Come on," Mark said. "How did she do it? I'll tell you who else was involved in this if you tell me how she tracked me down."

"You first," O'Reilly said.

"How do I know you'll hold up your side of the deal?"

"You don't. You'll just have to trust me."

Mark went on to tell them the names of the people who had a hand in the recent madness on the island and it took longer than O'Reilly expected it to. There were more people involved than he suspected. O'Reilly didn't keep to his part of the bargain. He decided he would let Mark Spring stew on how he was eventually caught. He would let it consume him in the years he was going to spend behind bars. It was the least he deserved.

CHAPTER FIFTY NINE

"Damn cat."

It was the third time O'Reilly had almost tripped over the ginger brute that morning. Bram hadn't left his side for a minute since coming home from the vets.

"What is it you want?" he asked. "There's food in your bowl – the back door is open, and I said you can sleep on the bed tonight. What more do you want from me?"

Bram replied with a pitiful meow.

"Don't give me that shite again. I'm not falling for that again."

"Who are you talking to?" Victoria asked from the doorway.

"The ginger squatter," O'Reilly said. "He's driving me mad."

"Are you ready? You're not exactly dressed for a bike ride."

"I'll get changed in a minute. I'm really looking forward to it."

This was an understatement. The recent investigation had been a consuming one, and O'Reilly needed something to take his mind off it. A cruise around the island on a motorbike would be just the ticket.

Five more people had been arrested. Mark Spring had spoken in great detail about their involvement, and he'd also talked at length about how he expected the chain of events to pan out. He'd sourced the mystery narcotic from an old friend in London. It was a new drug, and the friend promised him it wouldn't disappoint. Mark needed to be absolutely sure of this, so he devised the plan to test it at the Gottlieb summer party. He was impressed at how well the drug had worked, but he wasn't expecting to be on the receiving end of its effects.

That was the only thing Mark left to chance. He made sure there was no trail left behind him – he corresponded with his cohorts in person only, and he chose the locations carefully. He didn't think anything would lead the police to his door but, as O'Reilly pointed out, there was always something overlooked in a plot to commit murder. There was still a long slog ahead of them, but O'Reilly wasn't going to think about that right now.

He managed to slip away without Bram noticing and he suited up, ready for the bike ride. It had been a while since he'd worn the leathers, and they seemed bigger somehow. He decided that it was a sign – he needed to work harder to put back the weight he'd lost during his solidarity diet with Victoria.

He retrieved his helmet from the cupboard under the stairs and headed for the kitchen. Bram was sniffing his food bowl. He looked up at O'Reilly and stopped as if he'd been frozen in time.
"What's wrong now, cat?" O'Reilly asked him.
He tried the helmet on for size and as he did so Bram shot up into the air, shrieked and raced outside. O'Reilly started to laugh. He'd never seen such a comical reaction to a motorcycle helmet.

"All set?" Victoria asked.
"All set," O'Reilly confirmed. "I was thinking, would you mind if I kept the bike helmet on my bedside table from now on?"
Victoria gave him a curious glance. "Have you gone mad?"
"It appears so," O'Reilly said. "There's a lot of it about."

THE END

Printed in Great Britain
by Amazon